*Sometimes you have to get out
before you can get home*

I0663535

KIMBERLY SOESBEE

TOUCH

PUBLISHING

Published by Touch Publishing
P.O. Box 541495
Grand Prairie, Texas 75054
U.S.A.
www.TouchPublishingServices.com

To contact the author visit
www.KimberlySoesbee.com

Cover design by Touch Publishing

This is a work of fiction. Names, characters, businesses, places, team names, events, and incidents are either the products of the author's imagination or used in a fictitious manner.

Author photo by Andrew Lipsett
www.lipsettphotographygroup.com

FOR BEN

Chances

When the fielder loves his record
More than victory for his team,
Doubtful chances miss his glances
For his caution is extreme.

Going after every grounder
Means a slip-up here and there,
And in terror of an error
He will choose the chances fair.

Spotless records are enticing
In a ball game as in life,
And the cunning pick their running
To avoid the stony strife.

Many a mortal swaggers slowly
Down the years in proud parade,
Boasting to the meek and lowly
Of the slips he never made.

Well it is that wise commanders,
When they call for sterling men,
Place the workers o'er the shirkers
Though they err and err again.

Men who try and fall when trying
Try again and win at last,
Never brooding, never sighing
O'er the errors of the past.

— *William F. Kirk*

PROLOGUE
SEPTEMBER 11, 1988
PORT-AU-PRINCE, HAITI

There is a space that exists between the moment when all is right with the world and the moment all hell breaks loose—a tiny gap when things are neither good nor bad. Most people never notice this in-between time, when life is about to be changed forever. The rush from calm to chaos appears simultaneous, as the hand of the devil reaches out for destruction. For the astute, however, there is time in the gap to make a decision. The decision in the gap determines one's future.

"William! Tie your shoe!" Mama called to her eager son, as he loped like an ocelot after his father.

"No time! We must hurry," Father replied without looking over his shoulder.

William skipped faster, watching his father's long strides and trying his best to keep up. Sundays were undoubtedly his favorite day of the week. On these mornings, William savored buttoning his light blue shirt; tucking it carefully into the navy pants reserved for the holy day. It was a stark contrast to the rest of the week, when he rolled out of the house in whatever clothing he slept in. As fine as he felt in his clean shirt and slacks, nothing compared to the pride that welled in his chest as he slipped on his shiny black shoes. They made the Sunday outfit complete, and William knew how important it was to look his best before God. He briefly wondered if he should stop and tie the laces, so as not to fray them, but as his family rounded the last corner, he forgot all about it.

There was a church nearer to their home, but more Sundays than not these days, Father traveled his family the extra distance to hear the preaching of the Reverend Jean-Bertrand Aristide. The church steeple of Saint Jean-Bosco Catholic Church reached higher than the other buildings nearby, bringing the people closer to God. The sight today brought Father to a halt.

"Sweet Jesus. Would you look at that?" he mumbled to himself.

Mama came up alongside him. "Maybe we shouldn't go to mass today," she offered, as she saw what stopped his pace. "They say it isn't safe. You know, they caught a man trying to enter the church with a gun last week."

From the other side of Father, William studied the scene before them. He spied a row of armed guards at the barracks across the street. William counted fifteen men, faces covered with black fabric, cradling long-barreled guns at imposing angles before them. The rooftop held even more masked guards.

"Why so many soldiers, Father?" William asked.

"To guard the church, right?" William's older brother suggested. He took William's hand and they waited for Father's response. He was clearly considering the situation.

Several moments passed. William was nearly certain Father was going to turn them around for the long march home.

"No," Father said finally. "We will not let the *macoutes* keep us from church today."

William shuddered at the thought of *bogeymen*.

"Do you think macoutes are responsible for the attacks?" Mama asked with wide eyes. "If so, then we should turn around right now."

"No," Father repeated. "Change will never come if we show that we are afraid. We must be willing to be heard. We must reject the regime to find righteousness and love."

William had heard Father recount that phrase many times in the last few months. He was often filled with hope when he heard it, but today, hope was not the feeling stirring in his chest.

Mama sighed. "Well, let's get on with it, then." She reached behind Father, whose purposeful strides again set the pace, and grabbed William's other hand.

Miraculously, Father secured seats near the front of the church. He went into the pew first, followed by William, William's brother, and Mama at the aisle. Most of the other men were still standing outside, surveying the ominous presence of the police and armed guards. Although they looked dangerous, the general consensus was that the extra barrack guards were there to protect the priest-under-fire—the Reverend Jean-Bertrand Aristide.

The gong of the mass bell brought the men and waiting families inside. The parish was now packed.

"Why are so many people wearing white today?" William asked his Father.

"They wear white to show their opposition," he replied.

Henri Namphy, with a long history of serving Haiti's military, was the current president, having taken office after a coup not even three months ago. Haiti's commoners did not trust him.

"Why didn't we wear white?" William wondered.

Father didn't answer. If William could have seen inside Father's head, he would have known that Father wasn't as confident standing up to the military as he projected to his family. He worried about the recent attacks in the city, and even though his heart opposed the government, seeds of fear kept him from being too outspoken in places where he might be overheard.

"Shh!" Father said.

William obeyed. He inhaled deeply. Second to putting on his shiny shoes, the moment when his nostrils were assaulted with heavy incense was the next best part of Sunday. The priest walked slowly, swinging the brassy thurible over the heads of the parishioners. William nearly forgot to cross himself as they passed, so enthralled was he with breathing in the frankincense. As the priest and boat-bearer made their way to the right of the altar, Father Aristide entered from the left. A few people cheered and were quickly hushed by the more reverend church-goers.

Father Aristide stood confidently behind the altar. He

raised his hands in praise to God, looking up to the heavens. The air teemed with expectancy for booming prayers and words of blessing. Instead of a blessing from God, however, what the people got came straight from the devil. Pops of gunfire filled the air and screams echoed off the stone walls. Masked bogeymen invaded the sanctuary and caught everyone unaware.

William seemed not to exist in the activity swirling around him. He heard the pops. He saw the gunmen. He saw blood. He watched Father Aristide's protectors encompass him. He heard Mama scream, "Grab William!" as she clutched his brother's arm and dragged him toward the front of the church, towards the door that was used by the priests. His brother reached back to William, but a throng of bodies pushed between them. He saw his brother's head retreat farther from where he was still seated. He heard his mother scream again but could see her no longer.

He looked to his left. His father was slumped away from him, dark liquid trailing from his ear. William sat. Alone. Untouched. In-between. Somehow the chaos didn't swallow him. So he waited. He looked down at his untied black shoe, swinging his foot up and down in front of him. The thought that he couldn't wait until his feet could touch the floor like his brother's passed through his mind.

After what seemed like hours, he realized that it was getting more difficult to breathe. The gap was closing. Screams continued around him, and although he knew the commotion had not settled, he felt a sudden urge to seek a safer place. The stone altar at the front of the church beckoned to him. A purple banner adorned with gold pomegranates hung from the altar's front declaring in red Creole lettering:

Ou pare yon tab pou mwen devan je tout lènmi m' yo.
You prepare a table before me in the presence of my enemies.

William could not read, yet he knew the words were for him. No one bothered him as he crawled beneath the stone, shielded by the banner, and curled his knees into his chest. He hugged them tightly. The incense thurible had taken shelter under there as well, dropped by the fleeing priest. He slowly realized how very hot it was. He had coals in his chest, scalding him from within. Orange blaze surrounded him on all sides. No longer able to bear the attempts to breathe, he pushed his nose into the small opening of the thurible. It, too, was hot.

    I'll close my eyes and sleep, he thought, as frankincense filled his head.

Sam's ears pounded with the slap of his shoes on the pavement. Even through a crowd of people, he could snake his way expertly along, as if on an invisible track that only he could see. He knew Polo was close behind—he sensed it—but he also knew he would be the victor. This was his day, and Sam would neither slow nor quit until he reached the step of Elena's boutik. He arrived a full ten seconds ahead of Polo.

"Ha! You run like a girl!" Sam called happily as Polo slowed to a stop in front of the shop. "Hope you brought some money."

"Boys, boys," Elena scolded with a smile on her face. "You race like demons let out of a box! If you use all your energy, who will help me carry this garbage to the corner?" She swept her hand at the pile of boxes and bags of trash in front of the store.

"We can do it, Miss Elena," Sam promised. "Come on, Polo!"

Three trips back and forth to the garbage field were all it took, and Elena treated them to Coca-Colas and gave each boy his very own bag of nuts. Polo got off easy this time; the loser of the race home from school was supposed to buy the nuts, but Sam didn't mind. Neither boy could even remember the last time Elena accepted their money.

"Guess what, Miss Elena?" Sam asked, leaning against the doorframe as he shook the empty soda can upside down above his mouth.

"What?" she responded absently, straightening a rack of

brightly colored scarves.

"Next week I take my test!" The pride in Sam's voice could not be missed.

That got Elena's attention. She darted over and squeezed him tightly. "Samféyo! That is remarkable! This calls for chocolate!" She pulled a bar from the shelf and broke it into three pieces.

She was right. Making it through primary school was no small feat for a Haitian. The *examen* was the final step. Many of Sam's classmates attended school sporadically; finances, sickness, the need to care for little ones—all trumped education when it came down to it. Sam was one of the few whose papa sent him to school above doing other things. When Sam's mother died in childbirth, Eduard Bernard decided that he would ensure an education for his only son. Some of Sam's classmates were also sixteen years old, and still would not take the exam this year.

"Miss Elena, I am going to take the exam *next* year," Polo offered suggestively, hoping for more chocolate.

Elena smiled at Polo and handed him a bag of nuts to take home to his Ma. "And when you do, we will celebrate again!"

Sam and Polo waved goodbye to Elena and headed down the dirt path that lead to their neighborhood. Elena's store sat at the end of rue Lasségue; it was the last named street before the dirt paths began. Compared to Americans, Sam and his papa were poor—*who in Haiti isn't?*—but they had a small plot of land, a house built from cinderblock, and because Papa had a steady job, starvation wasn't a daily threat, the way it was for many others. They made do. Polo, on the other hand, had six siblings and a mother who spent every waking moment fighting to survive. Sam and Polo bumped fists and Polo trotted off. Sam picked up his own pace. He had a few minutes to visit with Jourdain before Papa arrived home from work.

"Alo, Jourdain!" Sam called through the screen door into Jourdain's house.

"Sam! Back here!" he heard in reply.

Sam walked around to the back of Jourdain's property.

From the road, Jourdain's home and land sat directly to the left of Sam's house. Jourdain was an entrepreneur by Haitian standards, who grew tobacco in his compound and sold his homemade cigars to tourists for five American dollars apiece. Last year, he employed Sam as a means to grow his business (and to help alleviate the persistent ache in his arthritic hands). At first, Sam's main job was to separate the tobacco leaves into three piles: leaves good for filler, leaves to use for binding, and leaves for wrapping. As Sam's eye for leaf quality developed and his fingers became nimbler, he was given more responsibilities. Now, he could roll and bind a cigar as expertly as Jourdain himself.

"Have a seat," Jourdain suggested.

The workbench creaked with Sam's weight. A modest stack of large dried leaves was piled between them. Jourdain methodically took one and slit the vein from its center. Inspection of each half determined which of the three uses it would have. The leaves had been hanging in Jourdain's drying barn for the past seven weeks. Sam knew this because he had harvested and bundled them in September. There was no one part of the cigar-making process that Sam liked better than another. It was all fulfilling. But the exchange of American dollars for cigars was definitely the part Sam liked the best.

"This was a good batch," Sam said, taking his own leaf and cutting tool to get to work. "Hardly any of the leaves had holes or tears."

"Yes," Jourdain agreed. "There are still six bundles hanging. They all look strong. Maybe we will charge six dollars each for these."

"Whatever you think best," Sam replied. "Last weekend Chindo had a table outside the airport, and his sign said ten dollars!"

Jourdain whistled. "I bet he went home with more cigars than he sold."

Sam shrugged. "He made some sales. But I went *inside* the airport to catch the blanc before they even got outside."

Jourdain smiled. "That's why I like you, Sam! You think

like a businessman. Like me."

"So will you take me to DR with you next weekend then?"

Once each month, Jourdain packed his truck and traveled to the Dominican Republic to sell boxes of cigars to store owners that he developed relationships with. He didn't publicize it, for fear of hurting his business in Haiti, but Jourdain was half-Dominican. His mother worked as a cleaning woman for one of the all-inclusive resorts near the Caribbean. His father, who had also been into tobacco growing, had met her while on a business trip. Once Jourdain was born, his mother let his father raise him on the family land in Port-au-Prince. Both of his parents were gone now, and because of his hard work, Jourdain's home was a veritable mansion compared to the shanties around him. An electric pole at the back of the property supplied power for both his home and the drying barn. Many years ago, before Sam was even born, Jourdain spliced the electricity to run to Sam's home as well. This made Sam and his dad much more fortunate than others in their neighborhood.

"Let's see what Eduard says," Jourdain answered.

"Oh, Papa will let me!" Sam said confidently. "I am going to be seventeen next month."

"Aren't you graduating primary school soon?"

"Yes! And after that, I will go to secondary school. Maybe then even to college. Did you know, the schools in the United States will pay you to go to college if you can play baseball?" When he was a mere five years old, Sam had proclaimed himself the biggest baseball fan in Haiti.

Jourdain raised his eyebrows. "Have you been practicing?"

"Oh, I've been practicing," Sam said slyly. He reached into his pocket and retrieved a cream-colored baseball with bright red stitches. "Papa bought me a new baseball last week. He said it was an early graduation gift. Polo and I throw around every day before school. We found some new kids to play with us on weekends. They aren't very good, but it's better than nothing. My arm is getting stronger."

"Good. You practice, keep going to school, and maybe you can kiss this place goodbye one day. Your arm will also get stronger if you keep working the tobacco leaves." Jourdain nodded to the pile. "Let's get these finished before your pa comes home."

They finished the pile and placed the deveined leaves back in the barn. Tomorrow they would begin cutting the filler. Sam made it home in time to warm the beans for dinner and have the pot ready when his papa came in the door. He went to bed that night with his belly full and dreaming about baseball.

The next week Sam took and passed his final primary school exam. He could not wait to share the news with Papa. When Papa came home from work, he found the dinner table set.

"Se bon majne!" Papa noted as he came through the door and smelled the goat stew warming on the stove.

"Yes, Papa! Tonight, we celebrate!" Sam said proudly. "Look!"

Sam brought Papa the thin white paper with bold black lettering declaring Samféyo Bernard as a graduate of primary school. Papa held it up to the light and studied it.

"Samféyo," he said at last, "this is wonderful. Congratulations, my son!"

Sam scooped the stew into bowls and placed sliced bread on the table. They sat together at their small two-chair table, and Papa closed his eyes to pray.

"Bondye gran. Bondye bon. Nou di Bondye mèsi pou manje sa a. Amèn."

"Amèn," Sam agreed. "How was work, Papa?"

Papa shrugged. "It was a one hundred twenty-five day."

One hundred twenty-five days were good days. Sam's father worked in the Rawlings baseball factory. Every baseball used in the Major League was hand-stitched together right there in Port-au-Prince. Papa's quota was to sew a minimum of one hundred twenty-five balls each day.

"That's good, Papa," Sam said. He noticed, though, that

Papa seemed heavy-hearted. "What's wrong?"

"Ah, another ball factory closed down," Papa said. "Last summer all of the American companies said over and over that they had no plans to leave Haiti. Pfft! Mantè! Liars!"

"Is it Rawlings?" Sam asked nervously.

"No. Not yet. I worry though, Sam. It is a matter of time. Our government has the American businessmen in an uproar. I saw the news down at Ricardo's. Avril is no better than Namphy. It makes them all nervous. And I am sure their new American president won't help us any more than the old one did."

"They have a new president?" Sam asked.

"Yes. Their election was two weeks ago. Mr. George Bush takes over in the new year."

"Will we ever get to vote for a president?" Sam wondered.

"Mwen pa konnen," Papa answered. "I do not know. But I hope one day it will work the way it should. I just wish the American businesses would see that we Haitians can do so much more."

"Papa, when I go to the United States to play baseball, I will make sure I tell the president about Haiti," Sam promised.

Papa smiled. "Let's get you through secondary school first, Samféyo."

Secondary school was not scheduled to begin until the end of January. Sam did not mind, as this gave him more time to work with Jourdain and to play ball. Papa agreed to let him accompany Jourdain on the December sales call to the Dominican. On the first Sunday in December, they loaded the cigar boxes behind the front seat of Jourdain's pickup truck. Haitian men—and sometimes women—were always looking for a ride to the border, so it did not take Sam long to get the word around Port-au-Prince that Jourdain was making the trip. Sam had twelve people lined up by eight o'clock in the morning. Sam collected the cash, and Jourdain let him keep one fourth of it. The fee Jourdain was left with more than covered what he needed for gas and any unexpected expenses that a drive across Haitian roads could bring. It wasn't uncommon to blow a tire (or two). Jourdain also relied on the passenger fees to cover the border guard bribe money.

"Ready?" Jourdain asked Sam, who had taken up the shotgun spot.

"Yes, sir!" Sam beamed from ear to ear. This was the most exciting thing that he could remember. Papa had taken him to Jacmel when he was younger to visit an uncle, but the memory was faint. The truck banged and rattled its way out of Port-au-Prince and along Route 8.

The lushness of the greenery was such a contrast to the dirty city streets that Sam could hardly believe this was Haiti. Rich, deep emerald leaves shone from the trees like they were polished with a spit cloth. When they stopped to remove a large branch from the road, Sam pulled one of the shiny green leaves off to study it.

"Why don't we have colors like this in Port-au-Prince?" he asked Jourdain once they were back in the truck.

"We do. The tobacco leaves we grow are green," Jourdain answered.

"I don't mean *our* plants. Of course our plants are green, we work hard on them. I mean the trees. Why don't the trees grow? Out here, the trees are doing just fine all on their own. Where are our trees?"

"Sam, tell me how we plant tobacco seeds," Jourdain instructed.

"What?" Sam asked.

"How do we plant the seeds? What do we do?"

"Umm. Well, first we clean the dirt. We take away any junk that's blown in. Then we rake it so it's not packed down all tight and stuff. Then we scatter the seeds across the top of the soil. Then we wait."

"What do we wait for?"

"To see which seeds will germinate." Sam was proud of himself for remembering the scientific word that Jourdain had taught him last summer.

"Why don't we push the seeds down into the dirt?"

"Because the seeds need light in order to sprout their shoots. But Jourdain, what does this—?"

"Just answer me! What do we do when they start to grow?"

Sam sighed. "We make sure the plants are not too close together. We move them someplace else if they are."

"Bon! You have been paying attention. Now here's the lesson. Sam, the people of Haiti are like tobacco seeds that no one cares for. No one removes the trash when it blows in. It stays put. Dirty. The government presses us down into the dirt, so all of our light is blocked out by their corrupt ways. Anyone who tries to bring light into Haiti is shut down, shut up, or shot. Our people can't grow because we are all bunched up together. We can't get out, either. The conditions get worse and worse and nobody—*no-bo-dy*—is doing a thing about it. Our trees don't grow healthy because our *people* can't grow healthy. There's no room. No light. Just trash and more trash. We can't get someplace else." Jourdain wiped the sweat from his forehead with his pocket bandana.

They rode in silence the rest of the way to the border, then continued on to Barahona. Sam smoothed his thumb over the slick surface of the leaf. He would get out. *He had to.* Education and baseball would lead him to his someplace else.

From a business vantage, the day was a success. After five delivery stops, Jourdain announced they had one more stop to make. La Fleur Boutique, he explained, was always his last stop of the trip. As Jourdain turned into the narrow alley behind a row of storefronts, Sam held his breath, expecting to hear the scrape of the side mirrors on the brick walls. But Jourdain expertly steered between the buildings and slid into a small parking spot behind a brightly painted lime and orange store.

"Jourdain! We don't have any more cigars," Sam said with concern. They'd delivered all they brought to the other shop owners.

"It's OK. Take some of your money and grab something

to eat," Jourdain suggested, as he got out of the truck. "The beach is across the road to the right. There are all kinds of grub huts. I need about an hour, and then I'll meet you back here." He winked at Sam and slipped into the back entrance of the store.

Sam stared in dumb silence at the swirly-girly lettering on the back door of the shop. The penny finally dropped. "Oh!" he said aloud. He snickered. He got out of the pickup and walked down the alley. At the crossroads, he spotted a silver food truck. "Chimi Burger," he read from the large black sign. The saliva that filled his mouth told him he would search no further for his lunch.

The burger bun had no hope of containing the mounds of onions and cabbage spilling out from its sides. Sam studied the meaty sandwich for a full minute before deciding how to tackle it. He finally scooped it up with his hands, opened his mouth as wide as he'd ever opened, and bit into the juicy deliciousness. Sauce dripped from the corners of his lips as his eyes widened with pleasure.

"Se sa!" he cried. "This is incredible!" He chased the burger down with a bottle of water.

It did not take him long to finish. Still licking the sauce from his fingers, Sam headed down the golden sandy beach. He took the baseball from his pocket, tossing it high in the air and catching it as he walked. It was thrilling to see the expanse of the open blue sky above his head. He tried to see if he could throw the ball high enough so as to lose sight of it. Even when he thought he lost it, his eye was drawn to the falling orb like a magnet.

"Yo man! Wanna play? We need a ninth," a voice called out in Spanish.

Sam looked up. A Latino boy wearing long shorts and a baseball cap called to him from the grass where the sand ended. He waved Sam over. Jourdain spoke Spanish to Sam as often as he spoke Creole. Sam had picked it up quickly when he was young, and he used it when peddling Jourdain's cigars. He was glad for it now.

"Quires que juegue?" Sam asked.

"Yes! We want you to play! Come on!" The kid held out his hand. "Arturo."

"Sam." They shook hands, and Sam followed him onto a crude ball diamond where seven players were scattered across the field. Another group was off to the side of the batter's box.

"This is Sam," Arturo called out to the guys. A chorus of *hellos* rang out around him.

"Man, do you have a glove?" someone asked.

"Nah, but I'll be alright. I can play without a glove," Sam assured.

Another boy whistled. "Whew! No glove! The kid's got cojones!" Several laughs.

"OK, Sam," Arturo pointed. "Right field."

Sam trotted out to the shallow right field, his heart pounding in his chest. The pitcher wound up and threw his version of a fastball. The kid wasn't bad. After two fouls and a strike, the batter knocked one high to left field. The fielder initially caught it, then the ball fell to the grass. Whoops from the other team brought their batter all the way around to second base.

The next batter grounded out to the short stop. The third popped one high in Sam's direction. All eyes were on the kid with no glove. Sam's left hand stretched above his head. He looked through his spread fingers into the sky to watch the ball. He knew it would hurt—he actually had *not* caught such a high pop fly bare-handed before—but his desire to show off for these fellow ball players outweighed the pain of the sting.

"Woo woo woo!" his team called out as the ball stayed put right where it landed. In Sam's hand.

Sam never had so much fun. He caught four more pop flies and threw out two runners at home plate. His palm throbbed like the devil, and he lost all track of time, but after the third inning played, he noticed Jourdain sitting on the hood of his truck in the dirt parking lot, watching. He waved, and Jourdain waved back. When the game was over, there were handshakes all around. No one said the score aloud, but Sam knew his team won eight to six.

Sam talked Jourdain's ears off about the game the whole way back to Port-au-Prince, stopping only briefly as they picked up some passengers at the border for a ride back to Haiti's capital.

"This is the greatest day ever," Sam declared.

CHAPTER 2

Even the crow of the rooster did not wake Sam the next morning. He might have stayed in bed all day, but his bladder forced him out. After cleaning his sore hands and splashing water on his face, Sam realized there were noises coming from Papa's room. Papa should have been at work.

"Papa?" Sam inquired, pushing the door open. Sam gently pulled the sheet back to see Papa's face. Even without touching him, Sam could feel the fever radiating from Papa's body. Papa was awake, but his unfocused eyes showed that he was not well. Sam got a small cloth from the kitchen and soaked it in cold water. The cool cloth across Papa's head would not be enough to break this fever.

"I'll get some aspirin, Papa. Be right back," Sam promised.

Papa's bicycle got Sam to Elena's in record time. Sam barged through the shop door.

"Miss Elena!" he called frantically. "Elena!"

She emerged from the back. "What is it, Sam?"

"Papa has a fever. Do you have any aspirin?"

"Oh, my. Yes!"

She went to a shelf behind her register which held various first-aid items. She selected a small yellow bottle and handed it to Sam. He took three hundred gourdes from his pocket and placed them on the counter. She pushed half of the money back at him. She also grabbed two water bottles from her cooler and placed them in a small bag.

"Go!" she ordered. "Take care of Eduard."

Papa was asleep when Sam returned. He roused long

enough to allow Sam to slide two aspirin between his dry lips, then he gulped down a full bottle of water.

"Thank you, son," he managed to say, and he lay back down on his bed.

Except for a brief trip to the bathroom and to take more aspirin, Papa slept the rest of the day. Before going to bed, Sam checked on him one last time. He was still feverish.

"Sam," Papa said. "You have to go to the factory tomorrow."

"What?" Sam asked. "You mean the baseball factory?"

"Yes," Papa said. "If I miss more than one day, they will give up my chair."

Papa had been sick before over the years; he'd never lost his job.

"After only one day?" Sam couldn't believe it.

Papa nodded. "Every morning there have been men lined up outside the plant. Men from the baseball factories that have closed. They are vultures. Waiting. Looking for open jobs. Last week three people were out sick. They all lost their jobs to the vultures. The boss made an announcement that if you miss more than one day, you're out."

"Ay! Papa! I don't know how to sew a baseball," Sam lamented.

"Sure, you do. I taught you," Papa said, referring to the baseball shell and red thread that he'd brought home last summer. He had shown Sam how to expertly create the one hundred eight double stitches needed to secure the two pieces of cowhide together over the shell. He'd made Sam do it over and over until he could bury the first and last stitches perfectly.

"I haven't practiced!" Sam said. "They'll fire me!"

"Go get the ball," Papa said calmly. "And reach into that box over there and get the thread."

Sam located the practice ball from the previous summer, the spool of waxy red thread, two needles, a tape measure, and scissors. He pulled a dining chair alongside Papa's bed.

"How many inches do you cut?" Papa asked.

"'Eighty-eight inches of thread." Sam surprised himself

by remembering the answer.

"Yes. Now, at the factory, the thread is on two big spools. One for each needle. You won't cut the length, you just have to know it by touch. That's why I make you cut it here at home. If you use more or less than eighty-eight inches, your stitches won't be pulled right. Understand?"

"I think so," Sam said cautiously. He measured and cut the thread.

"Good. Now thread the needles. The balls at the factory will be a little bit sticky. They coat them in glue to help the leather stay in place when you sew. For now, squeeze the ball between your knees to hold it steady."

Sam's hands miraculously conjured up the memory of the hours of practicing Papa enforced on him last summer. He recalled how to hide the first stitch by pushing the needles first through the stringed core of the ball, then he crisscrossed his needles through the holes. After just a little guidance from Papa how to bury the last stitch, Sam breathed easier. He did remember.

Papa closed his eyes. "I am tired, Sam. You will do fine. When you get there, ask for Michel. He will help you."

Sam did not sleep that night. The cows mooing outside, the goats bleating in the distance, and the threat of an angry boss screaming, "You're fired!" kept his mind from resting. What if he lost Papa's job? What would they do?

Before the rooster even crowed, Sam had washed, ate a bit of bread, checked on Papa, dispensed more aspirin, and then left home, steering the bicycle in the direction of the baseball plant. It was a twenty-minute ride, during which Sam replayed all of Papa's final instructions.

"The break bell will sound at 10:30. You have fifteen minutes. There is a shared bathroom between the different sections. Use the one by section ten. It is less crowded. At 12:40 the lunch bell will sound. You have thirty minutes for lunch. There are food vendors in the market across the road. Drink water. You'll need it. By lunchtime you should have around fifty

balls finished. If not, speed up. Another bell will sound at 3:00. Fifteen-minute break. The bell at 5:00 signals the end of the day. If you are not finished with the balls, you may stay until six, but no more."

The sight of the dark brown building looming ahead made Sam's stomach queasy as he rounded the last corner. The word Rawlings in colossal red script on the rooftop sign stared at him, as if it knew he did not belong. He hurriedly parked Papa's bicycle with the dozen or so others and scurried inside door three, just as Papa suggested. Although the building was the largest he'd ever stepped inside, he had no problem locating section eleven, and not a single person stopped him nor asked what he was doing there. He was early enough that only a few of the job seekers lurked outside the gates, and there were several women already seated at their sewing stations. A man walked past him, and Sam tapped his shoulder.

"Eskize m?" Sam asked quietly. "Are you Michel?"

"Yes," the man answered. "Who are you?"

"I am Samféyo Bernard. Eduard's son," Sam said. It felt clandestine.

Michel raised an eyebrow in question.

"My papa is sick. I am to take his chair, so the vultures do not steal his job," Sam explained.

Michel laughed and patted Sam on the back. "Ha-ha! You sound like Eduard! Come, I will show you where to sit."

Papa's workstation was right next to Michel's. They were surrounded by women.

"Why so many women?" Sam asked, still whispering.

"Sewing is mostly women's work," Michel explained. "There are just a few of us men in this section, but it is alright. We get our jobs done."

It didn't really answer Sam's question, but it would have to do. Michel pointed to a large barrel next to Sam's table. It was filled with balls of tightly wound white string. They were the balls that Sam would cover with leather and stitch.

"The barrel contains your quota for the day. The gluers get here very early and prepare the balls for the leather. They place them next to the tables so you can get right to work when you come in. You have to go get your piles of leather, though. Come."

Near the front of section eleven was a long worktable. A woman dispensed stacks of leather, precut in the oblong figure eight pattern that would wrap around the sticky string balls.

"They come in stacks of fifty. Two for each ball. You sign out here." He showed Sam a clipboard with numbered lines. "Eduard is number twenty-seven. Always sign on that line and use Eduard's name."

Sam took a stack of leathers and signed.

"Bon. They expect you to sign out five stacks each day for your quota."

They carried their leathers back to their workstations.

"After you finish sewing the ball, you put it in this barrel." Michel indicated an empty barrel on the other side of the worktable. He placed a hand on Sam's shoulder. "Do not worry, Samféyo. You will be fine. This is not as difficult as it sounds."

Sam managed to give him a weak smile and took his seat at his station. The needles were neatly laid in a small divot in the wood. Sam threaded the waxy red thread and took a deep breath. Retrieving a ball from the barrel and placing it between the spring-loaded holder was easy! He got his threaded needles and then realized he forgot to put the leather on the ball.

"Darn!" he muttered. He released the ball and wrapped two of the leathers around it. He placed it back in the cradle and tried again.

"Push the needle through the ball. Now the other. Cross them. Go through the hole. Pull. Now the other. Pull. Not too tight. Bon. Now again. Make it snug. Now again."

"Samféyo" Michel hissed.

"Wi?"

"Hush!"

Sam hadn't realized he was talking out loud. His face reddened, and he went back to work. The final stitch gave him the most trouble, but after a couple of tries, he was pretty happy with it. He showed it to Michel for inspection.

"Not bad!" Michel said. He pointed out a couple of areas where Sam could have pulled the stitch tighter. "You probably used two inches too much. I wouldn't put this one in the bin," Michel warned. "They will reject it."

"What do I do with it?" Sam wondered.

"Put it in the reject bucket under your table. If you have time at the end, you take it apart and fix it," Michel said.

Sam noticed the orange bucket beneath the workstation. With sadness, he placed the ball inside and determined that would be the only ball in the bucket that day!

He showed his next four attempts to Michel for inspection and all passed scrutiny. Confidence high, Sam worked right through the first break and all the way until lunchtime without stopping. When the lunch bell rang, he still had fourteen leathers in his second pile, so he knew he was not yet at fifty balls.

"Forty-three!" Sam said with disappointment. "Not counting my reject."

He considered working through lunch, but he knew he would need sustenance. Across the street from the factory was a small convenience store, much like Elena's. He purchased two bottles of water, a mango, and a bag of pistachios. He ate quickly and returned to his workstation ten minutes early. He got right back to sewing.

At five o'clock he still had ten balls to complete. When the six o'clock closing bell sounded, there were four leathers still in the pile.

"Time to go!" the floor manager called from the doorway. The few remaining workers immediately put their needles down and stood to leave. Sam noticed they left their unfinished leathers in a neat pile on their tables, so he did the same.

The bike ride home took every ounce of energy Sam had. His fingers ached around the handlebars, and his legs pedaled in protest. Elena was outside her shop as Sam rode by.

"Samféyo!" she called.

He stopped. "Wi? I am exhausted, Miss Elena. I worked in the factory today so Papa could rest."

"I know, Sam. I went by to check on Eduard. He told me. I gave him more aspirin."

"Thank you. Is he feeling better?" Sam asked hopefully.

Elena shook her head. "I am afraid not. His fever was high again. I made him some broth so he would not dehydrate. He is not well. Here." She handed him a brown bag. "For your dinner."

Sam took the bag and tried to smile. "Mesi."

"You are a good son, Samféyo," she called after him as he pedaled away.

Sam toyed with whether or not to tell Papa that he didn't make the quota. He knew lying was wrong, yet he did not want worry to make Papa feel worse.

"How did it go?" Papa asked sleepily when Sam came into his room.

"Michel was very helpful," Sam said truthfully. "He showed me everything to do."

"Bon," Papa said. He did not ask any other questions but rolled over and went back to sleep. Sam was grateful. He ate his meal and fell onto his bed, nearly asleep before his head hit the pillow.

A bright yellow note greeted him on his worktable the next morning. "Twenty-five" was scrawled across it in bright red lettering.

"What is this?" Sam asked Michel.

"That, my friend, is the number of baseballs you were short of quota yesterday."

"Twenty-five! But I only had four leathers left!" Sam protested.

"Then you must have had twenty-three rejects," Michel explained. "They go through the barrel every night. You have until Friday to make up the yellow notes or else they take money out of your pay."

"Help me, Jesus!" Sam exclaimed. "How am I going to make one hundred fifty balls today?"

"Hang in there, Sam. You can do it."

Sam worked nonstop all day. By six o'clock, he only had twelve balls left to sew. The next morning, however, the yellow note read "seventeen."

Michel patted his back. "Not too shabby! You'll get there."

By Friday at four-thirty, Sam—with more than a little help from Michel—had finished the day's quota plus all of his make-up balls. On payday, the workers lined the payroll waiting area while the final batches of balls were inspected. There were five different payroll windows, behind which sat the women who dispensed the wages once they received verification from the managers. Sam held his breath until he heard Papa's name called.

"Eduard Bernard!" the woman at Window One yelled. She handed Sam an envelope. "One day absent. Four days' pay," she stated flatly.

"Thank you," Sam said, taking the envelope through the small opening. His hand shook as he peeked inside. Twenty-four American dollars! He waved the envelope at Michel, smiling.

Michel gave him a thumbs up. "See you next week!"

On his bicycle ride home, Sam hoped there would not be a "next week" for him at the baseball factory. Although there had been no change in Papa's condition, Sam prayed that the weekend would bring a turn-around.

Early Saturday morning, Sam elbowed his way through the brightly colored muumuus of the Haitian peasant women in the marketplace to acquire what he thought would be a hearty breakfast for Papa. He procured six fresh eggs, a couple of oranges, ground coffee, and thick cream. By eight-thirty he was back home, frying the eggs with Spam that he managed to cut into thick chunks. Papa ate in the kitchen, but the effort wasn't easy, as the fever was still present. The scrambled eggs were good for them both. Sam tucked Papa back into bed with more aspirin and headed to Jourdain's.

"Alo zanmi!" Jourdain greeted Sam from the shed. "What are you doing here? Don't you want to find Polo and play some baseball today?"

"Of course I do!" Sam answered. "But I need to work. We have rolling to do today, yes?"

"Yes. Some rolling. But I would rather you take cigars to the airport. A plane from Miami lands at eleven. Sell them for six American dollars and you keep fifty cents each."

"How many do you have?" Sam asked.

"Forty."

Sam did the math. "Wow! That's twenty dollars!"

It was almost as much as he'd made working four days in the factory. But cigar-selling days were too few and far between to be counted on as regular income. His daily work for Jourdain only earned him twenty-five cents an hour. It was decent earnings for a teenaged boy, but clearly wouldn't suffice as the sole income for him and Papa, should it come to that. If Papa didn't get better, Sam would have no choice but to keep going to the factory.

Sam put the cigars in a shoulder bag and left for the airport. He didn't dare take Papa's bicycle, as there would be no safe place to stash it, so he jogged in order to make it there by ten-thirty to get a prime location for sales.

Chindo, another cigar peddler, had his table set up near the taxi cab stands. He didn't see Sam arrive, so Sam slipped into the airport and took up a position near the money exchange booth. In general, the airport security guards left peddlers like Sam alone unless a citizen complained. By ten after eleven, passengers began to mill around, waiting for their luggage. Sam held up a couple of cigars and said in near-perfect English, "Good Haitian cigars! Only six dollars!"

Sam had a system. He'd catch the eye of a blanc, then casually turn his head, as if he didn't really care. He'd hold the cigars up in the other direction and call out, "Haitian cigars! Hand rolled with the finest tobacco!"

The blanc would almost always come over to see what he had. Once they smelled the tobacco, they always bought. Within two quick hours, Sam was sold out. Before leaving the airport, he took his cut—twenty dollars—and exchanged it for Haitian gourdes. He would have liked to keep American cash, but he needed gourdes for the marketplace. Haitians who waved around American dollars were often found in the alleyways, mugged.

On the way home, he first stopped in the Giant Supermarket for their kitchen necessities. The more important stop was to a small pharmacy.

"Do you have any antibiotics?" he inquired of the man in the white coat.

"What is the problem?" The pharmacist leaned casually against the counter.

"It's my papa. He has a fever that has been coming and going all week. He is tired all the time. The fever gets really high."

"Ah," the pharmacist nodded. "It is possible he has some kind of infection. Are you giving him aspirin?"

"Several each day! They help a little, but the fever always comes back."

"OK. Then yes, you should try antibiotics." Behind his counter stood a dense wooden cabinet which he opened using a small key that dangled from a ball chain around his neck. He removed a large container and counted out fourteen impressively-sized white pills.

"Give him one in the morning and one at night. Every day for seven days. Make sure he has something in his stomach before he takes the pill." He dropped the pills into a small baggie and handed it to Sam. "Five hundred gourdes."

"Mesi!" Sam said gratefully. He paid the man and hurried off.

Sam gave Jourdain the money from the cigar sales before going home to Papa, who was feeling significantly worse than he was at breakfast. Sam made him a goat cheese sandwich and presented it to him, along with the first white pill.

"I can't eat this," Papa argued. "I am not hungry."

"Papa, please. You have to have food in your stomach to take the pill or you will get sicker."

"I don't need fancy drugs. I'll be fine." Papa turned over in bed and Sam was left looking at his back.

"I already bought them. They were expensive. Please take it." Sam sat on the edge of the bed. He rubbed Papa's back the way Papa would rub his when Sam was sick.

Papa looked over his shoulder at his pleading son. He loved that boy enough to choke down a goat cheese sandwich, followed up with a pill big enough for a cow. Sam said a prayer to Jesus that the pills would work quickly.

CHAPTER 3

Day by day the strength returned to Papa's legs as the antibiotics worked their magic on the fever. Sam sewed his quota in baseballs in his second week and triumphantly brought home thirty dollars the following Friday. What made him even more thrilled was that he had no rejects all week.

"No rejects?" Papa couldn't believe it. "It took me a month before I made it a week with no rejects. I knew you could do it."

"Papa, why didn't you tell me about the reject bucket and the yellow notes?" Sam asked.

Papa patted Sam's knee. "If I had, what would you have done differently?"

Sam thought about it. "Probably nothing."

Papa shook his head. "No, I think you would have had an even more miserable first day because all you would have worried about were the reject balls. How many did you sew that first day?"

"All but two."

"Wow! See? If you were worried about rejects and yellow notes, I bet you would not have done half that many. Besides," he smiled. "I knew Michel would take care of you."

"Thanks, Papa."

"I am feeling stronger, Samféyo. I think on Monday I will be ready to go back to work."

"That's good," Sam agreed, "because school starts in three weeks."

Papa smiled. "I am proud of you. Your mama would have

been proud, too."

Papa rarely mentioned Sam's mama. When Sam was younger, he asked about her all of time. But questions made Papa's eyes cloud over and heavy sadness fall upon him like rain. So eventually Sam had quit asking. Today, however, Papa's eyes shone. Sam took a risk and ventured a question.

"Did Mama go to school?" It was something Sam often wondered.

Papa nodded. "She did. She finished her primary and her secondary schooling. She planned to become a nurse."

"A nurse?" This was unexpected.

"She was very smart, your mama." His countenance trailed away, and Sam knew not to ask anything else. As Sam turned to clean up the kitchen, he heard Papa add, "She would have made a wonderful nurse." Sam smiled. He felt a connection to her that he'd never felt before.

The weekend flew past. Jourdain was busy with other things, so Sam spent Saturday playing baseball with Polo and some of the other neighborhood kids. None of them were as good as Sam, but even bad baseball was better than no baseball. By Monday morning, Papa declared himself ready to return to work. He hugged Sam extra tightly before he left.

"Thank you, son," Papa said.

"For what?"

"For taking care of me. You are much wiser than your sixteen years."

"Papa! I am going to be seventeen this week."

"I know. You are a young man," Papa said wistfully. Sam thought he detected a tear in Papa's eye. "Anyway, always know I am proud of you."

"Thanks, Papa." As Papa headed off on his bicycle, Sam called out after him, "No rejects!"

"No rejects!" Papa called back with a fist pump in the air, and he turned out of their yard onto the dirt path.

After finishing his beans and mango breakfast, Sam went

next door. There were more plants ready to harvest and piles of filler ready to be bound. Jourdain set him on the careful work of binding. It was tricky business. Bind too tightly, and the cigar won't draw for the smoker. A loose cigar will be difficult to keep lit or will unravel before the buyer can smoke it. Although the blanc who bought at the airport would likely never be return customers, Jourdain knew the importance of keeping his Dominican clients happy with his product. Complaints hurt business. Sam took the process very seriously because Jourdain took the process very seriously.

Sam had just put the floury paste on his fortieth cigar of the day, when he heard Elena calling his name.

"Over here!" he shouted. He secured the edge of the binding leaf.

Elena ran into Jourdain's yard. "Oh, Sam! Come quickly!" she cried frantically. "It's Eduard!"

Sam jumped up from the bench, knocking the newly rolled cigar to the dirt. "What happened?"

"Just come!" She hurried back to her moto, which sat idling in the dirt path. Sam followed and climbed on behind her.

"Where is he?" Jourdain asked.

"Hospital!" she barked over the engine noise. "There has been an accident."

"I'll meet you there," Jourdain promised, calling after the moto as it agitated the dirt and they sped away.

Elena was one of the rare women who dared take a motorbike on the chaotic streets of Port-au-Prince. Hot tears poured from Sam's eyes as they zipped along the streets. He clung to her waist. *An accident?* His cheeks were sticky and wet when they pulled up at the hospital.

"What happened?" he asked her again as they entered the Emergency Room. Elena seemed not to hear him. She clutched his hand and pulled him along, eyes darting around the room. She stopped a passing nurse.

"Eskize m? Where is Eduard Bernard?" she asked.

"Surgery," the nurse replied. "The information desk is there." She pointed them toward another nurse who gave more news. It was not good. Papa was swiped by a car while riding his bicycle to work, and after he fell, a truck ran him over. He was able to give someone his name before he lost consciousness. It had taken all morning to find someone who recognized Papa's name and knew the approximate area of town where he lived. A man came asking about him in Elena's shop, and she took it from there.

"He was hit by a truck?" Sam repeated what they'd heard. "Oh, Papa!"

They sat in two small metal chairs and waited for surgery to be over. Sam sobbed on Elena's shoulder for a long time. At some point Jourdain arrived and relieved Elena so she could go check on her shop. She promised to return soon. Jourdain brought two Coca-Colas with him and they sipped while they waited. Every so often Jourdain would ask at the desk how things were going, but there was no new information. At five o'clock in the evening, a white doctor wearing blue scrubs came into the waiting room and called out Eduard's name.

"Yes, we are here," Jourdain answered. He and Sam stood shakily and walked over to the doctor.

"My name is Doctor Brown," the man said. "Are you Mr. Bernard's son?"

Sam nodded.

"Your father was in a very bad accident. The truck that hit him rolled over his leg, crushing his tibia, fibula, and kneecap. We had hoped we could save it, but I am very sorry, we could not."

"I don't understand," Sam said. "Save what?"

The doctor sighed sympathetically. "His leg. We could not save his leg. We had to amputate it just above his knee."

A wave of nausea swept over Sam. A sea of blurry blue fabric was the last thing he saw before passing out.

"Sam. Samféyo," Elena's gentle voice called to him. He opened his eyes, blinking in the pale light. Her cool hand was on his forehead.

"Where am I?" he whispered.

"You fainted. We are at the hospital."

Sam looked around. He'd been laid out on a pink sofa in the waiting room. Elena kneeled on the floor beside him. He saw Jourdain talking to the nurse at the information desk.

"Papa?" he asked Elena.

"When you are feeling better, we can go see him," Elena explained. "He is recovering from surgery."

"I want to see him."

She helped him stand. The activity around him felt distant. Papa had taken him last year to a movie at the Cine Triomphe. The movie was called *Predator* and starred a very large American actor who led a group of military fighters against an alien monster. It was Sam's first time in a movie theater, and he'd marveled at the gigantic screen that made him feel like he was a part of the actual movie, even though he wasn't. That is how he felt in the waiting room. Very small. He'd been plunked into movie that was happening to someone else. The noise was hollow, and the voices echoed in his head. The room started spinning.

"Elena," he croaked from his dry throat.

"Sit down," Elena said, and she caught Sam as he fell back onto the sofa. "We will wait longer."

Jourdain brought Sam another Coca-Cola. The sugar helped. When Sam was ready to walk, they flanked him, holding his elbows. Papa was in a recovery room that held a dozen or so other beds burdened with patients. Some moaned, some slept, some sat upright with glazed-over eyes. The three of them crowded around Papa's bed, which was enclosed by translucent yellow curtains. A padded green chair had been placed in front of the heart monitor, like a sad companion for the equipment. Papa's eyes were closed, and his torso covered with a velvet blanket. From the end of the bed, Sam softly placed a hand on Papa's left foot. As the awareness hit him that there was no right foot underneath the blanket, a sob broke from Sam's throat. He choked it back and went around near Papa's face.

"Papa," he whispered. "I'm here."

Papa's eyes fluttered and opened thinly. A very small smile formed on his closed lips.

"It's OK, Papa," Sam said. Then a flood of panic washed over him. He started talking rapidly. "I will go to work for you tomorrow, Papa. You won't need to worry about anything. I promise. Just please get better, OK? The vultures won't get your job. I swear it!"

Jourdain put a hand on Sam's back, which slowed Sam's talking. Papa's fingers reached for Sam's. As he clutched Papa's hand in both of his, Sam noticed for the first time how large his own hands were in comparison to Papa's. In fact, he hardly realized that he'd grown taller than Papa in these last few months. He noticed it now; Papa looked so small laying in the narrow hospital bed. Silent tears streamed down both faces. They didn't say anything. They didn't need to.

It was after midnight when Jourdain took Sam home. No matter what Jourdain said, Sam was insistent that he would go to Rawlings the next day. Jourdain slept over so he could drive Sam to work. Sam hadn't realized it yet, but Papa's bicycle would not be there for him to use.

"I will pick you up at five o'clock," Jourdain said as Sam got out of the truck at the baseball factory the next morning. "We will go to the hospital then."

Sam nodded and closed the door. He took a deep breath and went inside. The day was long and the baseballs boring. Sam's pace was good, and his final pile of leathers was gone by four forty-five. Jourdain was outside, waiting.

"Hungry?" he asked as Sam got in. He offered Sam a meat sandwich, which Sam gobbled down on the way to the hospital.

Papa was sitting up in bed when they arrived. Bruises covered his face, scrapes lined his arms, a gash sliced across his hand—Sam had noticed none of these things the night before. A tray of food sat untouched before him.

"Papa, you must eat!" Sam scolded.

"Eh, I don't want it," Papa said. "I am glad to see you,

though." He acknowledged Jourdain. "Thank you for taking care of my son."

Jourdain nodded in reply. "My pleasure, friend. Do not worry about anything."

"They are sending over a woman from the American Red Cross later this week to take measurements for an artificial leg. They said someone filled out the paperwork on my behalf. You wouldn't know anything about that, would you?" He raised an eyebrow at Jourdain.

Jourdain smiled. "Elena. She went to the humanitarian offices this morning. She found a company in Florida that works with the Red Cross. They make prosthetics for Haitians. She pleaded on behalf of you and Sam. She talked to the right person at the right time, I suppose. God's Will be done."

"Please thank her for me. They said as soon as the wound heals, I can be fitted with the new leg." Papa's tired voice trailed off.

"We will let you sleep, Papa," Sam said, kissing his cheek. "I will come see you tomorrow after work."

As they pulled up at Sam's house, Jourdain said, "Elena and I left something for you in the house."

"What is it?" Sam wondered.

"Go and see."

A shiny orange bicycle propped against the wall greeted Sam as he entered his lonely home. It sported a huge blue bow and a note that read, "Happy Birthday from Jourdain, Elena, and Papa."

Sam hugged his bicycle and brought it into his bedroom with him so he could stare at it as he fell asleep.

The tires on Sam's bicycle floated effortlessly over the dirt paths and bumpy pavement on his way to Rawlings the next day. He was feeling good, until he found a yellow note with the number eight on it on his workstation. He sighed and got to business. He sewed furiously, finishing fifty-eight good balls by lunchtime. He treated himself to an ice cream bar and Coca-Cola from the convenience store. Not the best meal choices, but *se lavi*, it was his birthday!

Michel stopped Sam as he was leaving at the end of the day. He handed Sam an envelope. Inside were ten American dollars.

"Michel! I cannot take this," Sam protested, offering it back to him.

"Take it. I am sure you need it," Michel pushed the envelope back to Sam. "When I first started here, I fell way behind in my quota. There were many, many days where I ended up more than thirty balls short. Your papa stayed after work all the time to help me get caught up so I would not lose my job. He is a good man. Please. Take it!"

Sam felt it was the right thing to do. "Are you sure?"

"Wi. Goodbye, Sam. See you tomorrow."

Sam pedaled to the hospital and parked his bicycle among the others. Sam's looked like a fancy BMW compared to the rusty frames on the other bikes. Sam knew he would have to get a lock for it. In Haiti there was a saying: "Everyone rides your bicycle." Bikes are stolen so much that they often end up coming back around to the original owner. The poor just keep stealing from the poor. Sam did not want everyone to ride his bicycle. He would get a lock tomorrow.

Inside the hospital things were much busier than on previous nights. A bus crash had the emergency room buzzing with activity. Sam wound his way through the maze of hallways and found Papa in the same place he was the day before.

"Bonswa, Papa," Sam said.

"Bonswa, Son," Papa replied quietly. "Happy birthday."

Sam kissed Papa's cheek. It was very warm. "Are you feeling alright?" he asked. "Your cheek is hot."

"Fever," Papa said, his voice raspy and dry. "I told the nurse. She said she would bring me some aspirin, but that was a couple of hours ago." His words were slurred. Something was wrong.

"I will find someone," Sam declared. He had to go all the way back to the emergency room before he found a nurse busily writing something on a clipboard. He felt this was important enough to interrupt.

"Eskize m? My father is feverish and needs some aspirin please."

"Mmm-hmm, I'll be right there," she said absently.

"Please, miss! He is burning up!" Sam cried loudly. A few faces turned their way.

This caused her to look up. "Your father is not the only one here! I will get to him as soon as I can."

Sam's eyes welled with tears. "Please. He's already lost his leg. He is in pain. He was feeling better, but now he is so hot."

"The amputee? Mr. Bernard has fever?" she clarified. Sam nodded. She went to another nurse and said something Sam couldn't hear. They both took off quickly toward Papa's room. Sam followed.

One of the nurses took his blood pressure while the other checked his temperature. Sam stood nearby, unable to stop his tears. Papa was sweating and his eyes were closed. His chest heaved up and down like a dog panting for breath. A doctor arrived, checked the chart, and began shouting orders.

"We need a complete blood count on this patient," he said to one nurse. To the other he said, "See if anyone is in surgery five. If not, begin prepping it. If so, find me a surgery room!" While the doctor snapped things into action, Sam slipped into a trance. The hope he'd felt when he arrived had left him. What would come in its place, Sam did not yet know.

The doctor noticed Sam standing there. "Are you his son? I suspect there may be an infection in his body somewhere. I am hoping it is not sepsis. Go to the waiting room. I will find you when I know more."

Sam kissed his father's face one more time. "I love you, Papa."

"I love you, Samféyo," Papa whispered thinly.

The waiting room was unbearably crowded and hot. A thunderstorm rolled in, and all of the people who'd been waiting outside were suddenly inside. Sam leaned against a wall and closed his eyes. He must have dozed off because the next thing knew someone was shaking his shoulder.

"Samféyo." It was Jourdain. "What are you doing out here? Where's Eduard?"

"Surgery," Sam said.

"What happened?"

"He got a fever. The doctor is worried there might be infection in his blood."

Sam began to weep again. Jourdain stayed with him. They eventually were able to find seats, and Coca-Cola was once again Sam's dinner.

At eight o'clock he heard Papa's name. A different doctor, this one a young black man in dark maroon scrubs, looked around the waiting room. Sam and Jourdain walked toward him.

"We are here for Eduard Bernard," Jourdain told the doctor.

"I am so sorry," the doctor said. "Mister Bernard has died. We tried to save him, but there was a blood infection. It spread through to all of his organs. We tried to transfuse the blood and stop the spread, but it was too late. He is gone."

CHAPTER 4
SIX WEEKS LATER

The large-screen television in Ricardo's Bar was the most popular spot in Port-au-Prince for locals to connect with sports-related news. Actually, Ricardo's was a hot-spot for *any* news, but politics were not spoken of aloud in Ricardo's. It was rumored that Ricardo was a cousin to Colonel Joseph Baguidy, a high-ranking member in the police force. Colonel Baguidy was, at one time, the head of the Recherches Criminelles but had been removed from his position under reports of serious human rights violations. His demotion was an act of goodwill by the police chief, merely to appease the Inter-American Commission on Human Rights, not really because he thought Baguidy did anything wrong. Baguidy maintained considerable control within the police force in Port-au-Prince, and no Haitian man nor woman wanted to cross his path.

Through his connections, Ricardo had secured a much-coveted satellite dish. The dish enabled him to bring the world into his bar, which had two distinct serving areas. Ricardo kept the tele in the front tuned to sports and sports news. Low to mid-class Haitian men could kick back, drink beer or rum, and talk about how nothing ever changed in their lives. Ricardo's more prominent customers were granted access to the back room where conversations were short and purposeful. Lives were often *permanently* changed as a result of those meetings.

Sam's papa made it a point to drop in to Ricardo's every two or three days to catch the sports and see what other gossip was going around. He'd share the sports information with Sam and the gossip with Elena. She often knew more than Eduard did and could fill in the gaps or correct any misinformation.

Papa's death created many voids for Sam, and the lack of sports news was one more reminder that he was gone forever.

An elaborate funeral was an impossibility for Sam. A funeral director approached them in the emergency room, not even ten minutes after the doctor told them that Papa had died, and offered to provide a decent burial in a plain wooden coffin for seven hundred fifty dollars. Sam was too shocked to speak, and Jourdain nearly punched the man in the face right there in the hospital. The doctor said they would hold the body in the morgue for twenty-four hours to give Sam time to make a decision. If he did not return, Papa's body would be sent to a mass grave with all of the other unclaimed dead.

The next morning, while a mostly-comatose Sam dragged himself to the baseball factory, Jourdain spoke with the caretaker for the cemetery where Sam's mama was buried. He agreed to open her grave and put Eduard in with her for the small fee of one hundred dollars. On behalf of Sam, Jourdain made the arrangement and got the body to the cemetery.

The descending sun cast a mango-orange glow over the landscape as Eduard Bernard was placed in the coffin with his wife. *At least I'll know where to find him*, Sam thought, as he wiped his eyes and watched Jourdain hand over one hundred dollars of Papa's savings.

The weeks that followed were torturous for Sam. He did not dare tell anyone that Papa had passed. He continued to go to work in the baseball plant each day, with Michel under the assumption that Papa was recovering at home, perhaps one day to return. Sam never said anything to the contrary. Papa had a few friends at Ricardo's, regulars, but in Haiti, those kinds of friends weren't the type to come calling at the house. Sam doubted any of Papa's friends even knew exactly where he lived. Sam was aware that he and Papa had more things than most families, and now that he was alone, Sam couldn't risk anyone challenging him for his property. Orphans did not own homes in Haiti.

Jourdain was in agreement with that plan. He would honor his word to Eduard by protecting Sam as best as he could, and Jourdain insisted that keeping Sam safe meant keeping the news of Papa's death a secret. Even Polo believed that Sam's distant attitude was because of Papa's accident and on account of having to now work to earn the family income. Just as with Michel, Sam didn't contradict.

The end of January came and went and with it, Sam's hope of starting secondary school. Jourdain forced him to play baseball at least once each weekend, to keep his muscles active. One Saturday in February, Sam pushed back.

"Why do you make me play, Jourdain?" Sam said with anger he rarely showed. "It no longer matters. School started last week. My dreams have died."

"A dormant dream is not a dead dream," Jourdain retorted. "Your dream might be sleeping, but you must not let it go."

"That is the dumbest thing I've ever heard. Life, for me, is over."

"No, Sam," Jourdain said firmly. "Your life is still here. Papa passed away. You did not. And you dishonor his memory if you give up hope. That is not what he would have wanted. What were his last words to you?"

Sam wiped a tear and did not answer.

"He said, 'I love you.' That's what you told me. When you love someone, you want the best for them. Papa would want the best for you. Your best includes baseball and one day, education. It will come, Sam."

Sam didn't say anything but returned to his house and flopped onto Papa's bed. He lay there, staring at the ceiling and thinking about all of the things that happened in the last four months. He suddenly missed baseball. He missed the information about baseball and American sports that Papa used to get for him. He ached for some connection to the world outside of the baseball factory. He got up and decided to go to Ricardo's himself and make an attempt to reconnect with that part of his life.

He locked his bicycle to a post and with hesitancy walked

into Ricardo's. He'd never been in a bar before. It was early Sunday afternoon, so the place was mostly empty. On Saturdays, Ricardo's filled up early. Haitian men often drank their breakfast, went home to sleep the afternoon away, then returned around suppertime. Sundays were a touch more reserved. Glad for the lack of crowd, Sam took an empty seat facing the television at the bar.

"You want a beer?" the man behind the counter asked.

Sam caught sight of himself in the mirror behind the bar. Was that his seventeen-year-old face staring back at him? The wear and tear of the last few months made him look considerably older.

"No, thank you. A Coke please," he answered.

The man pulled a bottle of Coke from a cooler and opened it for Sam. "You want some chips?" he asked.

Sam nodded. "Sure."

The sports news was just coming on. A picture of a baseball player flashed on the screen.

"Can you turn it up?" Sam asked the bartender, who retrieved a small silver remote from under the bar and raised the volume so Sam could hear the announcer:

"... ruled in favor of the San Diego Padres yesterday in the arbitration case involving Walt Terrell. Terrell, a pitcher who was acquired during the off season from the Detroit Tigers, will earn $775,000 this year rather than the $941,000 he requested. Walt Terrell made $665,000 in 1988. With three decisions to go, the players and teams are tied, 5-5, in this winter's arbitration results."

The action clip that played on the screen while the announcer talked was of Terrell pitching to Mark McGwire in 1986. The young McGwire had broken the rookie home run record in 1987, Sam remembered. Terrell had pitched to McGwire when he hit his first-ever Major League home run. Papa had brought home a newspaper article about it at the time. *The American baseball players make so much money,* Sam thought.

The sports news then switched to coverage of the FIFA

World Youth Soccer Championships. Haitians love foutbòl, and when the game came on, Ricardo's started to fill. Even though it was only youth soccer, when soccer is your only national sport, you get excited for it. And the Haitians were ready for excitement. Brazil was playing Mali. Word got out in the street that Brazil was on, and several men of varying ages now sat at the bar. Sam's munched his chips and enjoyed the sense of comradeship. He was still lonely, but not alone. A guy that looked a bit like Polo sat at the stool next to him and nodded in greeting at Sam. He ordered a beer and basket of chips and when they arrived, he offered to share with Sam.

"Haven't seen you in here before," the stranger said.

Sam, unprepared for conversation, answered awkwardly. "I just came in to check out the tele."

"Foutbòl fan?"

"Who isn't? But I also like baseball," Sam said. He ordered another Coke.

"You don't like the rum in your Coke?" the stranger pressed.

Sam shook his head. "Nah. Just Coke."

The stranger considered this response. "I'm Raul."

"Sam."

Chips never tasted so good to Sam. When Brazil scored their first goal, Ricardo's erupted in cheers. *Haitians must be bigger Brazilian soccer fans than the Brazilians are*, Sam thought. Cássio, a defender, got his team on the board, and the Haitian fans were ecstatic. Some of the men produced Brazilian flags from their pockets and began running up and down the street, waving them like capes. Ricardo's filled up even more, and the noise level rose. When Brazil scored again, this time by midfielder Bismark, even Sam couldn't resist giving a few high fives. He was pulled into the excitement.

The afternoon wore on with three more Brazilian goals, two more Cokes, and another basket of chips. Sam was feeling happy for the first time since he played baseball with the guys in the Dominican. When the game wrapped up and Sam paid his bill, Raul held out his hand to shake.

"Will you be here tomorrow?" Raul asked. "The Americans are playing."

"I work until five," Sam explained.

"Ah! A working man. Where do you work?"

"Baseball plant," Sam stated.

Raul nodded. "That's good, friend. OK, well, maybe I'll see you around."

Sam did not go to Ricardo's after work the next day. He had promised Elena he would help her with chores. After hauling her garbage down the road, he fetched a large bucket of water and helped her wash the store. Floors, counters, windows, her little bathroom—if it could be washed, they washed it. Most things in Haiti were covered by a layer of dirt and grime. Elena's store was not one of them. Elena's husband passed away a few years ago from diphtheria. She dealt with her grief and fears by keeping things incredibly clean. She lived in a small apartment above the boutik, which she kept just as immaculate. She had a goat stew dinner waiting for them once the last countertop was wiped clean.

"Thank you, Elena," Sam said, breaking a piece of bread from the small loaf and running it around his bowl. "This is delicious."

"No, Samféyo. I should thank you. You do everything I need, and you never complain."

Sam shrugged. "I don't mind helping you. You've been like a—" He stopped short of the word "mother." His shoulders slumped.

"Ah, Sam," she said delicately. "I know it's hard. I didn't know your mama. But I know if I ever had a son, I would want him to be just like you."

They sat, letting their minds wander for a while.

"I went to Ricardo's yesterday," Sam said at last. It felt like a confession.

"Oh, really? What for?"

"I wanted to watch the tele," he said. Then he shook his head. "No, that's not it. I think I wanted to feel like Papa."

"You didn't drink any beer, did you?" Elena put her hands on her hips. Sam's papa was unyielding in his opinion about alcohol. He never touched it. And he'd always told Sam that the dreams of drunkards never came true.

"Of course not. Don't worry, Miss Elena. Even though I have no more dreams, I will not end up a drunk."

"Samféyo. Do not talk that way. You are destined for great things. You are young. Your future is stretched out in front of you. You'll find your way."

Sam wished he was as confident in his future as she was. He gave her a warm hug before heading home.

Tuesday at the plant was thread-check day. Back in January the managers began a new inspection. They declared that once each week they would pull a completed ball from each sewer's barrel, snip the thread, and unstitch it. The purpose was to measure the thread, checking it against the eighty-eight inches it was supposed to be. Haitians whose baseballs were not measuring up would be let go.

The American blanc who had come to deliver news of this new inspection lectured the Haitians on the need for consistency. *Leathers not secured with the exact needed tension could become defective during a baseball game*, he had said. In the Major League, defective balls were not acceptable. He went on to pontificate about how proud Rawlings was to be the supplier for all Major League games, and amidst the fierce competition in the industry, they needed their standards to be the highest.

It sounded good, but talk amongst the Haitians was that the real purpose of the inspection was to find opportunities to fire the Haitians—a first step in shutting down the plant. Haitian flaws could allow the blancs to justify closing Rawlings Haiti and move somewhere more politically stable. Rawlings already acquired land in Costa Rica; everyone knew it. One of the women asked the visiting blanc about Costa Rica. He insisted that yes, although they did begin to build a plant there, it was *not* so they could shut down in Haiti. This new plant, he explained, would *be in addition* to the work in Haiti. He used this point to reinforce the importance of consistency. The Haitians weren't buying it, yet there was nothing to be done.

So far, Sam was spot-on with his thread checks. He had an uncanny sense of exactly how tight to pull the stitches so as to use the perfect length of thread. This Tuesday's check was no different. Michel, however, was out of compliance for the second time in a row. He was put on notice.

During lunch, Michel lamented to Sam. "One and a half inches! That's all I was off. One and a half! The balls look just fine. They won't bust up during play. Those Americans just want to get rid of us." He spat in disgust and crumpled the blue slip of paper. "I can't lose this job, Sam."

Later Sam thought about what Michel said. It mirrored what he'd heard others talking about in the plant. Were the Americans really building up reasons to justify shutting down the factory? If so, what would he do? He came to the same conclusion as the others. For now, he could do nothing except ensure his eighty-eight inches were true.

Confident that Elena did not *dis*approve, the orange bicycle made a detour to Ricardo's before heading home. He was disappointed, however, as there were no baseball games in progress. Replay of the Daytona 500 was followed by a report about Pete Rose, who had met with the Commissioner to discuss an investigation into his gambling on baseball games. Sam knew Pete Rose was a great baseball player—destined for the Hall of Fame—but he didn't understand why the league was so bothered about gambling. Almost all of the men in Haiti gambled. Lotto booths dot every other corner, happily liberating the working men from their money. Port-au-Prince's bigshots strut the casinos, making deals and losing at cards. And Sam knew that Haitian men bet on the cocks three nights a week in fight circles across the city. *Everyone* gambled.

He sighed heavily as he recalled his one and only experience with cockfighting. It had been two years since he thought about the incident. Sam had overheard some older boys talking at school. Their dads had taken them to see a fight, and the way they spoke of it, it was the most exciting sport since soccer! Curious, Sam asked Papa if they could go. Papa curtly responded that Sam should never, ever go to a cockfight, and he should forget all about it. But a young Sam was foolhardy in his persistence for information. To quiet his curiosity, that Friday night, Papa took Sam to a part of Port-au-Prince he'd never seen.

They walked for more than a mile and came to a stop in front of a building painted with obnoxiously large green and red stripes. Sam felt like a grown-up as Papa paid the doorman five dollars and pushed their way through the boisterous throng of men drinking merrily and exchanging cash for tickets at the betting booth.

"Are we going to buy a ticket?" he asked Papa with a grin.

Papa shook his head. "Not until you get a good look at the roosters."

Papa guided him through to the large courtyard out back where men paraded in front of small wire cages, each of which imprisoned a mighty rooster that stomped and chattered nervously at their inspection. Sam squatted in front of one of the cages.

"Don't put your finger too close!" a man behind him warned. "You'll go home with one less pinky."

The men surrounding them laughed. Sam stood quickly.

"Maybe we should let the boy get nipped. Pedro fights harder if he tastes blood first!" another man chortled, as he took a swig of his beer. More laughter.

Sam looked around. Concrete blocks framed a neat circle at the center of the courtyard.

"What's going to happen, Papa?" Sam asked, his confidence replaced with a twinge of fear.

"Each rooster has a number. The official draws two numbers and those will go into the circle and fight. They repeat it with all of the roosters until there is one winner."

"How does a rooster win?" Sam asked, suspecting that he

already knew.

Papa looked his son eye-to-eye. "By killing its opponent."

Sam's curiosity about cockfighting melted like hot butter. They didn't belong here; Sam felt it in his bones.

"Can we leave, Papa?" Sam asked.

Papa smiled for the first time that evening. The lesson was learned. He took Sam's hand and they left in the same way they came, never speaking of it again.

That night came back to him vividly as he listened to the sportscasters speculate on Pete Rose's fate. The hungry look on the faces of the men waiting anxiously to see if they picked the victor flashed before his eyes. They were only there for the hope of a financial payout. *Was, perhaps, gambling a pastime with sinister motives?* He remembered something Papa often spoke: "Just because something is legal, Samféyo, that doesn't mean it is right." He'd long forgotten that adage, but it came to him now. Lost in his thoughts about Pete Rose, roosters, and Papa, Sam didn't notice his friend from the other day come into the bar. Raul took the seat next to Sam and had ordered his rum and cola before Sam noticed him.

"Oh! Alo," Sam said.

"Bonjou!" Raul answered. "How's it going, Sam?"

"It was a long day," Sam admitted.

"Sorry to hear that, friend," Raul said. "You know, as they say, *si travey te bon bagay, moun ruch la pran-l lontan.*"

Sam smiled at the saying. It was one Papa occasionally said at the end of a long day. *If work were easy, the rich would have grabbed onto it long ago.* Papa was everywhere this evening. Sam nodded in agreement. "Yes, that is true."

Raul leaned on his elbows on the bar. "What are you doing on Saturday?"

"Saturday? I have some work to do."

"All day?"

"No. Just until one," Sam replied. The next batch of cigars was ready to sell. He would be at the airport, waiting on the eleven a.m. from Miami. "Why?"

"Join me for a foutbòl game at the stadium. Aigle Noir is

playing Don Bosco."

Sam whistled. He had never been to a match at the stadium. He'd asked Papa to go several times, but somehow it never worked out. He jumped at the chance.

"Sure. What time?" he asked.

"Let's meet here at three," Raul suggested.

"Sounds good," Sam agreed. "I'll be here."

At that moment, six men wearing police uniforms walked purposefully into Ricardo's. Conversations stopped, but faces did not turn to stare. Men stood stiffly, waiting to see what would happen. The police had made several seemingly random and violent arrests in the last months and the growing fear among the Haitian common folk was that no one was safe anywhere. One of the officers nodded a greeting to the bartender, and the men walked straight through to the back room of Ricardo's. After a few long moments, conversations resumed.

Sam let out his breath. Raul was staring at him.

"OK, Sam. I'll see you Saturday," Raul said.

CHAPTER 5

I t took Sam only an hour and a half to sell out of the forty-five cigars that he'd brought to the airport. Chindo was nowhere to be seen, so Sam had the business all to himself. He even stood at the taxi stand for a while to see if the action was better there. It wasn't. He decided that he preferred to be inside the airport because at least it was shaded.

As soon as he exchanged his American dollars for gourdes, he hurried home to pay Jourdain.

"Why the rush?" Jourdain asked as Sam deposited the money and turned to race away.

"I am going to the stadium to watch a foutbòl game!" Sam said with pride.

"Hey, Sam! That's great," Jourdain said. "With Polo?"

"No. With a guy I met at Ricardo's. His name is Raul. He's really nice, and he already has the tickets!"

Jourdain nodded thoughtfully. "I'm glad you made a friend. Remember, don't give too much personal information.

"I know. I won't," Sam promised. "He thinks I am older."

"Well, why wouldn't he? You have to be nearly six feet tall."

Sam raised his chin. "You think so?"

"Probably. You are taller than I am now. But I am serious. Do not let anyone know where you live. And certainly don't tell anybody that you are on your own."

"I won't!" Sam said again. Then he smiled and ran off to Ricardo's.

Raul was not there yet, so Sam took up a seat. Sports

news was buzzing with the firing of the Dallas Cowboys' football coach. Sam had always thought the coach, Mr. Tom Landry, looked very distinguished in his beige fedora and blazer. He had not seen many American football games, but he knew none of the other coaches dressed as sharply as Coach Landry. If Sam had to pick an American football team to cheer on, it would be the Dallas Cowboys. Many Haitians, both girls and boys, had at least one National Football League team t-shirt in their meager wardrobes; Americans loved to donate their old sports shirts to the relief organizations. On days that the Red Cross handed out clothes, the little ones fought like dogs for the best sports shirts. Out of all of the teams promoted on t-shirts across Haiti's poor, the Dallas Cowboys outnumbered them all.

Just as Jerry Jones, the new owner of the Cowboys, was giving his press release, Raul sat down next to Sam. Sam had been facing the door and didn't see Raul enter, which made him think perhaps he came from the back room.

"Hey, friend, *sak pase?*" Raul said.

"Bonjou," Sam replied. "I didn't see you come in."

"Ah, I've been here for a little while," Raul said.

"Are you ready to go?" Sam asked.

"Let's have a beer first," Raul suggested. "We have some time." He signaled to the bartender. "Two beers!"

Sam was about to object, but the bartender had turned away and came right back with two bottles from the cooler. He'd opened them and put them on the counter. Sam's chest tightened.

Raul picked his bottle up and held it toward Sam in a toast. "Cheers."

Sam reluctantly mimicked the action and put his lips to the top of the bottle. He wouldn't call it a drink, exactly, it was more like he wet his top lip with the liquid. It was bitter.

"Well, alo, Sam!" He felt a hand on his shoulder. He turned. It was Jourdain.

"Oh! Alo, Jourdain," Sam stammered.

Jourdain held his hand out to Raul. "Alo. I'm Jourdain."

Raul smiled. "Nice to meet you. Are you a friend of

Sam's?"

"Wi," Jourdain said. "We are neighbors."

Raul nodded. "Bon. We are going to the foutbòl game. Care to join us?"

"No, no," Jourdain said. "I just came to watch a little tele. Then I have work to do."

"OK, friend," Raul said. "I'll be right back, Sam, then we will go." Raul headed to the bathroom.

Jourdain raised an eyebrow at Sam and glanced at the beer.

"He bought it! I tried to say no, but it was too late," Sam explained quickly. "I don't even want it." He held the beer out to Jourdain. "You drink it."

Jourdain shook his head. "Who is this guy, Sam? Do you even know?"

"He seems nice enough."

"Please be careful. I promised your papa I would take care of you."

Raul returned. "Ready to go, Sam?"

Sam nodded. "Sure. Can't wait." He put his beer down on the counter.

Jourdain asked, "Who's playing?"

"Aigle Noir against Don Bosco," Raul answered.

"Nice! Go Noir!" Jourdain cheered.

"Of course!" Raul said with a fist pump in the air.

"I'll see you later, Jourdain," Sam called as they left.

As they neared the stadium, they joined in step with droves of other Haitian men. The pace quickened and Sam's excitement grew. There was an even split between the number of people wearing red and black jerseys supporting Aigle Noir and yellow jerseys on the Don Bosco fans. Sam did not have an Aigle Noir shirt, but he had chosen a red t-shirt for the game. Raul wore an authentic Aigle Noir jersey, complete with genuine stitched patches.

Raul flashed the tickets as they entered the gate, and Sam followed him to their midfield seats. Sam was impressed. The seats were amazing and very close to the action. Fans sitting around them acknowledged Raul, as handshakes and back slaps were exchanged. Most were in jerseys like Raul's. The Bosco contingent were primarily seated along the north and south ends of the field, with the Aigle Noir fans sandwiched in-between. The players were just finishing up their warm-ups and heading off to prepare for game time.

"This is terrific, no?" Raul asked Sam.

"Incredible! I've always wanted to come to a game," Sam confessed.

"Why haven't you come before?"

Sam shrugged. "I never had the opportunity. School, work, other things."

Raul nodded. "I get it, man. It's OK! Here we are!" He patted Sam's shoulder as the players lined up to enter the field.

The announcer called out the starting eleven for each team. Spirit leaders waving flags raced among the players as their names were called. After each player was acknowledged, the stadium became silent as the national anthem began to play through the speakers. The sound was terrible, and the crackle of the speakers overpowered the cassette tape that played the music, but every Haitian, including Sam, belted out the words.

"For our country. For our forefathers. United let us march. Let there be no traitors in our ranks…"

As Sam sang these words, he wondered about Raul and the back room of Ricardo's. Only those who were politically connected were allowed in. Surely Raul wasn't tied up with the political evils? The government was doing everything it could to hold Haitians in a state of constant fear.

He forgot these thoughts as the anthem morphed into game play. The increase of noise level pushed out thoughts of anything except for sports. A group sitting to their left kept a constant chant of *"Hey oh, hey oooohh,"* and *"Olé, olé, olé,"* for the entire game. Their chants were accompanied by a drum beating rhythmically to whatever they sang out. It was the most frenzied wave of activity Sam had ever experienced. Fans shook flags and banners of all sizes, and every time one team or the other did something skillful, the place erupted in cheers. Sam absorbed it all, loving every minute. He couldn't help but wonder how this compared to the excitement in an American baseball stadium. He tried to imagine it. What would it be like to be on the field, knocking a baseball out of the park, or tagging a runner out at first base? Hearing your name called the way the fans cheered for Jean-Jacques or Maurice? Sam didn't even realize he was smiling until Raul pointed it out.

"Having fun, yes?" Raul said.

"Wi. Incredible!" Sam said.

"I'm going to get a couple of beers," Raul said.

"Can I get a Coke?" Sam asked.

"Sure! Be right back."

Sam chalked the Coke up as a victory. He knew, no matter what else happened, he had to stay true to his papa. He would not let him down. *The dreams of drunkards do not come true,* "he heard Papa say in his mind.

The game flew by so quickly. The Aigle Noir club bested the Don Bosco team by a score of three to two. It ended in a shoot-out, and Sam felt only mildly sorry for the Bosco goalie, who remained seated on the field with his head in his hands when it was over. The ball had shot to his left, as he dove right, ending the match.

Noir fans triumphantly marched from the stadium, singing "Olé, olé, olé," with their arms draped over one another's shoulders. Raul, who had five beers in him, slung his arm over Sam's shoulder as they headed out.

"So what do you think, my friend?" he asked. "Pretty great, huh?"

"I can't believe it! Thrilling!" Sam said.

Raul laughed. "Yes, yes! Thrilling, indeed!"

They walked back to Ricardo's. Sam was prepared to say goodbye there and continue his journey home, but Raul stopped him.

"Sam. Come on in for a minute."

"Ah, I really should be heading home. I have many things yet to do today," Sam said.

"It'll only be a minute," Raul stated. "Come."

Sam reluctantly followed Ricardo into the bar and prepared to have a seat. "No. This way," Raul urged. He led Sam to a round table near the door to the back room. "Sit here."

Raul went to the bar and brought back two Cokes. He set one in front of Sam. "No rum in yours," he winked.

Raul sat across from Sam and gulped his drink, which Sam correctly guessed had rum inside. "Sam, let me ask you a question. What do you think is the biggest problem our country has?"

Sam's stomach got knotty. Not knowing Raul's allegiances made answering either way potentially problematic.

"Haiti's biggest problem?" Sam repeated. "Man, I don't know. Haiti has a lot of problems. No national baseball team?" Sam laughed, trying to make light of a conversation that felt very heavy.

Raul chuckled. "Good one. But seriously."

Sam played his answer as safely as he could. "The commoners don't trust the government. The government feels it can't control the people."

Raul nodded. "So who is right?"

"It depends who you ask," Sam replied.

"What do you think?" Raul persisted.

Sam sighed. "My job is with a company that depends on the government. Haiti has to allow them to continue to operate here. If the Americans pull out of Haiti, I lose my job. I care about Haiti, and I also care about the Americans trusting in our politics so they won't leave. I need my job to survive. I guess I think the biggest problem is survival."

Raul liked that answer. "Yes! Survival! I couldn't have said it better. Do you think your company will survive here if our politics are unstable?"

Sam shook his head. Easy answer. "Nope," he said truthfully. "I think that's why so many are already pulling out. The uprising and infighting hurts us. Americans don't have the time to deal with rebellion. And they don't have to! There are a lot of other options for them. In Haiti, we have no other options.

We stay. They go."

"Exactly! I knew you were smart!" Raul pointed a finger at Sam as he said this. He took another swig of his rum and Coke.

Raul didn't say anything for several minutes. He stared at the television across the room, deep in thought. Sam was hopeful that the conversation was over. He was just about to stand to leave, when Raul looked at him again.

"Sam, have you ever wanted to do something about our country's situation?"

"Do something? I'm not sure what you mean," Sam answered.

"How long have you been working at the same job?" Raul asked.

"Um, I'm not sure. For a while now."

"You do the same thing every day. Work, eat, sleep. Survive. Right?"

"Yes. I also go to church on some Sundays and play ball whenever I can."

"You had never even been to a soccer game! I can't believe it. You deserve more."

"Raul, I'm not following. I am not unhappy. I just don't want the American companies to leave Haiti. That's all I meant," Sam explained.

"Yes, yes, I know. Sam, I don't even think you know what you are missing. You could have so much more! I want you to join with us."

There it was. "I'm not sure what you mean," Sam said hesitantly.

"What if I told you there was money and power in Haiti, and it could be yours? You wouldn't have to worry about the Americans, or your job, or surviving. Aren't you tired of fighting to survive?"

"You said, 'join us.' Join who?" Sam asked.

"Soulèvman Jèn Yo. We are an organized group of young people, dedicated to helping our government stabilize by doing our part."

"What do you do?" Sam asked, not sure he really wanted to know. It was the same feeling he had at the cockfighting ring.

"I'll tell you what," Raul said. "Why don't you meet up with me tomorrow morning and I'll show you what we do."

"Soulèvman Jèn Yo?" Jourdain repeated when Sam told him about his conversation with Raul. "I've never heard of them. But 'Youth Uprising' can't be good."

"What should I do?" Sam lamented. "I don't want to go. But he didn't leave me much choice. He told me where to go and what time to be there."

"Did he say what they were doing?" Jourdain asked.

"No. He just said that I would get to see first-hand how the Soulèvman Jèn Yo were going to save our country. He made it sound like they want the same thing we all want—a stable government so the world will have faith in Haiti."

"I just don't know, Sam," Jourdain said. "I have made it so far by keeping my nose down, working hard, and avoiding trouble. I don't know how to solve Haiti's problems, and I don't think anyone but God alone can save our country. And that hasn't happened yet."

"If I don't go, I think he will be really angry. I don't think I could ever go near Ricardo's again," Sam said. "But maybe if I go, I can see what he has to say and then tell him no thanks, and let things go back to normal."

Jourdain took a deep breath. "It's quite the predicament. Do what you think is best."

Sam stared at the ceiling for most of the night, worrying. Sometime before the rooster woke up, he knew he would be going to church before meeting up with Raul. If ever he needed God's help, it would be this day. St. Bernard's held a seven-thirty mass. He and his papa would go occasionally, and Sam was comfortable there. The service was over within the hour, and Sam had plenty of time to make his nine o'clock meeting with Raul. They weren't meeting at Ricardo's this time, but at a small tire shop on the west end of Port-au-Prince. The street was deserted, and Sam pulled his bike onto the porch of the tire shop and knocked loudly on the door.

"Back here, Sam," he heard Raul call from the rear of the building. A small walkway between the tire shop and the building next to it led the way to the yard. Raul and four others were sitting in metal folding chairs. They wore black pants and long-sleeved black t-shirts.

"Welcome, Sam," Raul said warmly. "Guys, this is Sam. He is here today to see if he wants to join us."

Sam gave them as friendly of a smile as he could. He'd made the decision to say as little as possible, get this over with, and go home having politely declined whatever it was that was being offered.

Before anything could happen, though, a thin boy with the deepest black skin Sam had ever seen ran into the yard from behind the buildings. He was significantly younger than Sam.

"Eskize m," he said breathlessly. "Raul, I need to speak with you right away."

Raul's eyes narrowed as he followed the boy into the tire shop. Sam stood awkwardly, shifting his weight back and forth, trying not to look at any of the other guys.

"Are you a believer, Sam?" one of the men asked.

"A believer?" Sam repeated.

"In our cause, man. Do you want to see Haiti grow?" he clarified.

"I do want to see Haiti grow," Sam said.

"Alright! Glad you're here," another said.

Sam fought the urge to ask how they planned to make Haiti grow. "Don't ask questions you don't want to know the answers to," Papa always said. It was sound advice, wholly fitting for this situation.

After long minutes Raul and the skinny kid came out of the shop. Raul's face was flushed, and the skinny kid looked afraid.

"Sam, I am so sorry. We have to reschedule today. Something of the utmost importance has come up."

Sam feigned disappointment. "Oh. Well, I completely

understand. No worries. We can get together another time. I'll see you later."

Sam turned quickly to go. He fought the urge to run as he walked between the buildings and back to his bicycle. He could hear Raul's voice rising as he explained the situation to the rest of his crew. He was not happy, whatever it was.

It wasn't until he was safely back at home and in Jourdain's yard explaining what had happened that he breathed a sigh of relief.

"You got lucky, Sam," Jourdain agreed.

"Maybe he will forget about the whole thing," Sam hoped.

"I doubt it," Jourdain said. "Anyone who is in a group called 'Youth Uprising' is not likely to pack their things and quit the cause. If I were you, I would avoid Ricardo's and find somewhere else to watch the sports."

Sam knew that was the smart thing to do. He was disappointed that his friendship with Raul would go no further. He really did have fun at the soccer game.

"You're right. Do you know where I can go?"

Jourdain smiled. "We will find somewhere. I promise."

Later that day, Sam met up with Polo and some of the other neighborhood kids to play baseball. Papa had given him a real wooden bat two years ago for his birthday. His glove was an authentic Rawlings. Up until three years ago, the factory produced gloves as well as baseballs, and Papa was able to buy one for Sam. Sam didn't mind sharing his most prized possessions with the others, especially when it allowed them to play real games together. Whoever played first base got to use the real glove; the others had makeshift mitts fashioned from cardboard. Sam had just hit a ball deep into the small grove of trees behind the lot where they played, when he saw Jourdain motioning for him to come over.

"Yes, Jourdain. What is it?" Sam asked. "Did you see that hit?"

"I saw it, Sam. Very good. Listen, I have some news."
Jourdain looked troubled.

"What? What's wrong?"

"General Avril sent troops to raid the ports again today.
There was a small ship leaving the docks that reportedly had
eight kilos of cocaine aboard. The police shot and killed three of
the men on board; two of them got away."

"Yeah, so?" Drug smuggling and shooting raids were not
uncommon. Avril had been putting on a big show of cracking
down on the smugglers so the world would see that he is
benefitting Haiti. Most everyone believed that he set up the
raids himself to make his administration look good.

"One of the men killed was Raul."

"What? Raul? Are you sure?" Sam was shocked.

Jourdain nodded. "My shipment of cedar boxes came in
for the cigars. While I was waiting for my crate to unload, I
heard the commotion on the next pier. I saw him with my own
eyes."

"I can't believe it! Cocaine? What if I had been there?"

"Apparently he didn't want you there. He sent you home,
remember?"

"I can't believe it," Sam said again.

Sadness filled Sam's chest as he processed this
information. *Raul was dead?*

"I really had fun at the soccer game," Sam said, more to
himself than to Jourdain. He sounded and felt like a little kid.

"I know, Sam," Jourdain said. "I'm sorry, buddy. Hey—
why don't you and I go to the next game?"

"Yeah, sure. That'd be great," Sam said, not feeling great
at all.

CHAPTER 6

J ourdain found a small place called D.J.'s tucked into the lobby of a hotel in downtown Port-au-Prince, not too far from the Rawlings plant. It served decent food, was clean, and the manager kept the tele tuned to sports. Jourdain and Sam sat together one night after work and watched the news from around the Caribbean islands. A feature about the Dominican Republic baseball league caught Sam's eye.

"Man," Sam said. "I sure wish Haiti had a baseball league. I'd get noticed for sure."

Jourdain agreed. "Yes, you would. I watched you play last week. You're pretty good. You hit well."

"Thanks. But I don't really have anyone pitching to me who can throw any heat. Tomás has a good arm, but still. I wonder how I'd do against somebody with real throwing power?"

"Hey," Jourdain said. "Next weekend I go back to Barahona. Want to come? Maybe your baseball buddies will be playing. You can get in on a game."

Sam had not gone back to the Dominican with Jourdain since the trip before Papa died.

"I'd like that. And I'll bring my glove this time!"

Saturday's weather was perfect for their trip. The back of Jourdain's truck was full of passengers by seven-thirty. Glove and ball on his lap, Sam was eager to get there. He didn't even know if the locals would be playing, but he'd prayed to Jesus every day since Jourdain asked him to go that the boys would be in the empty lot.

Jourdain dropped Sam off near the beach while he made his deliveries. With no sign of the players, Sam entertained himself by throwing his ball, splashing in the waves, and napping in the sand. Time passed. When hunger finally struck, he located the food truck and treated himself to another enormous chimi burger. He spotted a convenience store on the corner near the food truck, and his parched throat told him to grab a bottle of water. He took a water from the cooler and was considering the purchase of a small plastic snow globe for Elena, when he almost missed noticing the two boys around his age who'd entered the store. They were looking at the rack of chips, discussing which to buy. Sam recognized them as two of the guys that played on his team the last time he was there.

"Hey there!" Sam said with a wave. The boys looked up, surprised. "I'm Sam. I played baseball with you a few weeks ago."

They recognized him. "Oh, hey! Sam!" They all shook hands.

"Great to see you, man," one of the boys said. Sam remembered him to be Nick, the pitcher.

"Man, where've you been?" the other boy asked.

"What do you mean?" Sam asked, confused.

"We'd been looking for you! We wanted you to keep playing with us. You're really good," Nick answered.

"Oh! I live in—" Sam stopped. He felt a caution not to say he was from Port-au-Prince.

"You live where?" the other kid asked.

"I don't live in town here. I just come with my uncle sometimes when he does deliveries."

"Ah! OK," Nick said. "Do you want to play?"

"Yes! I even have my glove this time!" Sam held it up.

"Good! Let's go. The others should be showing up soon. They will be happy to see you."

Sam bought his water (leaving the snow globe behind), Nick bought a large bag of chicharron, and the boys headed toward the lot. Sam thanked Jesus at least five times along the way. He couldn't believe it! They had been *looking* for him!

"Do you play every week?" Sam asked the other boy, whose name was Ricco.

"Saturday and Sunday," Ricco answered. "Usually we get here around two."

A few other guys were already there, and when they saw Sam, they whooped and greeted him like a friend.

The regular first baseman did not show up, so Sam was allocated to the bag. If he couldn't play outfield, first base was the next best thing. He treated every position he played like it was the most important position on the field. He caught every out thrown his way and stopped the grounders that bounced his direction. The other team had a decent pitcher, so Sam finally felt like his at-bats were for real. He struck out twice, but then belted one for a grand slam, which put his team ahead for good.

Cheers and handshakes were passed around when the game was over, and most all of the guys called out, "See you next week!" as they departed.

"I don't think we'll be in town next week," he told Nick. "But if I can come back, I will."

"OK, Sam," Nick replied. "Anytime!"

Sam trotted over to Jourdain, who was perched on the truck, watching.

"That was quite the hit!" Jourdain praised. "Nicely done."

"Thanks!" Sam beamed. "It was so much fun. Can I come back with you next time?"

"Of course, Samféyo, you can always come!"

Sam and Jourdain worked hard to get the tobacco prepared and the cigars prepped and boxed into the new cedar boxes that Jourdain had purchased from Cuba. Sam cut filler and rolled leaves after coming home from the baseball plant each day, and often he worked long into the night. Elena would hand him a bagged dinner as he rode past her shop. He was determined to get back to the DR. The effort paid off, and they had another sales batch ready to go in three weeks' time.

Sam's game improved each time he played. He alternated between playing first base and right field, and to be honest, he wasn't sure which he preferred. His batting got better and better, and he experimented more with switch-hitting. Surprisingly he had equal skill on both sides of the plate. It added uniqueness to Sam that his Dominican friends appreciated.

He continued to play with Polo and the guys on the weekends in-between their DR trips. They were good weeks for Sam. The usually wet spring was drier than normal, but not so dry as to damage Jourdain's tobacco. On the contrary, the crops thrived. Sam's laser-focus on getting cigar boxes ready for sale so he could get back to DR was a great benefit to the plants, and there was more tobacco than ever.

D.J.'s proved to be a reliable place for Sam to watch summer baseball; he saw plenty of the Major League games and league games from around the Caribbean. In the little free time he allowed himself, he would steal away and catch whatever was on. Talk of Oakland being in a strong position to win their division buzzed the airwaves by summer's end. The biggest news of the summer, however, concerned Pete Rose.

Accusations turned to sanctions, and Rose was declared permanently ineligible to participate in Major League Baseball because of his gambling. The ruling frustrated Sam. As an athlete, Sam admired Rose. He wanted to be a switch-hitter like Rose, and Sam could see himself on the field in a variety of playing positions; versatile, also like Rose. He felt the loss of Rose's expulsion from the sport he loved. He had shifted his perspective from wondering why, in a country full of gamblers, Pete Rose was being picked on, to a position of disappointment that Rose couldn't have simply been satisfied with the success he had.

"Why would he need *more* money?" Sam whined. "He had it made!"

"I don't know, zanmi," Jourdain said. "Americans do what Americans do."

"He was the best! He won three World Series! Did you know that?"

"Yes, you told me," Jourdain assured. "And he got all kinds of awards."

"Gold gloves, MVPs, Sportsman of the Year—he's won everything!" Sam ranted. "If I become a baseball player in America, I'll follow all the rules."

"I'm sure you will, Sam," Jourdain said. "I'm sure you will."

At the beginning of September, Rawlings fired one hundred fifty workers. Anyone who failed the eighty-eight inches inspection at any point in the summer months was let go. Michel hugged Sam before heading out of the factory.

"I'm sorry, Michel," Sam said. "I hate this!"

"It's OK, Sam. My cousin might have a job for me with the telephone company. They need people to hook up the cable wires and stuff."

"Do you know how to do that?" Sam asked.

Michel shrugged. "I'll figure it out. Say hello to your papa for me."

Michel always asked about Papa's health. Initially it pained Sam to continue the lie, but eventually he grew dull to it. It was all part of survival.

Sam knew he had to make sure his eighty-eight inches stayed true. After the mass firing, managers declared that *anyone* who failed a red thread inspection would be immediately let go, and anyone who missed any work should not even bother to come back. Sam remained reliable. He always made quota, he always used the exact amount of red waxy thread on his leathers, and he always showed up.

To the world, conditions in Haiti seemed promising, with talk of a real election scheduled to happen in the next year. Within Haiti, however, the citizens lived on edge; fear gripping their hearts every time a policeman or dark-clothed stranger walked past. It no longer surprised anyone to hear stories of rapes, beatings, and, yes, random murders. Bodies were dumped on busy streets or on the steps of the government buildings—put on display to discourage any talk of public elections. The world turned a blind eye to the violence, but the baseball factories did not.

More manufacturers closed their Haitian doors, highlighting to Sam that it was only a matter of time until Rawlings followed suit, despite what "management" said. Tensions were high at the plant as the bosses found reasons to fire people on a daily basis. Too much time on break, talking instead of working, stitches not perfect—the Haitians could do no right anymore. Sam kept his head down, rarely took a lunch, and used not a centimeter more than eighty-eight inches of thread in his sewing.

One September evening, as Sam pedaled home from work, he heard a strange noise as he neared his neighborhood. It was a high-pitched squeak, almost like a whimper. He pedaled back and hopped off the bike to investigate.

"Hello?" Sam called into the greenery. "Is someone there?"

One of the bushes moved. Muffled sobs came from behind it. Sam peeked over the top of the brush and saw a small girl, lying in the dirt. She was naked, holding a strip of a rag to her face. Her legs and arms were striped with blood. Sam squatted next to her, unsure what to do.

"Can I help you?" he asked gently. "I won't hurt you. My name is Sam."

The girl moved her hands and Sam was able to see her face. It was Polo's sister Amelia.

"Oh, Amelia! It's me, Sam," he said. "It's OK. I'll help you."

Amelia's small face was streaked with tears. Sam removed his t-shirt to cover her up.

"Let me go get help. We'll take you to the doctor," Sam offered.

Amelia shook her head no and grabbed Sam's arm. Her crying became louder.

"Sam?" he heard a voice call. It was Elena.

"Miss Elena! Over here!" Sam called.

"What are you doing? I saw your bike lying by the path and—" Elena stopped when she saw Amelia. "What is this?"

"I heard her crying. I found her like this. What happened to her?"

"Poor baby," Elena said, kneeling down next to Amelia. "Let me help you on with this shirt. Sam, you go get her mother, then tell Jourdain to bring his truck."

"Yes, ma'am."

Sam rode hard to Polo's. Polo, his mom, and his three sisters lived in a small wooden shanty on a narrow strip of land. His older brothers left long ago. The shanty leaned against a concrete block wall, which helped to hold the structure upright. He explained what he knew of the situation to Amelia's mother and told her where to find her daughter.

"I can't leave dees babies!" she said in frustration, waving her hand across the yard. Her other children were playing in the dirt. "If dat girl got herself in trouble, she jus' gone hafta figure out how to get out." She turned her back on Sam and went inside.

Polo was stirring a pot of something that bubbled over their fire. "Mama!" he called after his mother. "Watch the stew. I'll go check on Amelia."

"Whatever!" came her reply.

Sam directed Polo where to find his sister, then continued on to Jourdain's house.

"Jourdain!" Sam called. "Jourdain! Come quickly!"

Jourdain and Sam brought the truck. They loaded a battered Amelia into the back. Elena cradled Amelia's head in her lap and Polo held her hand. Sam rode in the cab to the hospital, telling Jourdain what Amelia's mother had said. He couldn't understand how she could be so callous.

"She has a lot on her plate," Jourdain tried to explain. "I am sure she cares, she just can't do much about it."

"But she didn't even want to come see her own daughter!" Sam said with indignance. "How does a person just leave their child behind, maybe even to die?"

"God sent *you* to her, Sam. She needed someone. God knew you would help her."

Thankfully, it was a slow night at the hospital, and Amelia

was given a bed right away. She could not find her voice, but the doctor confirmed that she had been raped. There wasn't much he could really do. She was bruised, but nothing broken. At least not her bones, anyway. She clung to her brother's hand silently, and every few minutes a lonely tear trickled from her purple eye. She willingly took some aspirin and allowed Elena to hold an ice pack against her face, but she said nothing. Recognizing Amelia's pitiful state, the doctor said she could sleep in a hospital bed for the night. Elena declared that she would stay by her bedside, ushering everyone else out so Amelia could rest.

As Jourdain drove them home, Sam reflected how lucky they all were to have Elena. She was there for him when Papa was sick, and now she is there for Polo's sister. He wanted to do something nice for her.

All the next day Sam wondered about Amelia. He hoped that when Jourdain picked her up and brought her home, her mother would be kind to her. When the day's baseball quota was done, he pedaled to Elena's.

"Elena! Are you here?" Sam called as he entered the store.

She emerged from the back. "Bonswa, Sam. How was your day?"

"It was fine. How's Amelia?"

"Her soul is in pain. And her body. But she found her voice again, so that is good. She started talking in the wee hours of the night. I was half-asleep when I heard her tiny sound. She said two men in police uniforms hurt her. We cried, and I held her hand."

"You are so good to all of us, Miss Elena," Sam stated. "That poor girl."

"The darkness is closing in everywhere."

"Can I clean for you?" Sam asked. "We haven't cleaned in a month."

Elena smiled. "You are a good boy, Sam. Yes, I will allow you to help me clean, then we will eat meat sandwiches."

They worked quickly and ate even more quickly. They both were famished and exhausted. Sam felt good, though. Elena and Jourdain were his family now. He had to do his part for them, the way they did their part for him. It was a strange family trio, with no one of them really tied to the other by anything but friendship. Jourdain and Elena had no parental authority over Sam, yet he would do anything they asked of him. As he forced his legs to work the pedals along the last dirt road before arriving at his house he wondered, *did God put them in his life because He knew Papa would die?*

"Thank you, God," Sam said aloud.

Sam didn't hear the men enter his home. His sleep was so deep that he didn't even hear them enter his room, despite one of them tripping over Sam's shoes. It wasn't until a gloved hand covered his mouth and a small wooden club smacked him upside his head that he knew anything was wrong. A leathery finger slipped into his mouth and on instinct Sam bit down. Hard. The assailant screamed out in pain before his partner kicked Sam in the side. Sam's cry echoed off the walls.

Sam was tall, but not overly muscular, and had no chance of wiggling free against the stocky, armed attackers. But he tried. As they worked to maneuver Sam out of his room, his mouth got free, and he let out another cry for help. A second smack to the head made everything fuzzy. His body went limp, but he had a modicum of consciousness for what happened next.

He was being carried from his house.

At the door, a blinding flash of light came from outside.

There was a loud crack.

The man holding Sam's legs dropped them and collapsed to the ground.

The other man let go of Sam and reached for the gun tucked in his waistband.

An explosion. The man careened backwards.

Sam's body smacked the ground.

Pain.

Then nothing.

CHAPTER 7

Awareness faded in slowly. Then left. It remained a little longer each time, until eventually Sam's heavy eyes stayed open. His neck throbbed, and even if he wanted to move, he couldn't. He blinked, and the ceiling of his bedroom came into focus.

"Sam?" It was Elena's voice, but he could not see her. In his mind he answered her, but no words came from his mouth.

"It's OK, Sam," she said. "Don't move. Don't speak. Rest."

He felt the world fading out again and did not fight it. When consciousness returned, he tried moving a little. It hurt. He blinked and slowly turned his head.

"Hey, buddy," Jourdain said. Elena was not there.

"Ah," Sam whispered. His mouth was unbearably dry. Jourdain held a bottle of water to Sam's lips and let some trickle in. After several small sips, Sam tried speaking again. "What happened?"

"Don't worry about that now," Jourdain said. "Let's get you feeling better first. Don't worry. Elena and I won't leave you."

One or the other stayed with Sam for the next two days. They kept him on a regular aspirin regimen and kept a cold cloth on his tender, aching head. A knot the size of a small stone protruded from his skull, near his right ear.

"Please tell me what happened," Sam begged Jourdain. He was finally able to sit up in his bed and eat some porridge.

"What do you remember?" Jourdain asked.

"I helped Elena clean her shop. We ate dinner. I was so very tired. I came home and went right to bed. That's it."

"You don't remember the men?"

Sam thought for a moment. Nothing came to mind. "No."

Jourdain let out a big sigh. "This won't be easy to hear. Two men broke into your house. It seems their intent was to kidnap you—or at least to drag you somewhere else—I heard a scream and arrived as they were carrying you out the front door."

"Did you fight them?"

Jourdain pressed his lips together, trying to decide how to answer. "I shot them."

"You—shot them?"

Jourdain nodded.

"Are they—"

Jourdain nodded.

"Where—are they now?"

Jourdain shook his head. "It's better if you don't know. They aren't here, though."

"Who were they?"

"I went through their pockets and their vehicle—I found it parked down the road—I believe they were macoute."

"Macoute? What would they want with me?"

"I do not know. But Sam, I found a slip of paper in their truck. It had Raul's name on it."

A fist enclosed around Sam's heart. "That was months ago. Why me?"

It was an answer Jourdain did not know.

Elena helped Sam get cleaned up and changed out of his dirty clothes. It had been four days since the attack, and during that time she'd washed everything that could be washed and scrubbed the blood from the floor where the men were shot. The knot on Sam's head was decreasing and the stiffness in his neck loosening. Tight strips of cloth wrapped around his midsection would help Sam's bruised ribs heal back into their proper place. It appeared he would be alright. At least, until the next macoute came calling for him...

"What should I do?" he asked Jourdain and Elena as they ate dinner.

The two people he depended on the most looked at each other with worry.

"What?" Sam demanded to know their thoughts.

Elena reached across the table and took Sam's hand. "Samféyo. I think of you like a son. And I know Jourdain does too. We can't force you to do anything, but you are special to us. We had an idea."

Sam's eyes began to water. Something big was coming; he'd slipped into the gap where things were about to be changed. He nodded for her to continue. She squeezed his hand. "You are not safe here. If the macoute are after you, they will catch up with you eventually."

"Why would they be after me, though?" he asked.

"I'd been thinking about that," Jourdain said. "You said there were four other guys with Raul."

"Yes," Sam said.

"It's possible they have been looking for you to see what Raul told you. Or to recruit you to join with them. Or to see if you were involved in the raid," Jourdain suggested.

"But I wasn't!" Sam insisted.

"They don't know that," Jourdain said. "Regardless, they wanted to find you. Sam. I think you need to get away from here."

"Where can I go? I have no place else," Sam argued.

"I think you should go to Santo Domingo," Jourdain said.

"Santo Domingo? Why?" The capital of the Dominican Republic was a small step up from Port-au-Prince, but he had never been there, nor did he know anyone there. All he knew about Santo Domingo was... "Wait. Isn't that where the baseball academies are?"

Jourdain nodded. "Yes. If your dream of becoming a real baseball player ever will come true, then it has to start in Santo Domingo. It is time to try."

"They won't let me in any baseball academy. Will they? I'm not Dominican. I don't have any money. I don't have anything! I'm not even a real baseball player."

"I am flying there tomorrow. I have a connection who I

think can help us. Let me see what I can do, and then we'll work out the details. In the meantime, we think you should stay with Elena."

"I don't suppose I have my job at the baseball plant anymore," Sam sighed.

Elena, who was still holding Sam's hand, gave it another squeeze. "We'll help you, Samféyo, I promise."

Jourdain took off the next morning, while Sam packed his clothing into a green canvas duffel bag that had been Papa's. As a small boy, Sam admired the brown leather straps that encircled the bag; the softness of the leather made him feel rich. The bag itself never had a real adventure. As he zipped the bag, he realized he had been on an adventure ever since Papa died. A part of him knew he would be leaving Port-au-Prince. *Where would he go?* He dared not hope too hard that it would be to a baseball academy. But maybe…

There were some personal things in the house that, if he were to leave, he would take with him, but Elena didn't think he needed to worry about clearing things out just yet. Sam did, however, take the money pouch that contained his savings. He had been frugal over the months since Papa died and had a respectable amount of money saved up.

Elena seemed to think that they could sell Papa's house, which would bring in even more money for Sam's future. She had a connection in town—a relative who brokered deals for people like Sam, who were not wealthy but were a step above the poor. Sam wanted to wait and hear what Jourdain learned before making that decision.

Jourdain was gone for three days, leaving Sam on pins and needles the whole time. To keep busy, Sam worked the tobacco plants so things wouldn't fall behind. Once dusk crept in, he locked up the shed and hurried back to Elena's, looking over his shoulder the whole way. He never felt unsafe in Haiti. Until now. He chastised himself for ever going to Ricardo's in the first place. He wasn't a man. He didn't belong there.

"There is no use beating yourself up about it," Elena

countered one night when Sam lamented his choices. "Didn't your papa used to have a saying about that?"

"Yes. He'd say, 'Life is meant to be traveled forward, not backwards.'" Sam had almost forgotten that one.

"Keep your eyes forward, Sam. God has big plans for you."

They heard a knock on the shop door downstairs. They froze, uncertain whether to answer it. It was nearly ten o'clock at night. Then they heard the whistle.

"It's Jourdain!" Sam squealed, and he ran quickly to let him in. Sam bounced up the stairs after him, doing his best to control his anxiety.

In true Elena-fashion, she made them wait to talk until she had served hot tea and some thin cookie crisps that she had made that morning. When they were seated comfortably around her table, she indicated to Jourdain that he may proceed.

He began with a sigh, which Sam read as bad news.

"I knew it was a bad idea," Sam said dejectedly. He put his head down on his folded arms. "Thank you for trying, Jourdain."

"Now what makes you think I failed?" Jourdain stated firmly. "Have you no faith in me, boy?"

Sam lifted his head. Jourdain's stern look melted into a smile.

"Well, what happened?" Elena said impatiently. "Tell us!"

"OK, so my old friend Charlie is part of the coaching staff at Campo Las Palmas. He works with rookies."

"Campo Las Palmas? The Los Angeles Dodgers?" Sam's eyes grew wide.

"How do you know him?" Elena demanded. "Why didn't you mention this before?"

"Charlie's mother and my mother used to work at the same resort. We'd play together when my father took me to visit her. I lost track of him over the years. I didn't even know he was involved in baseball!" Jourdain said in apologetic response to Elena's stern look. "I ran into him last month during our trip to Barahona. He told me that he worked for the Dodgers' baseball academy. I got a little hope in my heart that maybe this could be good for Sam, but I wasn't sure how to approach it. Then with all that happened last week, I knew it was not coincidence that our paths had crossed!

"I went to the academy and we had lunch together. I asked him how it all worked. A few times each year they do open tryouts for the rookie team. They announce it in the paper a few days before, and dozens of youth show up. They run the players through a one-day screening. If they like you, they'll keep you a bit longer. He told me that most of the players are brought in by scouts. They've been playing in amateur leagues or in school leagues and want their shot. The scouts work the coaches' ears off endlessly on behalf of their players, hounding them at every chance they get to convince them that their kid is the best. He said it is extremely rare for a walk-up player without a scout to be good enough to make it from the try-outs because the good players are already on their radar. The academy has their own scouts pounding the lots, looking for talent."

"That doesn't sound good for me," Sam said.

"He said it is rare, but it is not impossible. I told him I knew of a boy who was young, talented, and in a bit of a jam. I asked what I needed to do in order to get you a tryout, Sam. Charlie said anyone can come to public tryouts, and because our mamas go way back, he would give Sam a solid look. He also told me the date of the next open tryout. It's scheduled for October 30, after the World Series is over."

"Woo-hoo!" Elena yelled! "That's wonderful!"

"Really! Oh wow!" Sam cried.

Elena and Sam both went around the table and hugged Jourdain.

"Now wait. There's more," Jourdain said. "Sit back down."

"I'll do anything!" Sam promised. "Just tell me."

"Charlie said you have to be at least sixteen years old and have a Dominican birth certificate in order to be signed as a rookie with the Academy."

Sam and Elena blinked in shock at Jourdain.

"I am not Dominican," Sam said.

Jourdain smiled. "That takes me to the second part of my trip. After I thanked Charlie and told him that we would be back, I visited another old friend."

From his pocket, Jourdain pulled a sheet of paper and handed it to Sam. Sam unfolded it.

"Gobienero De República Dominicana," he read. "Certificado de nacimiento. Lionel Albert Bierto. Santo Domingo. July 17, 1972."

"Jourdain. What is that?" Elena asked.

"It is a birth certificate for a seventeen-year-old boy. Sam speaks Spanish as well as a native. And his English is very good, too."

"But it says, 'Lionel.' Would I have to change my name?" Sam asked.

"That is a downside, my friend. You would be known as Lionel Bierto."

Sam processed this news. On the one hand, there is a slim chance that he could be accepted in the Baseball Academy! On the other, by doing so, he gives up his country, his home, and his identity.

"What should I do?" he asked Elena quietly.

She took his hand. "Son. I can't tell you what to do. This is your path. You must walk it."

Tears welled in his eyes. They teetered there for a moment, then spilled in long streaks down his face. "I don't know what to do."

"Why don't you think about it? You do not have to decide tonight. October 30 is four weeks away. If it's what you want, we'll help you get there."

"Can I think about it for a couple of days?" Sam asked.

"Yes, Samféyo," Elena patted his hand. "Pray. Think. And whatever you decide, we are here for you."

Sam rolled cigars for the entire next day to keep his hands busy while his mind was occupied elsewhere. This was the opportunity he would never have again. He was fully grounded in the reality that he likely would not be accepted. But should he try? Jourdain explained that if he was not accepted at tryouts, he had to wait for the next date. He had enough money to possibly find a place to live in Santo Domingo for a little while, but to find a job? Probably not. In the Dominican, boys played baseball *because* there were no jobs to be had. Baseball was the gleaming star in the sky that Dominican boys did everything to catch.

Sam tried to imagine owning the name Lionel. It meant 'young lion,' which was a good sign. He would need all the bravery in the world to survive this journey, should he decide to take it.

"Jourdain," he asked. "What if I don't get accepted?"

Jourdain put down the knife he was using to cut filler. "Well, Sam, if you are not accepted, we will figure out Plan B."

"Do you think anyone would believe I am an athlete?"

"Sam, you are over six feet tall now. You are growing fuzz on your lip. Your muscles are bulgy. Yes, you look like an athlete."

"If I sell the house and go, then don't make it, I won't have a home to return to."

Jourdain shook his head. "That isn't true. As long as Elena or I are alive, you will always have a home to come back to."

"What about the macoute?"

Jourdain sighed. "I don't know. Maybe after the elections next year life will be different. Maybe you can find a job in the Dominican and settle there. Maybe you will get accepted and become a Major League star in America. Nothing in life is certain, Sam. In the blink of an eye everything can change. All you can do is make the best decision with what is placed before you. You never know what a day will hold. The only thing certain is that God is good."

Sam continued rolling cigars. He had made up his mind.

"Jourdain."

"Yes, Sam?"

"Call me Lionel."

CHAPTER 8

Sissy Luba gathered her things and turned off the fan that dangled precariously from her ceiling. Its spin resembled that of a bike tire that's come loose from its axle. It would not have surprised her to see it wobble itself right from the ceiling and roll out the door. She thought, for the fourth time that week, that she needed to have someone come and secure it.

Hands on hips, she looked around for anything that needed tidying before calling it a day. Sissy was proud of the business she'd built. It was her baby. Eight years ago she'd lost her real baby and her husband in Hurricane Allen. Winds like no one but God alone had ever seen shredded their beloved city of Les Cayes. Angry waves swallowed everything in their path as Allen pushed a foamy wall of death over the town. Why she didn't go to a watery grave with her family, she still didn't understand. It was one of those questions she planned to ask her Maker, should she ever get the chance.

She noticed a smear of mud along the lemony-yellow painted wall near the door.

"That'll never do," she said, and she went to the bathroom to get a cleaning rag. When she returned a moment later, she was pleased to have a visitor.

"Elena!" she cried with glee. The two women hugged. "Hang on one moment."

Sissy wiped away the smudge and cleaned a good twelve inches around the spot for good measure.

"There!" she declared. "Now I can focus."

"I completely understand," Elena said. The two women

shared a propensity for cleanliness. "It's next to godliness."

"What can I do for you? Is your friend ready to sell?"

"It is a unique situation," Elena began. "The young man who owns the house must move. It is important that no one knows where he plans to go."

Sissy shrugged. The situation was about as unique as coconuts. "So the paperwork—" she prompted.

"Can the paperwork be done in Jourdain's name?" Elena asked cautiously.

"Jourdain Felix?"

"Wi. He is their neighbor. He has helped the family since the boy's mother died in childbirth. He and the father are – were – dear friends. This family has been through so much."

If it were anyone except Elena, Sissy would require verification of all these facts.

"No problem. I've been searching out potential buyers since you came to see me last week. I may have someone. Let me contact them tomorrow. How soon do we need this done?"

"As soon as possible."

"Wi. Can I see the house?"

"Come tomorrow morning."

Elena thanked God *and* Jesus for this good news as she rode her moto back to the boutik. She didn't doubt that Sissy would help, but she wasn't sure how quickly a buyer could be found. Sissy's husband had been Elena's brother. When he and Elena's sweet nephew were washed out to sea, Sissy moved to Port-au-Prince. She and Elena shared a bond that would never be broken—the heartache of family loss. Life's busy-ness kept them from seeing one another more than a couple of times each month, but their souls were intertwined. Trust would never be an issue.

First thing in the morning, Sam and Elena straightened up the house. It didn't need much—as Papa taught Sam the value of keeping things orderly. Sissy was quite pleased as she wrote down the room specifications.

"Very nice home, Sam," she said, approving. "Let me

make some phone calls. Come to my office tomorrow afternoon, OK?"

At four-thirty sharp the next day, Elena, Jourdain, and a nervous Sam visited Sissy's office. She waved them to sit down, as she was on the phone.

"Yes, sir," she said pleasantly. "I will see you on Monday. Au revoir!" She placed the phone receiver in its cradle. "I think we have a buyer!"

"Already?" Elena said in surprise.

"That's wonderful!" Jourdain declared. "Who?"

"It isn't firm yet, but the potential buyers are coming to town next week. That's a good sign. They are a Christian missions group looking for a house to use as lodging for visiting missionaries. They have a modest budget, and I think your house would be perfect. They loved the way it sounded and want to see it first-hand." Sissy sat back in her chair and folded her arms, a satisfied smile on her lips.

The three adults looked to Sam for reaction. His face was blank.

"What do you think, Sam?" Jourdain asked.

Elena put a hand on Sam's leg. "It's OK, Sam. We know it's a lot to take in."

Sam pressed his lips together tightly and closed his eyes. His deep breath was not one of hesitation, but of confidence.

"Let's do it!" he said boldly.

Sissy drew up paperwork for Jourdain Felix to sell the property to Calvary Hill Missions Group. She had everything but the price filled in when the two senior pastors and their wives arrived on Monday. The tour of the house and property did not take long, and Jourdain was the perfect host. The Americans liked the idea that Jourdain lived next door and even offered to pay him to be a property caretaker when the house was unoccupied. They agreed to the first price Sissy suggested, which had been padded a bit to allow room for negotiation. They wrote a check, payable to Jourdain, for the full amount. It was all done by six o'clock in the evening.

The Americans asked Jourdain if he could have the house cleared of personal belongings by Wednesday. They wanted to buy the meager furniture that the home had, and they gave Jourdain two hundred dollars in American cash for it all. It was a hundred fifty dollars more than it was worth, and Sam had a mere forty-eight hours left in the only home he'd ever known.

The next day, Elena took Sam to the Port-au-Prince shopping district. She insisted they revamp his wardrobe. Sam's clothes had always come from either street vendors or the humanitarian groups' distribution centers. Sam hadn't considered that he had no real clothes to take with him to Santo Domingo. Elena by-passed all of the usual places in Pétion-Ville and guided them to a large warehouse set behind a Caribbean Supermarket on rue Darguin. The warehouse reminded Sam of the airport. Sounds bounced off of the cement-block walls like hail and the racks were stuffed like an overcrowded city bus. Women and children wedged themselves between the racks. Everywhere Sam looked were clothes, clothes, and more clothes.

"I feel dizzy," Sam complained. "I can't breathe in here."

"We are not sending you into the world dressed like a bum from Haiti," Elena said firmly. "I know what to look for. Just follow me."

She forged a path toward the rear of the warehouse. As he pushed aside hangers and clothing, he realized there was loosely shaped order to the chaos. At six-foot-two, Sam saw clearly over the racks and could tell that they were entering a section of men's clothing. Elena pulled two pairs of jeans and handed them to Sam.

"32 x 34? Is that my size?" Sam asked.

She held them to his frame. "Yes," she declared. She proceeded to locate sweatpants, athletic shorts, t-shirts in various colors, two pairs of shoes, and a windbreaker. Next she grabbed a dozen pairs of underwear, socks, and a belt. She piled it all into Sam's arms.

"Now. Church clothes. Come."

She pressed through racks of women's negligees to the other end of the store which housed dressier clothing for men and women. One pair of black slacks, two button-up shirts, a lime-green tie, and a grey blazer later, she declared Sam ready to go.

"Is this all going to fit in my duffel bag?" Sam wondered.

"Next stop—suitcase!" she stated.

Near the payment counters was a small section of travel luggage. They chose a hard-cased black suitcase with wheels. When the woman rang it all up, Sam owed 9,000 gourdes. Elena offered the woman one of Sam's one-hundred-dollar bills, and the woman snatched it like a candy bar.

"Wow!" Sam said as he pulled his new suitcase full of clothes behind him. "This is incredible. I've never had so many things."

"We are not done yet. We must get you toiletries, Sam. You have to look *and* smell like you belong."

Sam smelled his armpit, then scrunched his nose. "Maybe you're right. Those ballplayers on television look very clean-cut."

A trip to the drugstore landed him a new toothbrush, toothpaste, deodorant, soap, and shampoo. They even picked out a small case to carry them in. Papa's electric razor would be something Sam kept always, and they purchased new blades to keep it in good condition.

"Now you're ready!" she announced.

As anxious as the crowded clothing store made him feel, going through the things in his home made him downright nauseous. It was easy to leave behind the furniture, but going through Papa's things brought a sadness he hadn't felt since Papa passed.

"Let's bag up the clothing first," Jourdain suggested. "Then we can see what's left."

Papa's old blue Dodgers baseball cap was like a friend to Sam, and it was the only thing in Papa's clothes bureau that he decided to keep. Memories of Papa throwing baseballs to Sam in the dirt lot flooded back as he held it, and he placed it on his head.

Papa had a ratty notebook, filled with various scribblings from over the years. Sam had seen it often, but he never dared leaf through it until after Papa died. A page written in delicate, careful script brought warmth to his heart. It was a mere grocery list, written by a woman he never had the chance to know, but it brought him peace. The notebook would go with him, as would the only two framed pictures in the house. One was of Papa and a pregnant Mama on the beach, and the other of Papa in his faithful Dodgers cap and ten-year-old Sam, proudly holding a baseball for the photographer to see. Papa had a small stack of other photos, which Sam placed carefully in an envelope. These were his treasures.

Jourdain was busy emptying the last dresser drawer, when he came across a tiny yellow envelope, no bigger than a business card. "What's this, Sam?" he asked.

"I've never seen it."

Jourdain handed it to Sam. There was something small and hard inside. Sam tore the edge and spilled the contents into his palm. He gasped. It was two perfect gold bands. They were exactly the same thin width, but one was larger than the other.

"Wedding rings!" Sam said with awe. He turned them over in his hand and examined them. "They are beautiful. Papa's and Mama's?" he questioned.

"I would suppose so," Jourdain replied. "I don't really remember seeing them wear them."

Sam took the photo of his parents from the box. "Look! Papa has his arms wrapped around Mama's stomach." The black and white photo was grainy, but their intertwined hands did appear to have wedding bands encircling the ring fingers.

Sam felt really happy for the first time all week. He put the rings back in the small envelope and tucked it away in his toiletry bag.

"Hey! What's this?" Jourdain pulled a box from under the bed.

"The baseball!" Sam said. "I definitely want to keep

that." Inside was the practice baseball that Sam sewed with Papa on the night before he went to Rawlings for the first time. He didn't have the waxy thread or needles anymore—he'd given them to Michel for practice. He wanted that ball though. Learning how to use exactly eighty-eight inches of thread was the key to his survival over these last months.

"Well then, that's about it!" Jourdain said. "Do you want to help me load the truck? We can take the garbage to the trash field."

Sam walked through the house one last time. He paused in Papa's bedroom. His birth coincided with his mother's death in that room. The thought creeped him out when he was younger. Not so much anymore. Birth and death were playmates in Haiti. If she were here, would he leave? Of course not. He'd likely still be in school and only dreaming of a chance to play baseball. Now, his chance was no longer a dream. "I won't blow it, Mama," he promised.

Figuring out how to get the check—made out to Jourdain—to Sam—who didn't have a bank account—wasn't as tricky as Sam thought it would be. After exploring several options, they decided to wait until they got to Santo Domingo, where they could open Sam a bank account using his new name and birth certificate. Then Jourdain would sign the check over to Sam and deposit it in his new account. Voila! A phone call by Sissy to BanReservas—the largest bank in the DR—confirmed that this process would work. She'd already called the Wells Fargo Bank in the United States and confirmed that the American's check was good for the funds. There should be no problems.

Sam's next challenge was to put some more muscles on his lanky body. Ever since Jourdain presented the opportunity to try out for the academy, Sam wore himself out nightly with push-ups, sit-ups, and squats. No matter what, he jogged five kilometers each morning. His ribs gave him surprisingly little pain, and something resembling muscles was developing on his bones. He prayed they were enough to make him look like an athlete. His efforts must have done some good, for Polo noticed a difference in Sam when Sam stopped in to say goodbye.

"You look different, man," Polo said.

"I've been building muscles," Sam joked, striking a body builder pose. Then he turned serious. "How's Amelia?"

"Not great. She won't go anywhere by herself. I can't blame her. It'll take time."

They were quiet for a moment. It was time to fill Polo in. "Polo, I have something to tell you…" For the next twenty minutes, Sam relayed everything that had gone on in the last nine months. From Papa's death, to Raul and the Soulèvman Jèn Yo, to the attempted kidnapping, to his plans to leave. For Polo's own safety, he didn't tell him where he planned to go or what his new name would be. (He also left out how much money he got for the house sale.)

"You're leaving?" Polo asked. "Like, forever?"

Sam shrugged. "I don't know. If things don't work out, I'll have to figure something out. For now, I don't know, yeah, I've got to go."

"Man," Polo hung his head. "Man." When he looked up a blush of sadness covered his face. "You're my homie. Like a brother."

Sam hugged Polo like he wished he could hug Papa one last time. He tried to squeeze Polo right through his skin and into his heart.

"I'll miss you," Sam said. "Brothers forever."

"Brothers forever," Polo agreed. "I'm sorry about your papa."

They shook hands; their secret handshake they'd come up with years ago. Sam wondered if he'd ever find another friend like Polo.

"I was wondering if you would mind keeping an eye on my bike while I'm gone? I mean, you can use it and all. And you can ride it over to Jourdain's house. Jourdain will need a new guy to help him roll cigars. He said if you were interested, he'd pay you. It's not a bad gig," Sam said.

"Really, man? Thanks!" Polo smiled. It helped Sam to

know Jourdain and Polo would have each other. It eased the pain of leaving. A little. He rubbed his hand over the orange crossbar of his bike one last time, then left it with Polo.

The goodbye to Elena was just as difficult. She was the glue to the broken pieces of his life over the last year. She didn't even try to keep her tears constrained. Her face was swollen, red, and snotty from the crying she started the night before.

"Oh, Sam! I am going to miss you. You are a huge piece of my heart," she sobbed, pulling him into a hug and clinging tightly to his back. Her face was buried in his chest. "I am so proud of you."

"I don't know how to ever repay you," Sam said. "I would have died without you and Jourdain."

"The Lord gives. The Lord takes away. When He took Eduard from you, He gave you to us. And you have been a gift to me, too, Sam. God never will give you more than you can handle, Samféyo. Remember that. When you feel like there is no one, ask Him to show you who is there for you. There will always be someone."

"I'll remember, Miss Elena. I promise.

Jourdain and Sam loaded the truck.

"Why are you sliding the check under the seat?" Sam asked Jourdain.

"I'm hiding it up in the seat springs. This check is substantial. We do not need a curious border guard finding it." Jourdain's nerves came through in a tone Sam hadn't heard before.

"Are you scared?" Sam asked.

"I'm being extra cautious," Jourdain said. After all, they were traveling with an unusually large check, a suitcase full of clothing, and a duffle bag of personal mementos. Even the least astute officer would know someone wasn't planning to return to Haiti. They stopped in town and picked up ten passengers for the trip. Barahona first, to sell boxes of cigars, then on to Santo Domingo. The adventure had begun.

CHAPTER 9

"**F**rom now on, you are Lionel Bierto," Jourdain reminded as they rolled toward the border. "We live in Barahona. I am your uncle."

"I got it," Lionel said.

The border guard was someone Jourdain knew, and he couldn't care less if the boy seated next to Jourdain was called Sam, Lionel, or Batman. No doubt it was a blessing. Jourdain had greased the guard's palm many times over the past couple of years. He accepted another moderate bribe, offering no trouble. He waved them along with a smile, bringing simultaneous sighs of relief from Jourdain and Lionel.

"Do all the guards take bribes?" Lionel asked.

"Every single one," Jourdain said. "They aren't paid well, and bribe money helps them survive."

"It's too bad that life is so hard," Lionel observed. The innocent statement dripped with truth. Survival was everyone's motive. Survival drove all decisions. Survival justified all behaviors. Even taking on a new identity.

Silence hung heavily in the cab, the young teen thinking about his future, Jourdain reflecting on his past. They delivered all of the cigars and brought in a record amount of money from sales. The late nights and long days working the tobacco plants paid off. Lionel's eyes widened when Jourdain gave him his share.

"So much? Are you sure?"

"Wi. This is it. Those plants will miss you greatly," Jourdain said.

"Don't forget about Polo. He can learn," he reminded.

Jourdain nodded. "Yes. I'll teach Polo. It won't be the same, though," he said wistfully.

Jourdain visited his friend at La Fleur while Lionel treated himself to a chimi burger. The Loro Tuerto Hotel provided them squishy beds and a clean-ish place to take a shower. There was no sleeping for Lionel; he counted ceiling tiles and listened to Jourdain's gruff snores all night long. He couldn't believe that tomorrow they were headed to Santo Domingo!

Two hundred seventeen kilometers east of Barahona lay the oldest city established by Europeans in the Western Hemisphere. Founded by the lesser-known Columbus brother, Bartholomew, Santo Domingo welcomes fewer tourists than other Dominican coast cities but houses more baseball talent than all of the other cities in the Dominican Republic combined.

The drive was easy, and as they passed through the cobblestoned streets of Santo Domingo, Jourdain and Lionel stopped for lunch at a small restaurant three streets in from the beach. The Good Day Café served simple sandwiches and fresh fruit, calming Lionel's ever-growing nerves.

"You doin' OK?" Jourdain asked, polishing off a roast beef hoagie.

"I've never felt like this about anything before," Lionel confessed. "My stomach is absolutely sick with nerves. I am one breath away from throwing up."

"You gotta calm it down," Jourdain warned. "I don't know much about baseball, but I know that nervous players make mistakes. You're going to need all your wits about you to play the best you've ever played. These guys have been playing hard for years. The competition is fierce."

"Thanks for the pep talk," Lionel said sarcastically.

"There's no candy-coating it," Jourdain said, opening his palms with a shrug. "This is it."

"I know," Lionel said. "Believe me. I haven't slept in two weeks."

"We've got to find a bank," Jourdain said. "Then maybe we can go to Campo and have a look around. Tryouts are early in the morning."

Opening a bank account for Lionel was a piece of cake, especially once the bank manager saw the size of his first deposit. After securing a hotel room, they drove to the ground of Campo Las Palmas to give Lionel his first glimpse at the place where his future would be decided in just a few short hours. It was dramatic to put that much pressure on it, Lionel knew, but that's how he felt. They parked the truck and strolled to the entrance of the compound. A dozen or so Dominican League players were engaged in afternoon batting practice on the field.

"Want to watch?" Jourdain asked.

"Yes! If they'll let us," Lionel replied.

"Are you a scout?" a sullen security guard asked as they approached.

"No," Jourdain answered. "We just want to watch. My nephew's trying out tomorrow."

A nod from the burly gatekeeper allowed them entrance. Lionel, who had never been in a real baseball park, felt like the proverbial fish out of water as they watched from the stands. He was getting a peek at something he only dreamed about or saw on television. These were real baseball players, playing with real equipment, in a real park. And tomorrow, he would be down there with them.

"Pay attention to what they're doing," Jourdain suggested. It was a needless directive. Lionel was taking it all in, at a level much deeper than the average fan.

For a while he stared only at the pitcher. He was older, probably a coach, tossing balls that he took from a large mesh barrel. One after another he pitched to the batter. Lionel watched the timing of the batting practice pitches. It was as regulated as a clock. Lionel counted the seconds between pitches. Eight seconds from the time the batter made contact to the time the pitcher released the next ball. The batter hit maybe forty balls, then with a nod of thanks to the pitcher, he stepped off and let the next guy go. This time, Lionel focused on the batter. He noted the distance of the batter's feet from the rubber and saw that he kept his feet perfectly parallel—not only to one another but also to the pitcher. This batter hit ten balls to left, ten up the center, and ten to right field in perfect succession. For his last swings he must have been aiming for the back fence because that's exactly where the balls went.

"Wow!" Lionel said appreciatively. "That was incredible."

Four more batters took their turns, then the players called it a day. After handshakes to the pitcher, they walked off the field.

"Got representatión?" a voice from behind them asked in Spanish.

"Que?" Jourdain responded.

"Representación," the stranger repeated. "For the kid. You're not a scout."

"Nah, I'm his uncle," Jourdain said. "And no, he doesn't have a scout."

The stranger handed him a card. "I'll represent him. You can't do anything around here without good representation."

"You've never seen him play," Jourdain accused. "How do you know he's any good?"

"What is he—six-foot-two? He's tall. He's got muscles. Lots of kids around here don't look so strong. He's a little skinny, but we can fatten him up."

"Nah, we good, man," Jourdain said, handing back the card. "But thank you."

"If you change your mind, they call me The Eagle. Ask anyone, they'll show you how to find me."

Once the stranger was far enough away so as not to hear, Lionel asked Jourdain why he didn't take the card.

"Charlie warned me about these guys. They call them buscóns. Most are thieves. They have no power to make the decision whether you are let into the academy. They just want a cut of any money you might get offered. You're too smart for that, Lionel. We don't need him. You'll show out tomorrow."

Lionel nodded, aware that there was much he didn't know.

Surprisingly, sleep was his friend that night. Stretching as he got out of bed the next morning, he was pleased to find that he felt strong and rested. His ribs had completely mended from the beating he took at the hands of the macoute, and his muscles felt loose. He warmed himself up with fifty push-ups and a few dozen sit-ups in the hotel room while Jourdain got himself dressed.

"I'm ready!" he declared, grabbing his glove and Papa's Dodgers cap. And they were off.

A handful of hopefuls were already clustered behind the backstop as Lionel walked onto the field ahead of Jourdain, who stopped in the restroom. Several more players were lined in front of a folding table, where a Dodger-capped Dominican added names to his clipboarded list.

"Name?" the man asked when it was Lionel's turn.

"Lionel Bierto," he answered, the words feeling thick in his mouth.

"Birthdate?"

Lionel paused. *What was it?* He couldn't remember his new birthdate.

"Son?" the man asked, looking skeptically at a sweating Lionel. "What's your birthdate?"

Lionel tried to picture the birth certificate. He could not.

"July 17, 1972," a voice said from behind. Jourdain came trotting up beside Lionel. "Charlie! How are you?"

"Jourdain!" The man stood, and they shook hands across the table. "Is this your boy?"

"Si," Jourdain answered in Spanish. "This is Lionel."

"Sorry, sir," Lionel apologized. "I'm a little nervous."

"No worries," Charlie answered. "I understand." He wrote down the birthday. "What positions do you play?"

"Outfield. First base," Lionel answered. That was an easy question.

"Lefty or right?"

"Both."

"No, I mean for batting. Left or right?" Charlie clarified.

"Yes, sir. I bat both sides," Lionel replied.

Charlie raised his eyebrows and wrote something on the

clipboard. "Wait over there with the others. We'll get going in a little while."

"Gracias," Lionel answered. He joined the other hopefuls. Jourdain stayed and spoke to Charlie for a few minutes more, then he headed to the stands, which were filling up rapidly. Open tryouts brought the neighborhoods into the academy.

It was hard not to notice the contingent of white men sitting behind the third base dugout.

"That's Ben Wade," a kid standing near him said, nodding toward an older guy in a tan suit.

"Ben Wade?" Lionel asked.

"He's in charge of scouting for the whole organization," the kid said in awe. "The man with the power."

Lionel nodded, watching the man chat casually. *"The man with the power,"* he said to himself. Some of the guys started jumping around to get loose. Lionel stepped away from the pack and went through a series of stretches. There was at least one other kid who appeared to match Lionel in height, but the rest were noticeably shorter in stature. Skinny arms, hungry faces. He dropped to the ground and did a few push-ups.

Wade was not the only man with power at Campo Las Palmas. A shrill whistle blew, and Charlie called for the tryouts to "Line up!" Many of the boys knew exactly what that meant, and they lined up side-by-side along the white chalk line that stretched between home plate and third base. Lionel fell in. A young boy, no more than ten, stood behind Charlie awaiting instructions. He wore a faded blue Dodger t-shirt and long shorts. Lionel grinned at him; the boy grinned back as if he knew a secret that none of the hopefuls knew. A few minutes later a growing murmur of interest could be heard through the stands behind them. The boys began to shift their feet, wanting badly to turn around, yet fighting to remain disciplined. Charlie looked over their heads into the bleachers. He nodded at whomever was back there. A minute later, a uniformed coach walked onto the field. Lionel felt the boys around him tense up. Lionel didn't yet know Ralph Avila's name, but he saw that the man oozed with importance. He stood before the lineup and spoke.

"Today, you will complete a series of tests. We will break you into three groups. Stay with your assigned group for the entire time. We expect that you stay focused and pay attention, so things run smoothly. If you can't stay focused, you will be asked to leave. You aren't here to joke around. We will inspect you, test you, and ask questions as you go through the drills. No arguing. You do what you are asked. There are coolers of water in the dugouts. Help yourselves as needed. Don't let yourself dehydrate. Got it?"

There were no questions. Avila walked away. Lionel counted twenty-nine boys present, and the first group's names were called. "Group One will bat," Charlie instructed, pointing to the on-deck circle. The boys went to their spot. As the first group of boys turned around, one of them exclaimed, "There's Tommy Lasorda!"

At that, every head in the line-up turned, and discipline went out the window! Even Lionel's. *Tommy Lasorda? Here?* The stomach butterflies did somersaults.

"All right, boys, get it together," Charlie called. The boys obeyed. He proceeded to call out the second group's names. Those boys were sent to fielding. Lionel's name was called in the third group. "Group Three will go to conditioning on the other field. Follow me."

Lionel's group had nine boys, of which he was the tallest. He couldn't resist a look back at Coach Lasorda as they left for the adjacent field where conditioning would be held. Lasorda was chatting with Mr. Wade. *Would he still be there when conditioning was over?* He wasn't sure if he should hope for or against that possibility.

The two coaches with Lionel's group didn't bother giving their names. Chalk marks in the grass designated a starting line and a finish line sixty yards away.

"You will run a timed sixty-yard sprint," the starting line coach said. "We will run through the line four times. Don't start until you hear the whistle from the coach at the finish line. After your last run, we will tell you your fastest time. Line up in the following order." He proceeded to call out the boys' names in the same order Charlie had called them. Lionel was fourth. Bending over to tighten his sneakers, he was grateful for the wherewithal from his furniture sale to purchase them. He noted a couple of the boys' sneakers were hanging on by torn leather and ratty shoelaces. One boy took his shoes off to run.

He set his glove in the grass and took his place in line. He bounced like a pogo stick to loosen his ankles. Through all the races home from school with Polo, no one had ever timed him before. He had no idea if he'd be an embarrassment or if he'd fit in. He prayed for the latter.

At his turn, he stood ready, waiting for the whistle. He stutter-stepped a bit on his take off but ran a straight shot for his sixty yards. Following the lead of the other boys, he trotted back to his place in line. He had scarcely caught his breath when it was his turn again. With a much better start, he willed his legs to go faster. He couldn't tell if his legs listened.

Between the second and third rounds, the coach gave an extra three-minute rest during which none of the boys spoke to one another. They saved their energy. When Lionel crossed the sixty-yard marker for the fourth time, he circled back to the coach to learn his time.

"Six-point-seven," the coach said with eyebrows raised.

Was that fast? Lionel had no idea if that was a good time. So he said the only thing he could think... "Thank you."

The coaches allowed a quick water break before explaining the next task—a three-hundred-yard sprint drill. They were to run sixty yards, touch the chalk line, sprint back to starting position, touch the starting line, and repeat until they had run five lengths.

"We are looking for a time under fifty-five seconds for this exercise," the coach said. "You will run in three groups. Numbers one through three, take your start."

Lionel watched the form of the sprinters in the first heat. He surmised that the key to keeping speed up was in the pivot. In his heat, the kid who started to his right was close behind him the entire sprint, but Lionel kept enough ahead to cross the finish easily before him. The other runner was at least five seconds behind.

"Forty-seven seconds," the coach told Lionel, who smiled in response.

For the next running drill, the players started on home plate. At the whistle, they were to round the bases to get to third as quickly as possible.

"Start out standing the direction you would face if you were batting," the coach instructed. "And no sliding. Stay on your feet."

The first boy tripped as he rounded second base, faceplanting in the dirt. He got up anyway and finished his run. The next kid stayed upright, but clearly was cautious rounding second base. The third ran straight through the first base bag, forgetting to head left to second. Once he realized his mistake, he took off, but the coach whistled him to stop.

"You ran out of the baseline," the coach called. "Get back in line."

The shaky starts of the first three runners unnerved Lionel. With a deep breath, he stood as if in a right-handed batter's stance. At the whistle he took off, rounding first easily, keeping his eye on the second base bag. As he neared it, he focused on the spot he wanted to tag and tapped it as he curved to third. He came to a stop on the bag, keeping his balance.

"That's the way," the coach encouraged. "You bat right?"

"I bat both, sir," Lionel said.

"Oh, yeah?" he said. "We'll see. Next time start the other side."

Lionel mirrored the run starting from a left-handed bat stance. He couldn't be sure, but it felt as fast as his first run. The coach nodded as he wrote on his clipboard.

When the running drills were over, the coaches timed the boys on push-ups and sit-ups. Lionel was one of six who did push-ups for the entire timed minute. The whole conditioning experience felt good, and he was glad to have it out of the way. But no matter how fast he ran, if he botched fielding and batting, it wouldn't matter one lick to the coaches.

Lionel's group was sent to fielding. All six of the coaches huddled together for a powwow to exchange clipboards and share initial impressions before beginning the next group's exercises. Coach Lasorda's imposing presence still graced the stands; Avila wandered from group to group, intensely watching. Lionel picked up on Avila's name from listening to the other boys' chatter. He noticed that Avila's demeanor toward certain players was more focused than with others. Lionel longed for Avila's attention; he had a feeling he wouldn't be asked to stay unless he commanded it somehow.

The fielding coaches explained that the players would rotate through all infield and outfield positions except for pitcher. They would play their given position until called to switch. First rotated to second, second to short, short to third, third to left, left to center, center to right, and right to the bye position. They would field the hits off the batters with the goal to play the ball to first as fast as possible. On a pop fly, the play was to go to second. Lionel was put at third to start. It's a long throw from third to first, requiring sharp precision. Fortunately for Lionel, the first batter pulled to right field consistently, and the second baseman and right fielder got the most workout off of him, allowing Lionel to relax and settle in.

In left and center, Lionel saw more action. He got the ball in quickly and cleanly, catching three pop flies and scooping up two grounders that got through. Avila took notice. He was ready to shine. When Lionel moved to right field, on the first pitch, the batter cracked it hard. The ball was headed over the wall, just behind Lionel. *Not today*, Lionel thought. With all the spring his legs could give, he leapt in the air, stopping the home run hit by catching the ball before it plunked over. The rest of his fielding squad whooped and cheered at the play. Lionel, not forgetting his goal, threw to the second baseman to stop a potential tag up from first base. He thought he saw Avila nod, but he couldn't be sure.

In the batter's box, Lionel struggled. Even at sixty miles per hour, the pitching coach threw harder than any of the kids in the dirt lots ever threw, and it took Lionel several strikes before getting a fair ball. Once he did, he was able to hit three more batting right-handed. None left the park, but his grounders were strong and went up and over the second base bag. The batting coach called for Lionel to switch sides. At lefty he did better, with only three strikes before he knocked one high and watched it bounce over the distracted center fielder's head.

They went through the batting order twice, and the second time through was treated like a real at-bat. Whereas most of the waiting boys were side-eyeing Tommy Lasorda in the stands, Lionel's eyes rarely left the pitcher. He'd been watching the release and anticipating the amount of time it took for the ball to get to the sweet spot at the plate. The pitcher was excruciatingly consistent and accurate. Lionel felt sure his timing would be better next time around. On his turn, he chose to bat left-handed. He took one strike just to be sure of the timing, and then with a deep breath and his eye on the ball, he swung for his second pitch with all he had. The crack of wood to leather was a sound he'd never heard before. He didn't need to wait for it to happen to know that ball was out of the park. It was by far the furthest hit any of them had seen that day. The hit caused enough commotion to bring Avila over to talk to the coaches. They glanced Lionel's way twice.

The hour-long wait while the coaches conferred was brutal. Some of the boys practiced pitching and hitting to one another, some stretched out on the grass, and some went to the stands to talk to their buscóns. Lasorda and Burns left the stands and were presumably wherever the coaches were having their discussions. Or maybe they weren't. Lionel couldn't be sure. He talked to Jourdain for a while, then, feeling anxious, made a pit stop into the bathrooms. When he came out, he could see that the coaches were re-entering the field area.

The players lined up again along the third base line. Quite unceremoniously, Avila called out, "Almora, Javier, Bierto. We want to talk to you. The rest of you, you can try out again next time. Thank you for coming out."

Twenty-six disheartened boys hung their heads and walked heavy-footed off the field. Lionel stood in place and watched them go. *How many times had they been there before?* he wondered. He didn't want to breathe. What were they going to say? Once the field was clear, Avila spoke.

"Boys, you've made it a tiny step further. You are not, I repeat, NOT, being offered any kind of contract at this time. We want to evaluate you more. We are giving you thirty days to show us what you got. You'll stay here at the academy and train with the rookies. We will feed you and make sure you've got a bed to sleep in, but you are not yet a rookie player. At the end of the thirty days, we will either talk contract, or we'll shake hands and send you away." He smiled. "It won't be easy. But you'll see if you've got the stuff. Most importantly, *we'll* see if you've got the stuff. If you do, we'll talk. Understand?"

Three glassy-eyed boys nodded.

"Good. Now, go home and get your things. Be back here for supper at six. You will meet with Charlie in the trainer's office tomorrow morning at seven for a complete physical evaluation by our team doctor. Don't be late."

CHAPTER 10

Saying goodbye to Jourdain was scary and painful. They kept it short, with Jourdain promising to be back in thirty days.

"You don't have to come check on me," Lionel said, with a tone that expressed the opposite.

"Sure, I do," Jourdain said, grinning. "Besides, I visited a few shops while I was here. I've got to bring 'em back some cigars."

"Hey! That's great," Lionel said, genuinely happy. "I can't believe this is happening."

Jourdain gave him a quick hug. "Take care. Work hard. Don't give them a reason to cut you. Whatever the others say or do, be the bigger man."

Lionel nodded. *"Don't give them a reason to cut you."* This would be his mantra.

From the first day, the rookies called Lionel and the two other guys the *tres farsantes*. It really didn't bother Lionel much; he felt like a "faker" anyway, posing as a seventeen-year-old Dominican ballplayer instead of the Haitian orphan that he was. The three new guys didn't spend much time with the rookies. Charlie and the other coaches took turns running them through endless drills, always in an area where the rookies weren't. Avila vetted them daily. He tested all three of them for pitching skills in the first week, after which he designated that José Javier was to train for two hours each day with the pitchers. They dropped into their beds each night exhausted. Even though everyone was busy, and everyone worked their tails off, several of the rookies took advantage of any time they were all in the same place to give the three boys grief. This often happened in the locker room after practice or in the dining hall. After two weeks' worth of taunts, one afternoon José Javier snapped back.

"The only thing fake around here is your talent!" he retorted, following one of the rookies' jeers.

Things fell silent. After several heavy seconds, the rookie, whose name was Frank Orza, reached out and knocked a pile of towels off of a bench. "Oh look, faker, you knocked the towels onto the floor. Guess you'd better pick them up."

Lionel saw José's hand tighten into a fist. He didn't move.

"Did you not hear me, estúpido?" Orza prodded.

That did it. José barreled over the bench and plowed his shoulder into Orza's chest, knocking both of them backward onto the concrete floor. Unfortunately, Orza was standing near the end of the row of lockers, and as they flew to their backs, his head hit a metal corner on the end locker before smacking onto the concrete. The pool of blood grew quickly from the unconscious rookie.

"Mierda!" another rookie yelled. "Get some help!"

Two guys ran out, leaving the stunned group unsure what to do.

"Get off him, idiota!" another rookie yelled, snatching the back of José's neck and yanking him up off the ground.

José pushed him away and stormed out of the locker room. A minute later, Charlie and another coach appeared behind the two guys who ran for help.

"What the hell happened here?" Charlie said, as they bent over Orza. "Get a towel!"

They held a towel to the back of his head, putting pressure on the wound. Orza, still unconscious, was wearing only his underwear. The other coach bolted back to the office to call an ambulance.

"Everybody, out!" Charlie instructed. "Except you, you, and you." He pointed to three other rookies. "Go on! Get out!" he screamed to the rest of them.

Lionel followed the group silently, grabbing his duffel

bag from the floor as they left.

"Man, he shouldn't have tackled him like that," someone said.

"Orza pushed it," another answered.

"Shut up, pendejo. New guy's gotta have control," a third responded.

The chatter continued as the group made their way to the dining hall. José wasn't there, and Lionel wondered if he should go look for him. He decided against it, opting to sit with the other *farsante*, Manny Almora.

"What do you think?" Manny asked.

Lionel shrugged. "We gotta keep our cool."

"Yeah," Manny nodded. They ate the rest of their dinner in silence, listening to the heated arguments from the rookies around them.

Lionel went to bed early; there was no news on Orza, and José was nowhere to be found. He knew the others were up late, talking about the incident, but he kept his blanket pulled over his head until he fell asleep.

At six a.m. Coach Ramos banged on the wall in Lionel's dormitory room. "Wake up! Be on the field in twenty minutes."

Lionel made it there in ten. By twenty after, the rookie team sat in the infield, waiting, with Lionel and Manny seated to the right of the group. At six thirty, the coaching staff showed up. Anger steamed from Avila's face.

"Gentlemen, I'm pissed," he began. "Orza has a concussion and is out indefinitely. Javier is gone. I don't know how this crap started, and I don't care. Don't let it happen again." He was looking at the rookies when he said this, then he turned his face to Lionel and Manny. "And you two!" He pointed an accusatory finger. "Keep your heads. If you can't hold it together now, you won't hold it together when the stakes are higher. This is as high as they might ever get for you. Don't screw it up."

With his lecture over, he marched from the field. Lionel was sure he could see smoke billowing from Coach's ears. Since the other coaches were still there, no one moved to get up.

The coaches conferred in a group, then Coach García, a batting coach, turned to them. "You are going to work your asses off today. Eat something. Get dressed. Be back in one hour." As they started to rise he added, "And gentlemen, I would *not* be late if I were you."

That morning's practice was the most brutal yet. Lionel and Manny were assimilated into the rookie group. The day began with an eight-mile run, through which Manny and a few of the others threw up. Lionel was one of the first five guys back, and Charlie gave him a thumbs up when he wrote his time on the clipboard. This was followed with drills, weights, and batting and fielding practice. At the lunch break, they were instructed to be on the field at two o'clock sharp, dressed in game gear.

"Game gear?" Manny asked Lionel as they ate their ham sandwiches. "We playing a game?"

"I don't know," Lionel answered. "I hope so. It feels like I haven't played in weeks."

"Yeah," Manny laughed. "This has been the longest two weeks of my life."

"But the greatest!" Lionel added.

"Definitely."

Hanging in the locker room were Dodger's jerseys for Lionel and Manny; Lionel's was white, and Manny's blue. They weren't exactly like the other players' uniforms, but Lionel and Manny didn't care. Lionel never had any kind of uniform before.

"Hey, man! I like this!" Manny said, spinning around for Lionel to see.

"Looking good!" Lionel said. "Your belt is twisted."

Manny fixed himself up while Lionel tightened his shoes. *This is it!* He thought as they made their way to the field.

Lionel spent the first three innings in the dugout. He didn't mind this, as it gave him time to watch the pitcher for the other team. He absorbed the movements, the quirks, and the actions of everyone, and with each play, he placed himself in the game, deciding how he would have reacted. When the coach called him to play right field in the top of the fourth inning, he was ready.

The first batter fouled out to left. The second knocked a grounder that got past the pitcher and second baseman, enabling the batter to land on first. The third player up hit two fouls into the far-right bleachers. Lionel heard the coach yell, "Straighten it out!" Lionel had a gut feeling the next one was heading his way. He punched his fist into his glove and bounced on his toes. He was ready.

Sure enough, the batter knocked it over the first baseman's head in a beautiful arc that ended in Lionel's glove. It was an easy one. Lionel kept his head and threw a bullet to the second baseman, preventing the tag-up. His team cheered for him.

The next batter brought them trouble, however, and hit a fastball so high out of the park, the center fielder had no chance of grabbing it. This put the other team up by two.

Lionel's place in the batting order was eighth, and the inning started out with the sixth batter, who got a double by dropping it over the left fielder's head. The left fielder bobbled it before the throw and nearly missed the cut-off. The seventh batter hit a sweet grounder that took a bad hop for the defense, allowing that batter to reach first base before the throw from right got there.

"Runners on first and second," Coach said to Lionel. "Can you bunt?"

"Bunt?" Lionel asked. "I've never bunted in a game." In truth, he'd never bunted anywhere.

"I want you to try," he replied. "Bat left and push the ball down the third base line."

"Third base?" Lionel clarified.

"Yes, son. Third base line. Gently push it along the third base line."

"I'll try, sir," Lionel said. Disappointment filled him. His first at-bat, and he was sure he'd get out. He noticed, though, that the third baseman was playing further back than normal, probably anticipating a line drive in his direction. Maybe the bunt would work.

Lionel took a deep breath and took his stance. What he knew about bunting was that it needed to be a surprise to the infield. He had one shot at this. He let the first pitch go by without even swinging, just to see what it looked like. Strike one. It was a curveball that dropped just before Lionel would have swung at it. *If he throws that pitch again,* Lionel thought, *maybe I can hit it.*

Before the next pitch, the pitcher made two failed attempts to get the runner at second out. On the next pitch, Lionel was ready. As the ball came towards him, he bent his knees, anticipating the curve ball. He guessed correctly and as gently as he could, he tapped the ball toward the third base line. It looked good initially, but unfortunately, it rolled over the line before reaching the third base bag.

"Foul," the ump called.

The coach indicated a time out and called Lionel over. "Not bad. We lost the element of surprise, so now I want you to swing for the fences."

The pitcher threw Lionel a high fastball, which sailed past him as he swung with gusto. It was his third strike. Lionel walked slowly back to the dugout. He sat on the bench and put his head in his hands.

"It's OK, man," another player said. "That was a good bunt. You'll get there. Buck up and cheer for your team."

A deep sacrifice fly on the next batter's part allowed the runners to advance. It's what the coach had wanted Lionel to do. But then the next batter dinged one to first base, ending the inning with the runners still on the bags.

The next inning went better for Lionel's team. Lionel caught another pop fly, and when his team went to bat, Jose Peréz hit a homerun. In the sixth inning, his team was still down by one, and Lionel came up to bat again.

"Just swing, kid," the coach said.

This time Lionel hit a grounder to third base. A wild throw by the third baseman to first allowed him to get on the bag. Even without the crazy throw, Lionel felt sure he would have gotten there first.

"Lucky break, kid," the first baseman said. Lionel didn't respond. He took a few steps toward second. It shocked him when the pitcher turned and suddenly threw it back to first. He was slow to react, and the pitcher threw him out.

"You're outta there!" the first baseman called after him. "Bye-bye!"

Lionel was furious with himself. The coach switched up the lineup again after the sixth inning, and that was the last Lionel played that game, which ended with the other team winning three to two.

"Enough already. You gotta shut up about it," Manny finally told Lionel at dinner.

Lionel had been going on and on about how stupid he was for getting caught napping. "Do you know how many at-bats and innings we gonna play? Too many to count. If you yammer on every time you get out, I'm gonna stuff my glove down your throat."

Lionel stopped talking. He knew Manny was right. These other guys had dozens, if not hundreds, of games under their belts. Nobody understood that this one scrimmage game was the single most important game Lionel ever played. But the games became a regular thing for the two wanna-bes. If there was anything good to come of José's attack on Orza, it was that the coaches brought Lionel and Manny into the rookie fold for the remainder of their thirty-day evaluation. Yes, they still had times of independent testing and drills, but they played every day with the team. And not one rookie even hinted at teasing the two new guys. Lionel settled in to the routine, not letting his frustration show when he got out, instead mentally processing his errors so as not to make the same one twice.

The Dominican Winter League had started in September, and many of the rookies had already been playing for their respective Dominican teams. Rookies who were not signed to a roster hoped to get noticed by the coaches during the practice games. Before his injury, Orza had been signed as a third baseman for Licey, one of the two Santo Domingo-based teams. His misfortune had opened up a coveted spot, which one of the other Dodger rookies was chosen to fill.

With just five days left in the thirty-day evaluation, Manny and Lionel were invited to go with the team one evening to watch Licey play the Estrellas Orientales of San Pedro de Macorís.

"Sure!" Manny said quickly. Lionel nodded.

One of the coaches drove the team bus to Quisqueya Stadium. Lionel sat with Manny on the ride, and they listened to the chatter about which Major League players were playing in the Winter League this year.

"I heard José DeLeón was pitching for Licey," one guy said.

"Nah, man, he went to the Venezuelan League this year," another replied.

"Venezuelan? Why would he do that?" someone else chimed in.

And on it went. Lionel couldn't wait for the game. Dominican players who made it to the Majors took great pride in coming home to show out for the Dominican crowds through the Winter League games. Here, they were heroes, some known to walk down the street handing out pesos to young fans. Most of them relished in the hometown spotlight. The addition of non-Dominicans from Major League teams, who were sent there to build skills or recover from injury, upped the quality of Winter League play from other rookie leagues. The Dominican Winter League is no joke. Players give all they've got, and the fans appreciate it. The rookies know if they aren't selected for a Winter League team, they have about three years of shelf-life before their chance is gone.

As the bus pulled up, Lionel got his first glimpse at Quisqueya Stadium. So many greats played here, and Lionel could taste his desire to be one of them. "Someday," he whispered to himself. He was keeping his head about him, working hard—they just had to give him a shot!

He followed the group into the stadium and at once was taken aback at the crowd presence. Rather, the *lack* of crowd presence. After the experience of the fútbol game with Raul in Port-u-Prince, Lionel figured the baseball game in Santo Domingo would be at least as intense, if not more! This was baseball! In comparison, it was not even close. Sure, there were fans clustered in the stands, but Lionel estimated the stands to only be about a third filled. The laid-back ambiance lent to more of a pick-up game than a fierce rivalry. The rookies trailed over to claim seats above the dugout of the Licey team. A few players waved hellos and good-natured insults to some of the rookies, then a call from the loudspeakers sent the teams to line up in front of their dugouts for the National Anthem.

"Quisqueyanos valientes alcemos; nuestro canto con viva emoción..."

As the others belted out the lyrics, Lionel realized he did not know the anthem; a problem he resolved to fix as soon as possible. After all, this was his homeland. At least, according to his birth certificate it was. As they took the field, he recognized a few of the players from around the academy. Many played for Licey, but several were decked out in the bright green of the Estrellas Orientales.

The teams were evenly matched through the first four innings. No score, and each time players were left stranded on base. As the top of the fifth got going, the large stadium lights suddenly went dark.

"Awwwww!" a collective lament rose from everyone in the stadium.

It was dusk, not quite evening, so the stadium was not pitch black, but the game definitely could not continue.

"What's going on?" Lionel asked Manny.

"What do you mean?" Manny asked.

"What happened to the lights?" Lionel asked.

"It's a brownout," Manny said.

"Brownout?" Lionel didn't get it.

"There ain't a Dominican anywhere who don't know about brownouts," Manny chided. "Where are you from?"

Panic filled Lionel's chest. "No, I mean, I know it's a brownout," he stammered. "I mean, don't they have back up lights? I've never been in this stadium."

"Oh. Right. I forget you're not from Santo Domingo," Manny said. "My dad brought me here lots. This happens all the time. Takes a while and they come back on."

Lionel kept quiet after that. No one else was fazed at the brownout. A couple of guys a few rows above them tried lighting some bunched-up newspaper on fire, until a guard yelled for them to cut it out. The players left their dugouts and convened on the field, chatting and lying in the grass as they waited.

"I'm going to go see if I can get something to drink," one of the rookies said. He headed out. Most of the others followed him.

"Want to go see what's up?" Manny asked Lionel.

Lionel shrugged. "Sure."

They found the guys drinking rum at the back of the stands. The coaches lectured the guys continually about staying away from strong drink and keeping out of trouble. Lionel moved away, opting to grab a Coke from a vendor and head back to his seat. Manny stayed with the rookies and took a swig of the bottle as it was passed around.

Lionel, feeling quite alone as he sipped his Coke, watched the inactivity on the field and contemplated his situation. In just a few days he would know his next steps. An offer with the rookie team? Released and alone on the streets of Santo Domingo? He knew Jourdain would come back to see him. He also knew he couldn't go back to Haiti. That part of his life was finished. His house belonged to someone else. His parents shared a wooden box. He was no longer part of that world. He was still in that in-between place, waiting for the next chapter to begin.

"Hey, son," a voice said. Ralph Avila sat down next to him. "Mind if I sit?"

"Yes, sir," Lionel said, shocked. "I mean, no, sir. I mean, please sit. I didn't know you were here."

Avila chuckled as he sat. "Good decision," he said, nodding at the Coke. "No rum?"

"No, sir," Lionel said. "I don't drink."

"Why not?" Avila asked.

Lionel decided the honest answer was the best one. "My papa always said, 'The dreams of drunkards do not come true.' I guess I don't want anything to interfere with my dreams."

Avila nodded. "That's good advice, kid."

They sat in silence for a while.

"Is your dad alive?" Avila eventually asked.

"No, sir," Lionel answered. "He isn't."

The stadium lights began to hum and brighten. A cheer rose from the lackadaisical crowd.

"I'll see you tomorrow, kid," Avila said, and he walked down, jumped onto the field, and went into the Licey dugout.

The rest of the game went quickly. The players definitely were not playing in top shape, their actions clumsy and the hits weak. Lionel felt quite certain he could have played on either team out there and showed out as a star. Mercifully, a lucky home run by one of the Licey players in the eighth inning kept the game from being scoreless. It was a disappointment, and Lionel could understand why perhaps the crowd was sparse. The rookies and Manny were tipsy and sluggish on the bus ride back. It was just as well. Lionel didn't feel like talking to anyone.

CHAPTER 11

Day thirty was finally upon him. As Lionel ate his breakfast, the young kid in the light blue t-shirt that carried Charlie's clipboard found him and handed him a folded note. He handed a second note to Manny.

"What's yours say?" Manny asked Lionel.

"Report to Coach Avila's office at eight forty-five. Yours?"

"Nine-fifteen," Manny said. "You got an hour. You gonna pack?"

"I don't know. I think I will. Just in case," Lionel said.

Lionel didn't want to pack. He didn't want to think that this was where his baseball dream ended. He played his heart out. He kept his cool under pressure. He did everything that was asked. Every time. If he was cut, it wouldn't be for lack of effort. There was comfort in that knowledge. If they didn't want him, it was straight up because he just wasn't good enough. Not because he didn't try.

He showered, brushed his teeth, and made himself presentable in a clean blue t-shirt, grey sweatpants, and Papa's Dodgers cap. Reluctantly, he put his personal things back into his suitcase and sat on his bed, waiting for the clock to catch up with his anxiety. At eight thirty he and Manny parted with a fist bump and Lionel left for his appointment. Lionel rapped on Avila's door right on time.

"Come on in," Avila called. He wasn't alone. Jourdain occupied a chair across from Avila's desk. He rose when Lionel entered.

"Jourdain!" Lionel said with surprise. They hugged.

"Hey, Lionel," Jourdain said. Lionel's mind raced. *Was*

this a good thing? he wondered.

"Please have a seat," Avila indicated the chair next to Jourdain. "I've asked your uncle to be here because I want to offer you a contract with our rookie team. I understand you have no other relatives, is that right?"

Lionel couldn't believe what he was hearing. *A contract?* "A contract?"

Avila smiled. "Yes, kid. A contract. We like what we see. You got good feet. You can catch anything. Bigger than that, your head is on right. That ain't something you can coach. We're gonna give you a six-month contract; seven hundred American dollars each month. At the end of that, if—IF—I want to sign you to my Summer League team, I'll make you a Summer League Dodger and you'll get a bonus. If you aren't ready, I'll decide then if you are worth hanging onto for another rookie year. You'll continue on at seven hundred dollars for six more months."

Lionel calculated the amount in his head. Four thousand two hundred dollars! To play baseball for six months?

"Do I live here?" Lionel asked.

"Yeah. Rookies stay here at the Academy. We keep a very tight schedule during the week. As you've seen."

Lionel nodded thoughtfully. Jourdain grinned like crazy. "What do you think?" he asked.

"Can we see the contract?" Lionel asked Avila.

It was in English. Lionel and Jourdain leaned in together to read it.

"You can read English?" Avila asked. Most couldn't.

"Yes, sir," Lionel replied.

"I'll be damned," Avila said under his breath.

Signing the contract released the Dodgers and any of its affiliates from any liability, *medical or otherwise*, for any injuries, *up to and including death*, that Lionel Albert Bierto might incur while participating in the sport of baseball as a representative of their organization. In signing, Lionel also acknowledged that he could be released at any time for behavior unbecoming of the Dominican Dodgers, as deemed by management or coaches. His signature also served as his guarantee that he would not use nor sell any illegal drugs.

It all looked good. Except for one thing.

"Sir," Lionel said. "This dollar amount is not calculated correctly."

"Where?" Avila asked gruffly.

"Right here," Lionel pointed. "The dollar amount on this line reads three thousand five hundred dollars to be paid by the end of the six months. It should be four thousand two hundred."

Avila had a look. "You're right," he acknowledged. "I'll be right back."

He took the paper, slamming his office door behind him. Coach Ruiz, the rookie team coach, was in the office adjacent to Avila's. Jourdain and Lionel could hear Avila screaming at him through the paper-thin walls.

"I told you not to do this shit again!" Avila bellowed. Ruiz's response was undetectable. "Let me see the paperwork!" Pause. "Right there! Four thousand two hundred!" Pause. "You going to pocket the rest?" Pause. "Rewrite this. Now!"

Lionel and Jourdain didn't say a word, but Jourdain put up his fist for Lionel to bump. "Good job," he whispered.

A few minutes later Avila reappeared. His face was red, but he was smiling. "Son, I am sorry. I want you to know, it was not my intent to cheat you."

"Sir, I didn't think—" Lionel stammered.

Avila held up his hand. "I know you didn't. Here is the new contract."

Lionel and Jourdain once again scanned the words. Noting everything appeared in order, Lionel signed his name where indicated. Jourdain followed suit on the line indicating a relative signature for players under age eighteen.

Avila handed Lionel his first check. "We hand out checks on the last day of the month. Congratulations, kid. You're one step closer. Take today off. Spend it with your uncle. We'll see you at eight a.m. tomorrow in the locker room."

Lionel stood and held his hand to Avila. They shook. "Mr. Avila, I will not let you down."

Once Lionel and Jourdain were outside, they whooped and hollered so much, the groundskeepers heard them over the roar of the lawnmowers.

"I can't believe it!" Lionel said over and over. "I can't believe it!"

"You're on your way!" Jourdain said proudly. "We knew you could do it."

"Want to see my dorm?" Lionel asked.

He gave Jourdain a tour of the grounds. Other rookies gave high fives and fist bumps as they passed, and when he got to the dorm room, there was a uniform folded neatly on Lionel's bed, complete with a new pair of cleats. Jourdain held the jersey by its shoulders so they could read the word *Bierto* stitched across the back.

Jourdain whistled his approval. "Hey, now! That's what I'm talking about! Number eleven. A good number." He held it up. "Would you look at this?"

"I wish Papa were here to see me," Lionel said. "I wish he knew how much I miss him."

Jourdain placed a reassuring hand on Lionel's shoulder. "He knows."

"Hey, hey, hey!" Manny called, coming into the locker room. "We made it, amigo!"

They slapped hands and congratulated one another. Lionel was relieved to see Manny still there. "Are your parents here?" he asked Manny.

"Si. They are waiting outside. With all my little brothers and sisters too. We are going to go to lunch and to put this check in the bank. I'll catch you later, brother." Manny grabbed his knapsack and headed out.

"Well, should we do that, too?" Jourdain asked. "Are you hungry?"

Lionel nodded. "And can we go to the beach today?"

Jourdain and Lionel cruised around like old times. They visited Jourdain's new cigar clients, delivering thirty-two boxes. Lionel nodded his approval at Polo's rolling techniques, and Jourdain filled him in on things happening around Port-au-

Prince. Elena was doing well; she and Sissy decided to take a trip to Jacmel. It made Lionel happy that Elena was spending more time with her sister-in-law. Jourdain also assured Lionel that Polo was helping Elena keep her shop clean.

When they stopped at the bank, Lionel deposited his check and also made a withdrawal. He handed Jourdain three hundred dollars.

"What's this?" Jourdain asked.

"One hundred for you. One hundred for Elena. One hundred for Polo."

Jourdain shook his head and handed two hundred back to Lionel. "Elena and I don't need your money. We love you, Samféyo, and we want you to save for your future."

Lionel smiled at the sound of his name. "You called me Samféyo."

"You'll always be Samféyo Bernard. No matter what your fancy Dodger jersey says."

"Will you give some money to Polo? If it wasn't for him practicing with me, I might not be here now. But don't tell him it was from me."

"Yes. Now, let's go enjoy the day."

It was much less scary for Lionel to say goodbye to Jourdain that evening. Jourdain promised to come back when he had his next delivery ready—and Lionel promised to keep working hard and not give the Dodgers a reason to cut him loose.

Manny and Lionel were prompt for their eight-a.m. locker room appointment. Printed labels bearing their names were taped to their previously generic lockers, officially marking the territory theirs. Inside hung two additional uniforms, five Dominican Dodgers t-shirts (three long-sleeved and two short), a blue windbreaker, and a ballcap.

"Oh, these are niiiiiice!" Manny swooned over his new gear.

"Good morning, gentlemen," Charlie entered the locker room with his enormous mug of coffee, which he set on a bench. "You found your gifts."

"Thank you, sir," Lionel said. "This is incredible!"

Charlie waved the thanks away with his hand. "You show a lot of promise and we are glad to have you. Keep working hard. You'll join up with the team this afternoon, but there are some things we need to do first. The team doc is going to give you each another physical. It will take most of the morning. Are you both up to date on all of your shots, vaccinations, that sort of thing?"

Manny and Lionel just stared in reply.

"OK, we'll get those done. Don't worry, no one shows up here current with their shots. We want to keep you boys as healthy as possible." Charlie scribbled notes on his ever-present clipboard then picked up his coffee. "Wear the long-sleeved blue t-shirt with grey pants. Meet me in the training room in ten minutes."

"Yes, sir!" they replied in unison.

The morning consisted of urine samples, pokes with needles, and groping hands. Lionel's leg lengths, wing span, head circumference, and hand sizes all were measured, then measured again. His hinged joints, ball-and-socket joints, and pivot joints were tested for fluidity of movement. The doctor looked into Lionel's eyes, throat, ears, and rear end. For a kid who'd never been to a doctor in his life, this exam made up for it.

"Alrighty, son, that's it," the doctor declared after every inch of Lionel was inspected at close range. As he left the examination room, Lionel rubbed his left arm. The Band-Aids on each of his triceps felt like badges of honor. The Dodgers *wanted* him. They cared enough for his health to vaccinate him against diseases which could hurt him. Sure, he knew they were merely protecting their investment, but *he* was the investment. He grinned like a fool.

The typical day for Lionel that winter went something like this:

6:30 – Wake up, two to three-mile run
7:30 – Breakfast
8:30 – Report to training room for taping, heat packs
9:30 – Clubhouse meeting
10:00 – Morning practice—fielding drills, pitchers' practice
12:30 – Lunch
1:30 – Afternoon practice—batting practice, baserunning
3:45 – Cool down, stretching, training room for ice packs
4:30 – Shower
5:00 – Mandatory English class
6:00 – Dinner and free time
10:30 – Players must be in their dorm rooms
11:00 – Lights out

Whereas many complained about the mundaneness, the structure was friendly to Lionel. The morning run was self-imposed; it cleared his mind and readied him for the day. In his evening free-time he did laundry, watched television, or read books. He did not go out much, but he also didn't consider himself a loner—on the contrary, guys were constantly coming and going around the academy.

On the morning of December 17, Lionel woke extra early. By the time his small, battery-operated alarm clock read five a.m., he was on the dirt trail for his morning run, knapsack strapped to his back. A mile or so from Campo Las Palmas was a clearing. Normally this was Lionel's turn-around point, today he made it his chapel. The clearing was an oddity on the face of the Dominican landscape. The surrounding flatland rose up suddenly to a gentle hill, at the top of which sat a rather large, table-like white rock. The sea was a good twelve miles away, but from there he could see the line of blue stretching into the horizon.

Upon the rock he opened his sack, gingerly removing the contents. The pages of Papa's notebook felt fragile in the morning heat, and he turned them until he located his mother's grocery list. *Eggs, bread, coffee, soap, cheese.* His index finger traced over the script, rewriting the words.

"Oh, Mama," he mused, great sadness filling his heart.

Next he removed the small framed photos and wondered again which beach his parents visited before he was born. The picture of him and Papa with the baseball brought tender tears from his eyes. "I wish you could see me, Papa," he whispered to the photo. He sniffled, then the sound of footfall on the grass behind him made his head whip around.

"It's OK, son, I didn't mean to startle you." A man had come up the small hill. He, too, wore a Dodgers t-shirt.

"Coach *Lasorda*?" Lionel said.

"Good morning," Tommy Lasorda replied. "What are you doing here?"

"I, um," Lionel wasn't sure how to answer. "I go for a run in the mornings."

"You're the new rookie," Lasorda affirmed.

"Yes, sir."

"Did you know this is my land?" he asked.

"I—what? Oh! No, I didn't. I'm so sorry," Lionel apologized, scrambling from the rock and gathering his things to put back in the knapsack.

Lasorda waved his hand and leaned on the rock. "Sit down, sit down. It's fine, son. If I'm in town, I generally come up here at this time to meditate. I had this spot made for such."

Lionel nodded thoughtfully. "It is beautiful."

"It is. What do you have there?" he asked, eyeing the pictures.

"Oh! These are my parents," he showed the picture. "Today is the anniversary of my papa's death. It is also the anniversary of my mother's death, although she died seventeen years before him. I was just thinking about them." It was also his own *real* birthday, but of course he couldn't tell Coach Lasorda that. So many things happened on December 17.

Coach Lasorda considered the picture for quite a while. "I'm sorry for your loss," he said quietly, handing the photo back. "And that one?"

Lionel handed him the other frame. "This is me and Papa." Papa would have been over the moon to know that Tommy Lasorda looked at his picture. Lionel's heaviness lifted somewhat at the thought.

"A Dodgers cap. He must have been a great man," Lasorda finally said.

"He was the best," Lionel agreed. "Papa used to say, 'Life is meant to be traveled forward, not backwards,' but sometimes I think it is important to reflect on the past."

Lasorda nodded. They sat in silence on the rock, eyes turned to the ocean and hearts reflecting.

The winter days passed quickly. A new rookie coach was brought in to replace Ruiz, and Lionel wondered if it had anything to do with the messed-up contract. Lionel gratefully deposited his monthly checks into his growing bank account, Jourdain paid regular visits every four to five weeks, and Lionel's skills in both the batting box and the outfield got better and better. On April 1, Lionel was summoned to Coach Avila's office.

"Have a look at this, Lionel," Avila instructed, handing him a folder. Inside was a contract. "We want to sign you to one of our Summer League teams. Effective immediately."

"My six months aren't up yet," Lionel pointed out.

"True, but Goméz was just called up to San Antonio, and I'm sure you'll hear soon enough that the Rangers signed Ahosta. I think you're the man to fill our now-empty right field spot. I want you here," he stated. "You'll see that I have included a four-thousand-seven-hundred-dollar bonus check for you. You'll also be bumped up to nine hundred a month." Lionel reviewed the contract. It contained all of the same releases of liability and promises that the other contract held. And more money. He looked up at Avila. "Thank you, Coach," he said, reaching for the pen.

Manny, who played second base, was given a contract also. He bragged about his fifty-dollar-a-month boost and thousand-dollar bonus, and Lionel didn't have the heart to tell him that it was nothing compared to his own increase. Lionel kept his check to himself, sharing the amount with no one except the teller at the bank, whose impressed nod was all the ego boost Lionel needed. He treated himself to a steak dinner and the new Teenage Mutant Ninja Turtles movie that night.

The Dodgers operated two teams in the Dominican Summer League that year. Lionel was placed as the right field starter on the Cibao Dodgers team. Manny was assigned to the San Pedro de Macoris Dodgers team. They lived and practiced together as one big happy family but parted ways at game time. The Cibao team was strong, but not quite consistent enough to beat the Pirates' Summer League team. Avila was disappointed—the Dodgers had won the league the year before—but the rookies all played well, so there wasn't too much to be angry about. Consistency comes with time.

"We'll get them next year," he said at the last game of the season. And that was it.

One late August day, Lionel was once again summoned to Avila's office. A man wearing a Licey ballcap stood to shake his hand. "John Roseboro," the man said.

"Nice to meet you," Lionel answered, and took a seat. He couldn't help but notice the World Series Champion ring on Roseboro's right hand.

"Lionel, Roseboro here is managing Licey this year. I've been talking to him about you, and he's watched a few practices. He wants you on his team," Avila stated, wasting no time with pleasantries. Lionel appreciated that about him.

"Really?" Lionel answered. "Wow." He wasn't expecting to get pulled to a winter team this year.

"What do you say, kid?" Roseboro asked.

"Is that OK with you, Coach?" Lionel asked Avila. He knew Coach Lasorda was Licey's manager for a while, but he didn't want to do anything without Avila's—and the Dodgers'—approval.

Avila laughed. "Are you kidding? It'll be good for you, kid. Get more experience. Work on your game sense. That's why you're here."

"Alright, then," Lionel agreed.

Roseboro indicated a contract on the desk. "You'll get one thousand dollars a month. A bonus if Licey wins the championship."

"You'll train here at the academy on your off-days, travel on your game days. Attend the team meetings as required," Avila explained.

"Sounds great!" Lionel beamed. He and Roseboro shook hands again. He didn't know who this man was, but he sensed he could learn a lot from him. The dream was alive.

CHAPTER 12

Manny was noticeably disappointed that he hadn't been chosen for a winter team. They talked about it the next day in the locker room, as they dressed for practice.

"I'm glad for you, bro," Manny said, tightening his sneakers. He lowered his voice so the other guys wouldn't hear. "But I sure can't wait for my turn. I'm at least as good as Rodriguez. He's playing for Estrellas."

"It'll come," Lionel said. "You know things can change fast around here."

"Yeah. Oh, hey, did you hear? They're holding tryouts today," Manny grinned. "Remember when that was us?"

"It wasn't so long ago," Lionel said. "Only one year."

"Yeah, we're pretty lucky," Manny said. He shrugged. "I guess I shouldn't complain. Another winter of practice won't kill me."

"My papa used to say there is no such thing as luck," Lionel said. "Hard work and God's grace drive us to our destination."

"Hey, Lionel, your papa sounds like he was a smart dude," Ramone Marcione, a pitcher for Licey, said, overhearing Lionel's statement.

"¡Vamos!" another player poked his head in the doorframe before Lionel could answer. "On the field in three!"

Lionel followed the rest of the guys to the outfield for stretching and warm-up. The wanna-bes were lined up on the third base line, listening to Charlie's welcoming instructions. As he trotted past, he noticed the last player in the line looked familiar. He paused.

"Arturo?" he questioned.

Arturo smiled and held his glove up in acknowledgement, then turned his attention back to Charlie.

Lionel went through the motions of practice that morning with his mind elsewhere. *What if he tells everyone my name is Sam?* he wondered repeatedly. It shouldn't have surprised him to see Arturo; Arturo was one of the best he saw when he played with the guys in Barahona. He tried and tried to come up with a plausible reason for the name change. *Maybe it won't come up,* he hoped.

After lunch, Lionel was due for a meeting with Licey at the Quisqueya Stadium locker room. Besides Lionel and Marcione, six other guys from the Dodgers rookie team also were signed with Licey, so they all rode over together. It was dinnertime when they returned, uniforms in hand, and they were all famished. Lionel grabbed his tray and found Manny.

"How'd the try-outs end up?" He tried not to sound anxious.

"Charlie took two guys. They aren't back yet with their things," Manny replied.

"Do you know their names?" Lionel asked.

"No idea," Manny replied, stuffing a forkful of sausage and rice into his mouth.

Lionel didn't have long to wonder if one of the new guys was Arturo. Within minutes Arturo came into the cafeteria. He immediately caught Lionel's eye and with a big smile, came over to join them.

"Sam! So good to see you," he said genuinely. They shook hands.

"Hello Arturo! This is Manny Almora," Lionel said.

"Congratulations, man!" Manny said. "Welcome to Campo Las Palmas."

"Thanks. I can't believe it. This was the second time I've tried out," Arturo explained. "I'm not surprised to see you here, Sam."

"Hey, why you keep calling him Sam?" Manny asked.

"This is Lionel Bierto."

Lionel laughed nervously. "Oh. Well, Sam is a nickname my family has for me. When I came here, I started going strictly by Lionel." It wasn't a total lie.

Manny looked at him sideways. "How do you get Sam as a nickname for Lionel?"

"I don't know, man. My papa used to call me Sam. He died so I can't really ask him, can I?" Anxiety made his voice much angrier than he'd intended.

"Hey, hey. Siento mucho, man. I didn't mean to upset you. It's cool," Manny said, throwing up his hands. "I didn't mean nothin' by it."

Lionel shook his head. He felt like a turd. "Naw, it's good."

Silence stretched longer than was comfortable.

"So," Arturo said finally. "Guess what, Sam—Lionel —sorry. The other guy they took is Nick."

"That's great!" Lionel said sincerely. "Where is he?"

"He'll be here soon," Arturo said. "His parents took him to get some toothpaste and shampoo or something. He'll be here when they're done shopping. I don't really think he expected to make it."

"He has a good arm," Lionel recalled.

"Yeah. I think that's what they liked. When they heard he was a pitcher, they made him throw a bunch to test his speed. He said he clocked eighty-three."

Manny whistled. "Daaaanng."

"Yeah. I was just glad to have a friendly face here with me. But now that I see you're here too, I'm even more relieved," he said to Lionel.

"This place is no joke," Lionel admitted. "The next thirty days will be exhausting. The best advice I can give you is something my uncle told me. Work hard. Don't give them a reason to cut you."

Arturo nodded.

In the locker room the next morning, Nick greeted Lionel with a big hug and a, "*Lionel!* Great to see you!" Lionel smiled;

glad Arturo spared him from having to have the awkward *Sam vs. Lionel conversation* with Nick. He introduced Arturo and Nick to the rest of the guys. These were the first wanna-bes invited for a thirty-day evaluation since Lionel's group came through almost a year ago. With the picture of Frank Orza's bleeding head still painted on everyone's minds, no one dared called the new guys "fakers" or take any other cheap shots at them. Avila instructed them to be one big happy family and by God, that's what they were going to be.

From what Lionel could see, Arturo and Nick worked their tails off. Nick trained with the pitchers, and on days Lionel trained at the Academy, he could see that Nick's arm was getting stronger. What he struggled with was control.

"If I can't straighten out, they're gonna cut me," he moaned in the locker room one day after practice.

"Don't put so much pressure on yourself, man," Lionel said. "You have to relax."

Relaxing wasn't in Nick's playbook. He threw strikes all day when it was just him and the catcher. Once a batter took his stand, however, he let his mind take over his body. Fortunately, Avila and the other coaches liked Nick's potential enough to sign both of them to a six-month contract, just like they did for Lionel and Manny. The guys celebrated with steak dinners and a movie—an American blockbuster about a little kid whose family went on vacation and left him home alone had just come to the Palacio Cine. Several of the other players joined them, and it became a real party. Afterwards, some of the older guys wanted to hit the clubs.

"Come on, man, let's have some fun," Manny prodded Lionel, when Lionel said he was heading back to the dorm.

"I can't. I want to go for a run in the morning, and we have a ten-thirty meeting at Licey," Lionel declined.

"We got permission for late curfew from Charlie," another guy said. "Don't be un perdedor!"

"Yeah, don't be a loser. Celebrate with us," Arturo said. "Let's dance with some chicas!" He shook his hips to make his point.

Manny laughed. "I could use me a chica!"

Music from a club down the block beckoned the boisterous band of ballplayers. Even though a line trailed the sidewalk, the bouncer recognized the Licey players, and the group was ushered inside quickly, not even having to pay the cover charge.

"Look at that, bro! We got it made," Manny nudged Lionel.

Inside, they scattered. Manny and Nick headed toward the bar. Arturo followed the older guys through the dim lighting toward the booths that aligned the back wall. Lionel weaved his way to an inconspicuous spot near the dance floor to figure out what one was supposed to do in a club. He didn't want to admit to anyone that he'd never been. With the same scrutiny that he observed a new pitcher on the mound, he took it all in, making mental notes.

"Hey papi," a voice cooed behind him. A petite waitress with long hair bouncing in curls around her shoulders smiled up at him. Even in her sparkly platform shoes she barely came up to his chest. "Can I get you a drink?"

"No, gracias," he answered, trying to avoid staring at the cleavage which she clearly wanted him to see.

"Ah, come on, papi, not even one little drink?" she purred, tilting her head and showing a row of perfect white teeth.

"Um, maybe a Coke?" he suggested. "No alcohol in it please."

She grimaced her disappointment. "Yeah, OK. Be right back."

He handed her a five-dollar bill in exchange for his Coca-Cola. She stuffed it into the front of her low-cut dress and moved on. From the time he was a little kid making his way through the Haitian street markets, Lionel always enjoyed people-watching. The club opened up a whole new world of it. The encounter with the waitress, as common as it appeared to be, made his heart beat a little faster. No female had *ever* batted her eyelashes at him.

The dancers were fascinating. Shamelessly short skirts

barely covered the things he thought a skirt was supposed to cover, and the cleavage on the waitress was tame compared to the jounce going on across the lighted floor. The guys wore shiny silk shirts open to their navels; their shiny black shoes let them glide along the tiles effortlessly.

"You like what you see?" He hadn't noticed the girl standing in front of him. He grinned, having no idea what an appropriate response would be. "I'm Rosa," she said.

"Lionel," he replied.

"You want to dance with me, Lionel?" she asked.

"I—I'm not much of a dancer," he said.

"It's OK, papi, I'll teach you," she said. She finessed the empty glass easily from his hand and set it on a table. Entwining his arm with hers, she pulled him through an opening in the brass railing that outlined the perimeter of the dance floor and snaked her way to the center. They faced each other for a moment, and then she allowed her hands to circle his waist. Pressing on the small of his back, her hands moved to the beat of the music, teaching his stiff hips what to do. Unsure of where to place his own hands, he set them awkwardly on her shoulders.

"No, no, Lionel," she scolded. She moved his hands to her backside, pulling him very close. The top of her head was just below his chin. The scent of coconut and jasmine floated from her hair and filled his nostrils.

"Wow," he breathed. She laughed in reply.

Each song morphed into the next, so there was no break in the music, just a gentle shift in tempo. After several upbeat salsas that left him breathless, the music slowed to a smooth bachata. Lionel felt the sweat adhere his t-shirt to his back. He was embarrassed, but Rosa appeared not to notice. She clung to him, eyes closed, body swaying and pulsating with the beat. When the second bachata ended, he leaned in and said, "Can we get something to drink?"

She broke away reluctantly and stepped through the crowd and off the dance floor. He asked what she wanted to drink, and with a wave of her hand she stated with a huff,

"Mamajuana."

"Mamajuana?" he repeated.

She nodded. He pushed his way up to the bar, where Manny and Nick stood. Manny slammed down a rum shot.

"Hey! There he is," Manny shouted over the noise, slapping Lionel on the shoulder. "You got yourself a chicaaaa!" He dragged out the last syllable with a shake of his hips and arms raised.

If Lionel's face wasn't already red from dancing, the guys would have noticed the blush. "It's nothing," he said, giving Manny a playful shove. He ordered Rosa's drink and got himself a water. When he returned to the place he'd left her, she was nowhere to be found. His eyes scanned the dance floor until he found her, body pressed against a short rotund Latino wearing a grey suit. The guy had one hand boldly fixed on her right breast, and she didn't mind at all.

"Well, I'll be," Lionel mused. Truth be told, he was grateful for the encounter to be over. The dance pushed him way out of his comfort zone. He returned to his friends and plunked the mamajuana heavily on the counter. "Here you go, fellas. On me."

Manny nearly fell over making a grab for the glass. He took a big pull on the straw. "Did you know—" he said with a drunken slur, "this drink is an afro-dilly-o?"

"A what?" Lionel said.

"An afro-dildo."

"A what?" Nick repeated.

"You know—the thing that makes you…" he used his pointer finger to mimic an erection.

"An aphrodisiac?" Nick said.

Manny doubled over in laughter. "Yeah. An afro-dilly-ack!"

"I think maybe it's time for us to get you home," Lionel said.

"But what about your chica?" he said loudly. "We need to get Lionel a chica!"

A couple of ladies at a nearby table looked over in

disgust. Lionel gave them an apologetic smile. "Where's Arturo?" he asked Nick.

"He went that way with some of the other guys," he said. "Haven't seen him since we got here."

"Should we tell him we're leaving?" Lionel wondered.

Nick shrugged. "I don't know. I'm sure he'll be fine."

Lionel hesitated. Manny needed to get home. Arturo was with other players. "OK, let's go."

They supported Manny on either side. Hushing him did no good. He belted out Gloria Estefan at the top of his lungs as they led him outside. Lionel signaled a taxicab. By the time they arrived back at Campo Las Palmas, Manny was subdued and complaining of a stomachache.

"Quick, let's get him to the showers," Lionel suggested. They barely got him stripped down and under the cold water when he vomited all over the tile wall.

"Man! That's disgusting!" Nick yelled, jumping backward. Manny followed it up with a few more heaves, emptying the liquor and parts of his steak dinner into the drain.

Lionel thought he would throw up from the smell, but he kept his cool by breathing through his mouth. They cleaned Manny up and guided him to his bunk, where he fell face-first, naked. Lionel couldn't resist grabbing a black marker from his knapsack and drawing a smiley face on Manny's right butt cheek. They chuckled and covered him with a blanket before heading to bed themselves.

"Lionel, wake up!" Nick hissed in his ear, shaking him out of his dreams.

"Wha—oh, Nick. What's up?" Lionel grumbled, rolling over.

"Arturo didn't come home," Nick whispered.

Lionel rubbed his eyes and sat up. "What?"

"He didn't come back," Nick said. "His bed is empty."

"What time is it?" Lionel asked.

"Eight."

"Crap," Lionel said, sitting up and rubbing his eyes. "Are

the others back?"

"I don't know," Nick said. "I don't really know who to look for."

Lionel threw on some sweatpants and did a survey of the room. There were five or six other beds that did not appear to have been slept in.

"Well, he's not alone," Lionel said. "Others are missing too. I hope they come back soon. We have a ten-thirty clubhouse meeting at Quisqueya and some of them are supposed to be there."

Breakfast in the cafeteria was served until eight-thirty each morning. Lionel and Nick hurried to the dining room, opting to leave Manny in the same position he passed out the night before. By nine forty-five, none of the missing ballplayers, including Arturo, had shown up. The other guys had noticed the six missing players and speculation to their whereabouts drifted around.

"After the movie we went to Zona Fuente," Lionel explained again. "Manny drank too much, so we got him home. The others were still there when we left."

"How could you leave your brothers, man?" another player, Miguel Cintos, yelled at Lionel.

"Hey! I am not a babysitter. I didn't even want to go to the stupid club!" Lionel retorted.

"Calm down," Marcione said. "Bierto is right. He's not their babysitter. They're all older than he is. Sounds like he was the only one with any sense. Back off." He directed his words to Cintos, who threw his hands up in the air and stormed off. "Come on, Bierto," Marcione said. "We gotta get to the stadium."

The Licey players took one of the Academy vans and left for Santo Domingo to make their ten-thirty meeting, three players short. Roseboro was furious when they arrived.

"Where in the hell are the other players?" he demanded.

"We don't know, sir," Marcione admitted. "They went out last night and didn't make it back."

Roseboro chewed his bottom lip, considering this news.

"OK, then," he said slowly. "I'll be right back." The other coaches followed him into his office.

The Tigres del Licey sat silently in the locker room, waiting. It was unprecedented for a group of guys to simply no-show for a team meeting; especially this early in the season, when all were vying for position. In ten minutes, Roseboro returned.

"Here's the line-up for tomorrow's game: Berroa, Cabrera, Reyes, Bell, Cedeño, Bierto, Rodriguez, Hernandez batting for Marcione, Suarez."

Even though they'd played six games so far as a team, this was the first time Lionel's name was called in the starting line-up. Notably missing were two of the guys unaccounted for, one of whom was supposed to have been in Lionel's place.

Roseboro continued his instructions. "We're playing the Águilas. Their starting pitcher is Peréz. He's a Southpaw. He favors the slider and the cut fastball, but don't rule out the change-up. He likes to toy with the runners, so stay alive on the bags."

Eighteen heads nodded their understanding.

"Bierto, you'll be in left field. Bora, you go right. Hernandez center. Got it?"

"Yes, coach," they answered.

"Marcione, I want to meet with you, Rojas, Tapia, and Guzmán. The rest of you, head out to the field. Light workout. Ten laps. Fielding practice. Get used to each other."

The team moved out, leaving Roseboro to consult with his pitching squad. Lionel didn't like left field, but he was in no position to voice his opinion. He was glad to be there. They ran the bases ten times through, then the starters took up their positions to get acquainted with each other's throwing techniques and stances. One of the batting coaches smacked balls to each player ten times in succession, starting with Lionel. Once each player had two sets of ten balls hit to him, the coach hit to random locations· and they all had to stay on their toes.

Lionel detected a pattern. By studying the position of the

coach's head and where his eyes looked immediately before hitting, he was able to discern the ball's final destination. By the end of the practice, he was predicting perfectly the drop spot for coach's hits; even knowing whether coach was going to drop it short in the outfield or go for a long one. Lionel felt great as the van headed back to Campo Las Palmas. He was ready.

CHAPTER 13

Things weren't going so well back at camp. The six missing players showed up—bedraggled and hungover—at twelve-thirty. A displeased Avila awaited them in the dormitory. According to Manny, he hauled them all into the showers and made them stand under cold water for fifteen minutes. Then he told them to get dressed and meet him on the field, where they ran the bases until they puked—which apparently didn't take long. Arturo held out the longest, as he wasn't really hungover. He was more of a lost puppy in the whole incident. After they left the club, the guys had taken a cab to a remote house owned by one of the Major Leaguers and Arturo was virtually trapped there. He didn't know where he was and had no money with which to get back to the Academy. Avila gave him a pass after hearing his story but chewed his butt out about making better decisions. Arturo was contrite and continued to take the punishment with the others, even though Avila had excused him, an act which earned him respect among the players.

The three Licey players learned that they were to be docked a week's pay and were suspended for the next five games. Rumor was that Roseboro wanted to can them, but Avila convinced him otherwise. The two other guys were players for the San Pedro de Macorís team. It was up in the air what would happen to them. That evening, Avila and the other Dodger coaches called an after-dinner meeting.

"You are members of the Dominican Republic Dodgers organization," Avila started solemnly. "You are not Yankees, or

Rangers, or the Pittsburgh Pirates." Several boos went up upon mention of the Pirates. "This Academy is the crème de la crème. We don't want to be the best in the Dominican. We want to be the best in the entire Caribbean. We take pride that the Winter League takes more Dodgers players than any other. We take pride that our greats play and win in the Caribbean. We take pride when you go on to the United States to play, like Pedro Guerrero or Raúl Mondesí or even Sammy Sosa." Several cheers went up at the mention of Sosa, a Winter League player who had signed to the Majors last year with the Rangers and was now a member of the Chicago White Sox.

"Listen. You are not guaranteed a spot in the Major Leagues just because you play here. You might get called up to the minors. You might get as high as Double-A or Triple-A ball. But it is going to be the best of the best of you who make the Show. There is no room for any *decisión estúpida* like several of you made last night. I tell you time and time again that you have to be better than that. There's nothing wrong with having fun. But if you can't keep your heads about you, and you get drunk—or even worse—and you can't make it home? Well, this will be the end of the line for you. Baseball doesn't need more *idiotas* who know how to drink. The world has enough of those. Baseball needs more men of integrity, who are willing to hold the line.

"I was pissed last year when your collective stupidity ended up with Orzo getting hurt. I was pissed this morning when Roseboro—a three-time World Series Champion—called to tell me that three of my guys didn't show up. I was even more pissed when Eduardo Antun called to tell me that two of my guys missed the bus for San Pedro. I do not want to be pissed again. Am I understood?"

"Yes, sir," every player in the room declared.

Avila and the other coaches left.

Lionel had his best game yet at Quisqueya Stadium the following night against the Águilas Cibaeñas. He not only fielded cleanly, he saved two balls from going over the back fence. On offense, he went two for four at bat, scoring both times on home runs by the designated hitter who followed him in the line-up. Marcione pitched exceptionally well, with a no-hitter going till the eighth inning. Overall, Roseboro was pleased. So much so, that he kept the same line-up for the next five games, except for giving his pitchers their rest.

When the five-game suspension was up, Lionel expected Guerro to reclaim his place in the line-up. Roseboro saw things differently. He allowed Guerro to play in the next series, against the Toros, but unfortunately for Guerro, he bobbled a couple of easy plays and had horrible at-bats, resulting in Lionel finding himself back in left field entering their next series against the Leones del Escogido. The Leones were managed by the famous Felipe Alou and were not only the reigning Winter League Champions, they were the current Caribbean World Series Champions. Roseboro wanted to beat them badly in this three-game stint.

As they took the field for the first afternoon game, Lionel was shocked to see the stands nearly full. They'd had some good crowds, but nothing compared to this. Both teams claimed Santo Domingo as their home city and Quisqueya as home field. A coin flip declared the Leones as home team.

Lionel studied the pitcher, looking for patterns and tells. He'd picked up a small spiral notebook—much like Papa's—in which he wrote down his reviews of the teams, and specifically the pitchers, he came up against. He brought it to every game.

In his first at-bat, he fouled two out of play, then got caught swinging at a change-up. Not a great start. He fielded well, though, and by the third inning the game was still scoreless, and Lionel was up again. He was pretty sure he had detected a slightly different foot stance when the pitcher was going to throw a fastball. The first two pitches were junk, thrown high and wide, and Lionel didn't budge. Then he saw the ever-so-minute left foot shift and correctly guessed a fastball was headed his way. He swung hard and it sailed over the left fielder's head, dropping in the back field near the fence. He made it around to second, driving in a runner. Once again, the designated hitter didn't disappoint and homered on his at-bat, bringing Lionel in. The Tigres held on to their three-run lead, earning a solid win.

They dropped the second game in the series to the Leones, but it was a close one. Tied at four-all, the teams played two extra innings before a bad pitching call by Licey enabled the Leones' strongest hitter to knock one out, ending the game.

On the third afternoon, things swung their way again, and the determined Tigres whipped the Leones soundly with a final score of six to zero.

Roseboro was thrilled.

As the season trudged along, Roseboro's Tigres became the team to be reckoned with. In mid-December, they were at the top of the pack going into the playoffs. The eighteen-game playoff series between them, the Leones, the Estrellas, and the Toros concluded with the two teams from Santo Domingo headed to the best of nine series to determine the Winter League Champions.

"Bierto, you've got a phone call," one of the guys called to Lionel, as he sat on the couch in the community room reading a book one evening. The telephone in the community room was for anyone's use, and family members could reach out between six and nine o'clock p.m.

"Hello?" Lionel said into the receiver.

"Samféyo?" a female voice said.

"Elena! It's me!" Lionel answered.

"It's so good to hear your voice," Elena said. "I've missed you."

"I miss you, too. How's the store?"

"I got a new shipment of scarves. They are neon colors and have animal prints on them. The ladies of Haiti are going wild for them," she said. "How are you?"

"I'm great. It's so much work, but I really love it," Lionel stated. "Hey, guess what? We made it to the Winter League Championship game. It starts this weekend."

"I know! That's why I am calling. Jourdain, Sissy, and I

are coming to watch you play. Can you get the tickets for us?"

"Are you kidding? Yes! When will you be here?"

"We will come on Friday. Can we have dinner with you?" she asked.

"Of course. I will see you Friday!"

Thursday and Friday were light practice days. Roseboro wanted the guys to be at full strength for Saturday's first game against the Leones del Escogido. Lionel's fan club picked him up at five thirty and they headed into Santo Domingo to Lionel's favorite steak restaurant.

"I'm so glad you guys are here," he said sincerely. "I really have missed you."

It had been eight weeks since Jourdain had come through town. Lionel asked how his business was going.

"Rolling the cigars is taking longer than I want it to," Jourdain admitted. "I can't keep up with the high demand."

"Isn't Polo helping you?" Lionel asked.

"Less and less," Jourdain said. "He is always off running errands or doing something else. He just isn't interested anymore. He won't even go to the airport for me."

Lionel was truly sorry to hear this, as he'd hoped Polo would see a good thing and take the opportunity to help himself financially.

"Don't be sad, Lionel," Jourdain reassured. "I am doing just fine. It is just going to take me longer. You know?"

"I'm helping out now, too," Elena interjected. "So is Sissy. We'll get things moving again at top speed."

Jourdain smiled. "Yes, yes. The power sisters here are going to become cigar gurus." Sissy and Elena nodded in agreement. Lionel knew they would all be OK, he wondered about Polo though.

Lionel insisted on paying for their dinner, and Jourdain respectfully allowed him the honor. He gave them their tickets and big hugs when they dropped him off at eight-thirty, in plenty of time to get a good rest.

"We'll be cheering for you!" Elena promised.

The first game of the Championship Series was set to begin at one o'clock. Lionel skipped his morning run, ate a decent breakfast, and made sure he had all of his gear when the bus came at ten-thirty sharp. He couldn't believe the activity surrounding the stadium. It was a far cry from the Leones-Tigres season match-up. There were so many vendors, it was like being back in the Port-au-Prince marketplace. Police presence was notable, as officers bearing M-16 rifles marched boldly along the sidewalks, keeping a keen eye out for anyone who might bear a weapon into the stadium.

"Holy cow," he said, eyeing a particularly angry-faced officer. "I hope they don't have to use those today."

Marcione leaned over and looked out of the bus window, unfazed. "Sometimes they do, but let's hope not today."

"This is nothing like the season games," Lionel said.

"Everybody comes out for the Championships," Marcione replied. "Especially when it is all Santo Domingo!"

Stepping inside the stadium was like stepping into a carnival. In the brief walk to the locker room, Lionel saw a juggler, a magician, and a sword-swallower! Kids tried to beg money from the ballplayers as they pushed through the crowd by offering to carry their duffle bags, but security quickly corralled the children away.

"Go on, urchin!" one guard barked gruffly to the small boy who wanted to carry Lionel's bag. He grabbed his arm and flung the boy into the crowd, where he landed on the ground. Lionel started to break away to help him up, but Marcione gently guided him to continue on to the locker room.

"We have to go. Welcome to the championships!" Marcione said.

Roseboro's locker room pep talk was pointed. "Let's win this."

Warm-ups were brief; a few throws loosening up the arm and back muscles, jogging in place, stretching the hamstrings. Roseboro and Alou shook hands and before Lionel knew it, they were lined on the baseline for the playing of the tinniest recording of the National Anthem Lionel had ever heard.

All nine playoff games would be played right there in Quisqueya, and Licey's domination of the playoffs earned them home team advantage for the first three games of the series. As they took the field to begin the first inning, Lionel still felt stiff, with the blood not flowing properly through his muscles just yet. He threw his glove to the ground and dropped, completing twenty-five push-ups right there in left field! The crowd's noise level rose considerably. He popped back to his feet confused, then realized the entire lower section just off the third base line was hollering encouragement and pointing at him. He raised his glove in salute and grinned. This elicited even more applause.

As the first batter took his place, Lionel was sure he could hear Elena's voice rise above the others, cheering him on. He bounced around on his toes, ready to move. The first batter struck out. The second got on base with a single up the middle. The third batter fouled two off into the stands his way, and he was ready for the fly ball that came on the next hit. He fielded it cleanly. By the fifth batter, the inning was over, leaving two men stranded.

The bottom of the first went similarly for Licey. No score.

Lionel got on base in the second inning and was moved around the bags by his teammates. They ended the second inning up by two and stayed on top. Everything about the rest of game went Licey's way, infuriating the Leones. In the top of the ninth, when the last batter for the Leones struck out, he flung his bat so hard at the fence pole, it splintered. Escogido left the field quickly, and Roseboro encouraged the Tigres to keep the on-field celebration short.

Because it was an afternoon game, Lionel was able to have dinner again with Jourdain, Elena, and Sissy. They oohed and aahed over how professionally he carried himself on the field and of course, how proud they were of him. Elena sported a Licey ballcap and t-shirt that she purchased at the stadium.

"Oh, Samféyo," she said. "Your papa would be so proud of you."

Lionel smiled weakly. "Thanks."

"What is wrong? You don't seem so happy," Sissy noted.

Lionel shrugged. "When I first arrived here, the older guys called us *fakers*. They were trying to get under our skin and make us feel we don't really belong here. Like we weren't good enough. You know?"

"Oh, but you are good enough," Elena said.

"Maybe so, but I *am* a faker. I'm not Lionel Bierto. I don't even know who that is! I just don't think Papa would be proud of me for pretending to be somebody I am not."

Jourdain patted Lionel's hand. "I understand what you are saying. You need to remember though that you were in a tough spot. Men came after your life! Macoute! I think Papa would be proud of you for taking a chance and doing something that took a lot of courage. I promised him I would protect you. If you need to blame someone, blame me. I got the birth certificate. I found a way out for you. But you did the brave stuff."

"I ran away," Lionel said. "Brave men don't run away."

"Being brave doesn't mean you endanger your life," Elena corrected. "Brave men make hard decisions every day. You bravely worked in that factory. You bravely helped your papa. You bravely walked into a place where you did not know anyone, and you earned a spot that hundreds—thousands—of boys want. You did that with what you are made of. Inside. No matter what you are called to the outside world, it's what is inside of you that is brave."

Lionel pushed the food around his plate with his fork and thought about this. "I hear you," he said finally.

"You played great tonight. Enjoy the success that comes your way," Jourdain added.

They stayed for the game the following afternoon, but between the boutik, the cigars, and Sissy's real estate business, they had to return to Haiti. If they had been able to stay and watch, however, they would have seen the Tigres del Licey sweep the Leones del Escogido in five straight games, earning them the title of Dominican Winter League Champions. Lionel and his team would be heading off to the Caribbean League

World Series, which was to be played this year in Miami

"Hey, Push-ups! We're going to Miami!" Marcione poked him in the shoulder on the bus ride home from the stadium following their final win. "This is going to be fantástico!"

Lionel grinned. After the first game, the crowd demanded push-ups from him in the first inning of the next game. They chanted, "Push-*ups*! Push-*ups*! Push-*ups*!" And once he figured out what they wanted, he happily obliged. The vigor of the push-ups prepared him for play. He started doing a few before every inning, which pleased the fans greatly.

"Have you been to Miami?" Lionel asked Marcione.

"Nah, man, this will be my first time. I can't wait! This is what's it's all about. Getting to travel. To see the world. To get out of the DR." He sat back in his seat and closed his eyes. A big smile crossed his face.

Lionel leaned his head against the bus window and watched the landscape. They rolled past a shoeless, shirtless boy picking through a garbage bin. *Most likely all he'll ever know is right here*, Lionel thought. The boy lifted his head as they went by, looking longingly at the bus.

CHAPTER 14

On February 1, Lionel Bierto, sixteen teammates, four coaches, and Ralph Avila were dropped off at the Las Américas Airport. Only Lionel and seven other players had never been on an airplane. A mashup of excitement, nervousness, and sheer terror coursed Lionel's veins as they navigated the airport procedures. The travel-veterans did their best to make the other guys less anxious, but it was clear some of them were going to need a lot more than hand-holding to get through their first plane flight.

Lionel carried the baseball that Papa had given him in his jacket pocket. He kept a hand on it, gaining comfort from smoothing his thumb over the red-threaded stitches. However, the sight of the airplane brought a lump to his throat that he could not swallow down. He sat quickly in the nearest seat and put his head between his knees.

"Take deep breaths, son," Avila said. "Stay here, I'll be right back."

A few minutes later, Avila returned and handed Lionel a glass with ice and brown liquid in it. "Drink this," he ordered.

"I—don't—drink, sir," Lionel said between breaths, head still between his knees.

"Look, kid, I admire your principles greatly. But I have been around long enough to know that if you don't drink this, you will not be able to get on that plane," Avila ordered. "Now, drink."

Lionel sat up slowly and took the glass of rum from Avila. He took a sip. It was thick and coated his throat. He took another sip. That sip was kind of sweet, and he felt he could venture a deep breath. He inhaled. He exhaled. He took a mouthful of rum and swallowed it with purpose.

"There you go," Avila said. "Finish that up and let's get on this plane."

Lionel swigged the rest down. "Woah!" he said, eyes widening. "That's a rush."

Avila laughed. "Yeah. Let's go."

The rum caused Lionel to fall asleep, rendering him mercifully unconscious for the two-and-a-half-hour plane flight.

"Sleepyhead, wake up!" Marcione shook his shoulder. "We're landed."

Lionel rubbed his groggy eyes. As he stepped from the staircase onto the tarmac, a flood of warmth ran through him—and it wasn't the Miami heat nor the rum. He was on American soil! He made it somewhere that most Haitians only dream about. The feeling was bigger than his chest could hold. He wanted to savor the moment longer, but the line behind him didn't allow it.

"Keep it moving, Push-ups!" one of the guys called from the plane.

Avila used a courtesy phone to contact the hotel, and within twenty minutes the team piled themselves, ballbags, and luggage into two hotel shuttle vans. Everyone didn't fit, so Lionel and four others stayed behind and waited for a van to circle back for them.

On the nine-mile trip to the hotel, Lionel noticed the streets of Miami, although very different from Haiti, were not much different from Santo Domingo. Kids bicycled in the streets, ladies walked with babies bouncing on their hips, Latino men congregated in front of auto shops, tattoo studios, and corner bars. The cars were a bit nicer. The storefronts were in better shape. But overall, it had the atmosphere of a Dominican town. There was a sense of home to it.

The Howard Johnson on 10th Avenue was six stories tall, and the ballplayers invaded the entire sixth floor. Lionel squeezed into the elevator with the other guys and his stomach did a flip as the small metal box rose. He couldn't imagine how it carried them all. Eagerly, he stepped out and carried his bag to the room he was to share with Henry Rodriguez, another outfielder who would be starting in the game.

He tried the door handle. It didn't budge.

"Use the key," Rodriguez instructed from behind him.

"They didn't give me a key," Lionel said.

"In your hand! In that little envelope," Rodriguez said with frustration.

"There's no key in here. Just the room number written on paper and a plastic card."

"The card is the key, estúpido. Move out of the way." Rodriguez pushed Lionel aside and pulled out his own key. He slid it into a thin opening on the door. Click! And Rodriguez turned the handle.

"Geez," Lionel muttered under his breath.

Rodriguez laughed. "It's OK, man. I didn't know what to do the first time, either."

Rodriguez claimed the bed closest to the bathroom. Lionel plunked his suitcase on the other bed and pulled back the curtains.

"Look at this!" he said with surprise. "I can see for miles."

"You really haven't been anywhere, have you?" Rodriguez said, though not unkindly.

Lionel shook his head, still in disbelief. Rodriguez laughed. "Come on, Push-ups. We have a team meeting down in the lobby."

The Tigres crowded into a conference room that was meant to hold maybe half the number that were in there. Lionel leaned against the back wall, arms folded across his chest, sweat beads forming on his forehead.

Coach Roseboro gave them the rundown. "It's warm in here, so I'll be quick. Miami Stadium is less than a mile away. We put you two to a hotel room instead of three or four, which means we have no money to hire buses. So, you're walking back and forth to the stadium. I figured you'd rather have your own beds." Heads nodded all around. "Good. You have the rest of today off. Don't do anything stupid. Tomorrow, we get the field between nine and eleven to practice. Let's meet in the lobby at eight-thirty to walk over. Bueno?" More head nods and affirmatives. "Alright. We play Puerto Rico on February 5th. They're doing things a little differently this year. We play all three of the other teams in the first round. The team with the best record gets to skip the semifinals and will play a three-game series against the winner of the semis. I want that to be us."

"Why the change, Coach?" Bell asked.

"I don't know. Lastly, there is a banquet when it's over. You need to wear a suit."

Grumbles and groans went up from everyone.

"I didn't bring no suit!" Rodriguez said. Everyone agreed.

"I know, I know. I didn't either. No one told me about it. But we gotta go. So, between now and then, find a suit. I'll get the hotel to shuttle you guys over to the mall. That's it for now. Have a great day, gentlemen. Make good choices."

"So what are you going to do tonight?" Rodriguez asked Lionel. Lionel had taken a nice afternoon nap, showered, and was putting on his jeans and a button-up shirt.

"I don't know. I'm getting hungry though."

"Bell convinced the hotel van driver to take some of us to Miami Beach. If you want to tag along, should be a good time."

"Yeah, thanks," Lionel said.

Any resemblance to Santo Domingo certainly didn't carry over to the flash and bling of Miami Beach. The pack of Tigres turned heads as they strolled the boardwalk. Those who recognized them to be baseball players ran over for autographs.

"Locals know the Caribbean players all arrived today. I bet they're hanging out all over Miami tonight, waiting to catch some autographs," Rodriguez said. A group of kids assaulted them with notepads, baseballs, and markers.

"Juegas al béisbol?" a little one holding up a baseball and

a marker asked Lionel. He was surprised to see it was a girl. A long black ponytail flowed from the back of a blue and red Atlanta Braves cap, which hung slightly over shy brown eyes.

He squatted down to see her face. "Yes, I play baseball."

"You famous?" she asked, retracting the offered ball, as if to consider that she might want to know this answer before gaining his signature.

"Not yet. But I will be," Lionel said with a laugh.

"Do you play for the Braves?" she persisted inquisitively.

He laughed again. "No. I play for the Tigres. Maybe one day I'll play for the Braves."

"Hm. OK, then. Will you sign my baseball?" She offered it to him.

He was glad to have been deemed worthy. He turned the dirty baseball over in his hand. Stamped onto the leather were the words MADE IN HAITI.

He traced his finger over the small black lettering.

"Is something wrong?" the girl asked.

"Nah. You know, my papa used to sew baseballs like this," he stated.

"Really?" she said. "My papa fixes cars. Here's the marker."

He scrawled his name. Lionel Bierto. As an afterthought, he added a scripted "S" near the HAITI stamp.

"What's that?" she asked.

"It's for my papa," he answered, giving her treasure back to her.

She nodded. "Thanks, mister," she said. "I'll watch for you on T.V." She turned to another player in the group.

The guys signed a dozen or so autographs before politely moving on to find a club in which they could have dinner. Lionel added his "S" to each ball he signed. He sighed and thought about his time sewing baseballs. Six weeks ago, Rawlings closed the Haiti plant. The HAITI balls would soon become COSTA RICA balls. The same blanc who stood before the Haitian factory workers and assured that the new Costa Rican plant was not going to replace the Port-au-Prince plant held a press conference during which he bashed the political climate of Haiti and said, although they were very sorry for the seven hundred Haitians that would be put out of work, the unrest made it necessary for Rawlings to review other sites for sourcing their baseballs. Lionel saw the news report on the television in the community room at the Academy. He was so upset for his fellow coworkers that night, he threw the book he was reading across the room and stormed out, hot tears in his eyes for all that Haiti continued to lose.

Manny had followed him out into the Dominican night. "What's wrong, hermano?"

"I had relatives that worked at that plant," Lionel confessed, wiping his eyes with the back of his hand.

"In Haiti?" Manny said, incredulous.

Lionel nodded. "Don't tell anyone," he said.

The Dominican Republic and Haiti are the Hatfields and McCoys of the Caribbean. Their bloody feud, which has raged on and off since the 17th century, is so bitter that a Haitian's very life could be in danger if he is caught in the wrong place in the Dominican. And the same holds true for Dominicans in Haiti. The two nations may share the island of Hispanola, but they also share a fierce sense of identity and desire for dominion. As such, in the Dominican, Haitians—or those with Haitian relatives—are seen as "less-than."

"I won't tell," Manny promised. "I've never been over the border. You?"

Lionel nodded. "Yeah. I've been there."

"Is it as bad as here?"

"Worse."

Manny whistled. "I saw on the news there was another explosion. Five dead and a whole bunch injured."

Lionel stared up at the evening sky, wondering what would become of all of the women in Section Eleven.

He remembered that evening now, as he wandered the streets of Miami, and hoped his former coworkers could find some measure of success in their lives, as he had. But for the life of him, he could not imagine what that would look like.

After their morning practice the next day, the Tigres stayed to watch the Venezuelans, who were earmarked as the team to beat. Each of the four countries in the series got a two-hour window to practice.

"They don't look so tough," Marcione stated, as they sat in the bleachers.

Lionel scrutinized the pitchers, watching for nuances that gave away their strategy. He jotted in his notebook.

"What do you write in that thing?" Marcione asked.

"My observations," Lionel answered without looking up.

"Observations about what?"

"Pitchers mostly."

"Pitchers? What about the pitchers?" Marcione reached over and grabbed Lionel's book. He flipped through the pages. "Figuero shifts his back foot before throwing a sinker?"

"Yup."

"Do I do anything?"

"You shrug your right shoulder slightly if you are going to throw a fastball."

"Eso es loco!" he was indignant.

"Every time," Lionel stated confidently.

Marcione thought that over. He looked through the book some more. "This is really smart."

"My papa used to say, 'The horse is prepared for the day of battle,'" Lionel said.

The Tigres *were* prepared. In their first game, they faced an impressive line-up of Major League stars and surprisingly bested the Cangrejeros de Santurce from Puerto Rico eight to two. They walked to a local Cubano restaurant for dinner and turned in early.

The good night's rest paid off, as they soundly blanked Mexico and then destroyed the Venezuelans. Roseboro and Avila were pleased with the Dominican dominance and the opportunity to skip the semifinals, jumping right to the championship game.

"Our pitching is hot!" Bell stated in their team meeting,

high fiving Rojas and Tapia.

"Bats aren't bad either!" Reyes said. "The Cardenales can suck it!"

"Yeah—twelve to one ain't no joke!" Tapia said.

"So who do you think we'll play in the series?" Rodriguez asked.

"Puerto Rico's got Delgado, Aquino, and Lemke. They're tough, Roseboro said.

"Yeah, we're tougher," Cedeño retorted. More high fives.

"Hey Push-ups! Nice grab out there," Rojas said to Lionel, referring to a save he made at the back fence against Randy Knorr of Venezuela.

"Thanks. Felt good," Lionel replied.

Avila came in and the meeting fell to order. "OK, hermanos," he said. "We're going to watch all of the semifinal games, so we are ready for whatever comes at us, si?" Nods all around. "We're bringing it home this year."

Home. Lionel wished that could be true. He'd love to play and have the win show the world that a Haitian has baseball talent. But, he reminded himself, his home now was the Dominican. Baseball and Haiti would never go together.

In the next couple of days, Lionel acquired his first formal suit—courtesy of H&M clothing store in Miami Beach, watched the Cardinales de Lara of Venezuela beat both the Puerto Rican and Mexican teams, and—the most exciting thing of all—went for his first *real* swim in the hotel swimming pool. Splashing around the Port-au-Prince Bay in Menelas once or twice each summer was the only swimming experience Lionel had up to that point. He was so enthralled with the pool, he got himself a pair of blue OP swimming trunks with sharks all over them from a surf shop near the hotel.

"Looking good!" Rodriguez admired, as Lionel modeled his new trunks.

"You think so?" Lionel spun around. "I like these. I might wear them every day."

Swimming in the pool was the single most relaxing thing

Lionel had ever done. He even went for an early morning swim on the day of their first game in the championship.

The series against Venezuela could hardly be called a competition. The Tigres del Licey whooped the Cardinales soundly in the first two games, with scores of thirteen to four and thirteen to one, respectively. In doing so, they not only won the 1991 Caribbean League Championship, they won with a perfect record.

At the banquet, Lionel beamed with pride as Coach Roseboro won the Manager of the Year award, and several of his teammates received accolades. He accepted his miniature version of the championship team trophy and posed for the team picture.

"Hey, Coach, can I get a copy of that picture?" Lionel asked Roseboro.

"Yeah, son, I'll get you a copy," Roseboro laughed.

Six weeks later, back at the Academy, when Lionel returned to his bunk after a particularly long and grueling practice, perched on his pillow was a framed 8 x 10 photo of the Tigres del Licey, looking sharp in suits and ties, proudly holding their trophies. A note was taped to the picture:

Thanks for playing your heart out! –Roseboro

Sweat had pooled in the creases of Lionel's elbows and in the small of his back before he even reached the turn-around point on his morning run. It had to be eighty-five degrees already. Thankfully he had his hand to his face to wipe the sweat from his eyes when the tip of his shoe caught on a jagged rock, pulling away at the rubber sole, causing him to spill, face-first, into the gravel. His hand protected his face, but his knees took a beating on the rocks.

"Aye!" he yowled. He lay on his back on the path, knees pulled to his chest. He pressed his hands down hard on his knee caps, as if to hold the pain inside. When he realized he had no choice but to get up and limp back to the Academy, he sat up slowly to inspect the damage. Forearms scraped. Left shoe torn. Knees bloody. Great.

His left knee took the worst of the fall. When he put pressure on his leg, it felt like it would give out from under him. It was a slow mile back to the Academy, and Lionel went directly to the trainer's room, hoping someone would be there to help him out.

"Hey Bierto," Dan said, as Lionel limped in. "What's going on?"

"I wiped out on my run," Lionel explained. "My knee hurts like a son-of-a-gun."

"Hop up," Dan instructed. Lionel got himself on the table. Dan cleaned up the scrapes, then felt around Lionel's kneecap. Lionel winced.

"Did I break anything?" Lionel asked.

"Your knee?" Dan chuckled. "No, it's not broken. I think

you just tweaked the ligament a little bit. There's only a small bit of swelling building up here. Let's sit with an ice pack for twenty minutes. I'll tape you up for practice. Then let's ice pack again right after practice today. Just take it easy on the running for a couple of days. Should be fine."

Lionel leaned back against the wall on the training table, leg outstretched, ice pack cradling his kneecap. Avila caught sight of him through the window and came into the training room.

"What happened?" he asked gruffly.

"Don't worry, Coach," Lionel said. "I just took a spill on my morning run. Dan said I'll be fine."

"Is that true?" Avila asked Dan.

"Yeah, he'll be fine. He should go easy running for a day or two. That's it."

Avila harrumphed. "You know you leave next Friday," he reminded.

"I know, Coach. I'll be fine," Lionel reassured.

"You better. Bakersfield is lucky to have you again. You'll be ready for Double-A or Triple-A ball in no time. Hell, you're probably ready now, but there isn't a spot yet."

"I wish we'd made the championships last year," Lionel said. "That would have helped."

Avila brushed that aside. "Nah. California League was tough last year. You played hard. Keep doing that. Keep your nose clean. I don't throw this around much, but I think you'll get there eventually." He patted Lionel's leg. "Get that knee healed."

Dan was right. Lionel's knee was tender for a couple of days, but by the time he packed for training camp, it was just fine. Last summer he'd been drafted to play for the Bakersfield Blaze—the Dodger's Single-A team. He was headed back there this summer, too, but first, Dodger's management was bringing all of the A, AA, and AAA players to Los Angeles for an unprecedented whole-group meeting before spring training.

Lionel packed his clothing in the large suitcase he'd

gotten in Haiti and his more personal items in the smaller suitcase that he'd picked up last summer on his first trip to the United States. He played with Bakersfield all summer and then came home to the Academy for Winter League. Licey didn't win the Series this past year, but his own personal stats improved tremendously. Manny would be playing summer ball for the Dominican Dodgers team again this year. He sat on Lionel's bed while he packed.

"It's not the same without you here," he said. "You get to go party it up in California, with all the sun goddesses throwing themselves at your feet."

Lionel laughed. "It's not like that at all, man. It's just like here. Ride the bus to the game. Play your butt off. Sleep in a crappy hotel. Repeat."

"Yeah, whatever. I hear stories about the California girls," Manny said. He picked up Lionel's papa's notebook out of his suitcase. A folded piece of thin white paper fell out. He opened it. "Samféyo Bernard? What is this?"

Lionel's head snapped around at the mention of his real name. "Hey! Let me see that!"

Manny handed it over. Lionel looked wistfully at the paper.

"A relative?" Manny asked.

Lionel nodded. "Something like that."

"Siento mucho," Manny said.

Lionel tucked his primary school completion certificate back in the notebook and placed it in the inner zipper of the suitcase. He'd thought several times about finding a way he could finish his schooling—at least to get a secondary education. He hoped maybe this summer he'd be able to look into it more. He finished packing and left Manny with a hug.

"See you in the fall, hermano," Lionel said.

The flight to Los Angeles required a quick stopover in Miami. Lionel carried a small bottle of rum when he traveled, which gave him the courage to get on the airplanes. It was the only alcohol he touched, even resisting the temptations that surfaced continually at the California parties last summer. He wasn't entirely truthful with Manny. A couple of the Bakersfield players had nice homes and loved to throw poolside cookouts when the team had a day off or an early game. There were usually at least a few girls there, looking for a good time. There was one girl in particular that Lionel danced with a few times, but when dancing turned to kissing, she asked him to take her to one of the bedrooms and he broke the connection off.

"A real man knows how to respect a woman," Papa told him when he turned fifteen. "And that means you wait until marriage to take a girl to bed." Haiti was full of young girls having babies. Not by choice, either. In Haiti, girls are often forced into sex. In the rest of the world, however, Lionel found that women were more than willing to give up their sexuality. He planned to keep himself pure; which wasn't easy for a twenty-year-old.

Marcione and three others traveled with Lionel from the Dominican. At the airport, two dozen other players met up with them, and the organization sent a bus to fetch them all. He'd been down to Los Angeles to watch the Dodgers play when the schedule allowed it—but this was the first time he was invited *officially* to Dodger Stadium.

"Bierto!" He heard his name called as they walked out onto the field. It was Juan Castro, a Mexican player from the Great Falls Dodgers who'd been moved up to Bakersfield for this season. Marianna, the administrative assistant for Bakersfield, had found them an apartment to share for the summer. It was furnished, cheap, and would be a perfect spot to crash when they were in town.

"Hola!" Lionel said, putting down his luggage. He shook hands with his friend.

"Come on! A bunch of us are over here," Castro said.

A large tarp covered the infield, and folding chairs, set in rows of forty across with an aisle down the center, faced a raised stage upon which the Dodger logo hung proudly from the front of an acrylic podium. A line of empty seats waited behind the podium for the guests of honor to arrive. In the spectator chairs, Bakersfield, San Antonio, Albuquerque, and the big-league guys—the Major League Dodgers—all had quadrants claimed for their teams. Near the dugout a long row of tables held beverages and snacks. Lionel took a Coke and bag of Lays and found a seat with his teammates.

"...never done anything like this before," one of the guys was saying.

"Maybe he's retiring," someone else offered.

"Lasorda? Never," another player said. "Besides, they wouldn't call all of us here for that. It don't make no sense."

Men continued to roll in, and within the next hour, nearly every seat was filled. Lionel was just as curious as the others as to the purpose for the meeting, but he hadn't been around long enough to even know what to speculate. A hush came across the field as Tommy Lasorda and a dozen others stepped onto the stage. The managers were in their team uniforms. The men in suits, Lionel presumed, were club owners and other very important persons. Marcione nudged him and pointed.

"That's the owner. O'Malley," he said as one of the suits walked to the podium. A round of applause rose up from the teams.

Mr. O'Malley smiled and waited for the claps to die down. "Well, now! Thank you, gentlemen," he said. "Welcome to the 1992 baseball season!" Another round of cheers went up. "We, at the Los Angeles Dodgers, are thrilled to have you as part of our organization. I'm glad to see so many smiling faces. I hope you are just as happy to be here as we are to have you. As Tommy here always says, 'If you don't love the Dodgers, there is a good chance you won't get into heaven.'" Laughter rose up from the guys. "I want to introduce to you the managers for our affiliate teams this year. Tom Beyers for Bakersfield. Jerry Royster for San Antonio. Bill Russell here for Albuquerque."

After each name, the manager tipped his hat to the crowd and the guys clapped politely; getting rowdier when their respective team names were called.

"And last but certainly not least, Mr. Tommy Lasorda for

the Los Angeles Dodgers." The loudest cheers were reserved for Lasorda, who came to the podium and shook O'Malley's hand. O'Malley took a seat and Lasorda faced the group.

"I bet you dollars to doughnuts you guys are going crazy trying to figure out why in the world we brought all of you here today." A murmur of agreement went up from the group. "As far as I can tell, no Major League team has ever brought its Minor League affiliate teams together in one place like this. We could have done this meeting in your hometowns. It would have been a lot cheaper for Mr. O'Malley and me to make one of those fancy video-taped messages and send a tape out to all of you to play at a team meeting. But we wanted you to be here to hear this message. Look around, gentlemen." He stretched out his arms, inviting the men to look around the stadium. He gave a moment for them to do so, taking in their surroundings.

"Look at those banners. Sandy Koufax. Roy Campanella. Jackie Robinson," he punctuated Jackie's name with a fist pump. "The first Dodgers to have their numbers retired. Then Gilliam. Drysdale. Snider. Men who came before you. Men who paved the way for future Dodger greatness. I don't care if you are slugging it out at Single A, Double A, Triple A, or you make it to the Big Show. You bear a piece of the legacy these men—and many others—left behind when you signed on to be a part of the Dodgers.

"On April 15, 1947, the Brooklyn Dodgers did something no other team was ready to do. They allowed a black man to put on a Major League team uniform. Jackie Robinson wore that uniform better than most. He did the world a favor by agreeing to put it on. But before Jackie Robinson wore the Dodgers' colors, he did something the majority of you sitting here are doing. He put on farm league colors and slugged it out in the pits. You guys know—there's way more minor league players than there are guys who make The Show. And there are countless young boys out there all across the world dreaming of their shot in the minors. Hear me, men. When Branch Rickey brought Robinson up to his farm team, he didn't know what the outcome would be. But he knew Robinson had integrity. Yeah, the talent was there, too," he chuckled. "But it was Robinson's integrity that made him stand out just as much as his ball skills. Our call to you today is one of integrity.

"Every one of you knows that there is a storm brewing in Los Angeles. This business with Rodney King last year threw a match into a box of dynamite. The box is smoldering. And in the coming weeks, there's going to be a decision made about the case. The dynamite could start to blow. The purpose for this meeting is so you men can hear this straight from our lips. You are not—I repeat—you are not to talk to the press about the Rodney King case. You guys playing out in San Antonio or New Mexico, you can be sure some po-dunk news idiot is going to want to ask you what you think of the Los Angeles Rodney King case. You Bakersfield boys and of course LA guys—I betcha a hundred bucks every interview is going to have some question about your opinion on the matter. They're going to ask you because this is happening in our city." He paused here, looking directly into the eyes of several men.

"Integrity, gentlemen. We are not the judge and jury. You probably have your own strong opinions on the matter. I know I do. But here's the thing. As a Los Angeles Dodger or a Dodger affiliate, you will represent this organization with professionalism and integrity. Whether you wear the colors of a Single-A, Two-A, or Three-A team. No matter if you play right here in Dodger Stadium. You will not comment on the matter to the media! When you are out in public, you will not run drunken mouths about Rodney King. Stick to baseball. Be all about baseball. The rest will sort itself out. You be about baseball." He pointed emphatically to the crowd and said it a third time. "You be all about baseball. Are there any questions?"

"Will the Dodgers release a statement?" a voice from the Major League players' group asked.

Lasorda nodded. "We will maintain what we've said all along. We are thankful for the difficult job that our law enforcement officers have. We trust our country's judicial system. We love our city and the people of Los Angeles. All people of every color."

Lionel absorbed this information. Sure, he saw the news last year and knew that Rodney King was beaten horribly after running from the police on a traffic stop. Did he think much else about it? Honestly, no. He wondered why the Dodgers felt this message was so important to deliver in person. Would the press really care what the ball players thought about the whole thing?

"Of course they will!" Marcione answered when Lionel asked him that question after the formal part of the meeting was over. "They want to get your words and twist them all up so that the ball club is brought into the hype and muck of it all. They hope to catch a player off-guard and have someone say something stupid that will make Los Angeles look even more stupid."

"Even in Bakersfield?" Lionel asked.

"They wouldn't have brought us all here if they didn't think so." He indicated the group of Dodger big wigs who were standing around talking to players near the podium. "They must be concerned if they spent all of this money to tell us to our faces."

Rumors floated through the crowd that one of the Dodger players was having a get-together at his house later that evening. Most of the guys had reservations at the Best Western in Chinatown, including Lionel. He and Marcione were sharing a room for the next two nights before heading up to Bakersfield. Marcione went to find the address for the party, while Lionel waited. He observed Tommy Lasorda talking with a group of guys and grinned with a slight wave when Coach Lasorda caught his eye. To Lionel's surprise, Lasorda excused himself and walked over to where Lionel stood.

"Hello," he said, holding out his hand for Lionel to shake. "You are my Dominican morning jogger."

"Yes, sir," Lionel said. "Thank you for having me here."

"Playing for Bakersfield, right?" Coach Lasorda said.

"Yes, sir," Lionel said, shocked that he knew.

"I know the guys I want to keep an eye on," Lasorda replied, catching the tone in Lionel's voice. "Especially my

Dominicans."

Lionel nodded. "I'll do you proud, sir."

Lasorda clapped Lionel on the back. "I know you will, son. You are one of those with integrity that I spoke of."

Marcione returned and held out his hand. "Hey, thanks Coach Lasorda," he said. They shook hands.

"Work hard, boys. Remember, baseball is like driving. It's the one who gets home safely that counts." He laughed at his own joke and moved along.

Lionel and Marcione checked into their hotel. Even though he was tired from the long day of travel and the time change, Lionel agreed to go with Marcione to the party. "Just for a couple of hours," he warned.

"That's it. I promise," Marcione said.

The cab ride cost them fifty dollars—which they split with Castro and Salcedo, another Bakersfield player. The cab let them out at the foot of a long driveway that snaked up a steep hill. The driveway ended at a modern white house that stretched out on a plateau which overlooked the neighborhood below.

They took it in as they caught their breaths from the uphill walk.

Castro whistled. "This place costs some pesos!"

"Brother's got bank," Salcedo said. "They signed him to a five-year deal."

"How much?"

"Two point five per."

"Nice," Castro said, appreciatively. "This is gonna be me one day, boys. I'll have you all over and we'll dance all night."

Two players Lionel recognized from the Albuquerque team walked up the drive.

"You guys going in?" one of them asked.

"Yeah, just admiring the view from up here," Castro answered. They followed the guys inside, and Lionel found himself in the largest living room he'd ever seen. People clustered everywhere, talking, laughing, and drinking. Through the bodies, Lionel could see that the room was generously outfitted with poofy white couches, soft white carpeting, and mirrored bobbles. Even the large paintings that adorned the walls were abstracts in varying shades of white. He found himself thinking Elena would like the cleanliness of this décor.

"Piazza!" someone yelled to one of the Albuquerque guys. "You made it! Come on—let's go outside."

They were led through the living room into a kitchen that exploded with color. Lionel felt he suddenly walked into a completely different home. Oversized brown Spanish tiles covered the floor. The walls were lavished with bright yellow paint that almost hurt to look at, and the countertop was inset with glossy green and blue tiles that formed patterns you might see in a Mayan temple. Mexican pottery filled the corners and sat atop the thick wooden cabinetry. Clusters of deep red and orange paper-mâché chili peppers dangled from the ceiling.

"Wow," Marcione said, taking in the onslaught of color. "This is something."

The back deck was even bigger than the living room. A bartender served drinks while music blared from speakers mounted to the house. Lionel opted for his usual and walked over to the glass railing to take in the view.

"Nice, yeah?" a player leaning on the rail next to him said.

"Definitely," Lionel replied, taking a sip of his Coke.

"I'm Pete," the guy said.

"Lionel."

"Just Coke?" Pete asked, nodding to Lionel's drink.

"Yeah. I don't drink," Lionel replied.

Pete held up his own drink to toast. "I drink Diet Coke. Less calories," he said, laughing, and the two tapped cans.

"So where are you from, Lionel?" he asked.

"Santo Domingo," Lionel replied. "I play for Bakersfield."

"Awesome. I'm from Ohio. What position?"

"Outfield. You?"

"I play a little bit of everywhere," he said. He was about to expand, but some guys nearby started arguing, and Pete stepped in to break it up. He sent them separate ways, then turned back to Lionel.

"Sorry, Lionel. I gotta keep an eye on my man. He gets excitable when he drinks."

Lionel nodded knowingly. The previous summer he learned quickly how players get to acting when they've had too much to drink—or worse, when someone brings out heavier substances. Pete was full of stories from around the minors, and Lionel could have listened to him all night. As it was, they only talked for about thirty minutes when suddenly the music cranked way up.

"Jump around!" someone screamed, and the deck became a dance floor. As House of Pain thumped from the speakers, fifty or so bodies started bouncing to the beat. Lionel backed up to find some breathing room and unfortunately moved into a prime spot to witness what happened next. Miguel Cruz—the player Pete shooed away from the argument—came back onto the deck when he heard the song and gave a war cry that could be heard above the music.

"Oh yeaaaahhhh! Jump around! Jump! Jump! Jump around!" he yelled, jumping with purpose. He pinballed off of a few people, then stomped right onto the foot of the guy he'd been arguing with earlier.

"Hey, pendejo! Get off of me!" the guy yelled, shoving Cruz in the other direction. Cruz, whose balance was impaired, fell heavily onto a small coffee table that was part of the wicker deck furniture. The problem for Cruz was that the wicker frame was not very strong, so the glass tabletop shattered when Cruz fell onto it. He put his hands out to catch himself, which resulted in one of the most horrific things Lionel had ever—or will ever—see. Cruz's face and hands hit the table at about the same time, causing the glass to break in three separate places.

When his left hand went through the glass, the sharp edge that angled upward pushed through Cruz's cheek, tearing the flesh and lodging into his face. Both of his hands were badly torn, and the screaming and chaos that ensued would give Lionel nightmares for weeks.

"Somebody dial 9-1-1!" Lionel heard someone yell before he threw up over the side of the railing.

CHAPTER 16

Lionel's stomach was in knots outside the coaches' offices at Dodger Stadium. For the life of him he couldn't figure out why they sent for him—of all people—to talk about what happened the previous night. Cruz had been taken by ambulance to a hospital. There were so many people heading to the hospital, Lionel and Marcione felt they would be in the way, so they called a cab to take them back to the hotel. There was no doubt Cruz wouldn't be playing baseball anytime soon. His hands were shredded, and his face? Well, Lionel could only imagine the plastic surgery in store for him.

The door opened. "Bierto. Come on in," Bill Russell, the coach of the Dukes, said.

Inside the office was Coach Lasorda, Bill Russell, Tom Beyers, and Jerry Royster. He took the empty chair.

"Good morning, son," Lasorda said. "Do you know why you're here?"

"No, sir," he said.

"I heard you saw what happened last night," Lasorda said. "It was pretty bad?"

"Yes, sir. It was awful," Lionel affirmed. "Just awful."

"I saw Cruz this morning. He is unable to talk and is scheduled for surgery later today. They have him on pretty strong pain meds," Lasorda said. Lionel nodded solemnly. "Son, I need to ask you something, and I need a truthful answer. Did Cruz fall on his own accord? Or was he pushed?"

Lionel's stomach twisted. He saw the other guy shove Cruz. He also knew Cruz deserved it. He certainly didn't deserve what happened to his face, but that wasn't the other guy's fault. *Was it?* He didn't want to be a snitch. He *couldn't* be a snitch. He shifted in his chair.

Bill Russell saw his discomfort. "Bierto. These guys aren't even on your team. They won't know we talked to you."

"But *I'll* know," Lionel answered. "And we're all Dodgers in some way, aren't we?" He looked down at his lap.

The coaches looked at one another. Lasorda rubbed his chin thoughtfully, mulling that question over. "Can you wait outside for a minute?" he asked Lionel.

Lionel went back to the hallway. Did he just screw up his chances with the Dodgers? It was a really long minute that stretched into ten, then twenty. He was invited back in.

"We are inclined to think that what happened last night was accidental. That no one intended to hurt Cruz," Lasorda said.

Lionel nodded his agreement. "Yes, sir. I believe that."

Lasorda sat back in his large leather chair and folded his hands behind his head. He was quiet long enough to make Lionel squirm in his seat again, but then he said, "Cruz played outfield for the Dukes. We're moving you up to take his spot."

"The Dukes?" Lionel said incredulously. "Triple A?"

"Yes," Bill Russell confirmed. "We'll do the paperwork and have it ready for you to sign later today. In the meantime, Cheryl from our office in Albuquerque is waiting for your phone call. She will get you an apartment and take care of a plane ticket and all that business."

"Um, OK," Lionel said. He was going to ask, "Are you sure?" but thought better of it.

"Integrity, kid," Lasorda said with a wink.

The next three days went by in a blur. Cheryl's magic touch handled every detail with such smoothness that Lionel had nothing to do but show up at the airport and get on the plane. He was so excited, he didn't even need the rum. In fact, after what happened at the party, he was pretty sure he never wanted the rum again.

His new apartment in Albuquerque was a tiny studio

above a family-owned Mexican restaurant. The furniture was made to look like thick wooden crates—durable, heavy, and not super-comfortable. The tiny couch didn't even allow for him to stretch out, as it was only two thick foam cushions across. But it did have a coffee table on which he could kick up his feet to watch the twenty-one-inch television. A partitioning wall separated the living area from the sleeping space. The bedroom furniture had the same crated look as the living room, with a wooden bed frame, a six-drawer chest, and a small nightstand. It wasn't fancy, but it was his. And it was tidy.

He had two free days in Albuquerque before reporting to spring training. He got acquainted with the town, found the closest grocery store, and even purchased an orange mountain bicycle for himself from a small sports store on Gold Avenue. It was a two-mile ride from his apartment to the stadium—the perfect distance.

On his first bike ride to the Albuquerque Sports Stadium he realized he was going to have to wear a bandana to cover his nose and mouth. Albuquerque was a dusty place. Several guys were arriving when he did, and friendly nods and greetings from everyone made him feel welcome. The locker room was bigger than what they had in Bakersfield, which made sense since the stadium was three times the size of Sam Lynn Ballpark and almost thirty years newer. He found his name etched into a bronze-plated sign above one of the lockers.

One of the players from the party, Mike Piazza, had the locker next to Lionel's and he greeted him. "Hey, good to see you man," he said warmly.

"Hey," Lionel replied with caution. He knew he was only there because of what happened to Cruz, and he wondered how many of the others knew it too. Would they look at him as an imposter? As someone who didn't belong? He hoped not. He would just have to show them on the field that he did belong.

"You're Bierto?" Piazza asked.

"Si. Lionel Bierto," he answered.

"You play outfield?"

"Si," Lionel answered.

Piazza nodded. "Catch 'em every time. Get 'em in fast," he advised. "Outfield errors cost runs."

Lionel nodded. He knew that well. He'd only committed four errors last season, but he remembered each in painstaking detail, having played and replayed the error in his mind until he had a sense of what caused it and what could have been done to avoid it.

Practice began with a team meeting, during which Coach Russell talked only briefly about Cruz's unfortunate accident and said they would keep everyone posted on his recovery.

"We play Las Vegas in four weeks," he instructed, as he handed out a thick packet. "This here is our full schedule, including practices. I expect you to find time to supplement our team practice with weight training. I've marked the times the weight room here will be open, but I know some of you like to go the Gold's Gym or that Bally Fitness place. Just make sure you're lifting every day when we aren't traveling or playing.

"For you new guys. When we travel by bus, you can wear comfortable clothes. If we are flying, blazer and tie. Be on time. If the bus leaves at seven, be here at six-thirty. I will leave you behind. You will not get paid for days missed if I leave you behind. You'll get your per-diem money handed to you in an envelope as we leave. You do not need to turn in receipts, but I would strongly recommend you keep them. Do not buy alcohol or cigarettes with your per-diem money.

"Erik, Angela, step up here please." Two young people in University of New Mexico polo shirts stood up next to Coach Russell. "This here is Erik Hudak and Angela Voss. They are graduates of UNM Sports Sciences. They are interning with us this season as our trainers. Training room schedule is in your packets. Respect their time.

"Today we'll have batting and fielding practice and position meetings. I want to see my pitchers first. The rest of you get on out there."

There were eight outfielders on the roster. They took turns fielding balls from batting practice until it was their turn to meet with Coach Russell. Lionel played at both left and right and felt strong.

"We'll decide who we'll start in outfield the week before the first game," Coach explained. "Cook, I know you started last year, but you're all pretty equal in talent, so we have to see how it all shakes out. Cook, Bierto, Ashley—play left. Rodriguez, Mondesí, you guys play right. The others play center."

The player he referenced, Garrett Cook, didn't look thrilled with this news. As they left the meeting, he said loud enough for Lionel to hear, "I'm not losing my starter spot to no new guy."

Cook's locker was across from Lionel's. If there was one player on the Dukes who was not friendly to Lionel, it was Cook. Whether on account of the battle for starting position or because of Cruz, Lionel wasn't sure. He'd heard talk that Cook and Cruz had been pretty good friends—roommates in their days with San Antonio.

"Don't worry about him," Billy Ashley said one day after a practice game when Coach pulled Cook to put in Lionel. Cook flung his cleats with force into his locker and shoved past Lionel on his way out. "He came back from the winter break angry. He's acting that way to everyone."

"I'm just doing my best out there," Lionel said. "I'm not trying to piss anyone off."

"You're fine," Ashley assured. "His poppa is related to some big shot with the Dodgers and he's just trying to make a name for himself. He thinks because he's connected, he shouldn't have to work for nothin'."

"Success don't come free," Piazza said, walking in on the tail end of the conversation.

When the time came for Coach to post the starting line-up, Lionel didn't expect to see his name on the list, so he wasn't disappointed when it wasn't there. His batting wasn't as strong as some of the other outfielders; although his defensive skills were as good, if not better. Ashley would start at left for their first game against the Las Vegas Stars.

Even though the Blaze had their share of phenomenal pitchers, Lionel was blown away by the meteors thrown in this league. They were in a whole other stratosphere from the California League pitchers. In the first two weeks of play, he didn't even know what to write in his notebook. He just took it all in. Russell made it standard practice to start either Ashley or Cook and then put Lionel in for the last two innings of each game, giving him the chance to show what he could do. He fielded everything that came his way, but his batting lulled somewhere around .165.

"Keep working, kid," Russell reassured after every game. "You'll get there."

On April 29, the Dukes played Calgary in an evening game. They bested the Cannons with a score of six to four. It was a good win for them, but as Coach Russell came into the locker room, he didn't look happy.

"What's wrong, Coach?" Piazza asked.

All eyes turned to Coach Russell.

"The officers were acquitted today," he said solemnly. "In the King case. Los Angeles is under attack."

"Attack?" someone called out. "By who?"

"Its own citizens," Coach said. "They are rioting in the streets. It's a mess."

Someone suggested they gather to pray. The team grouped together, held hands, and Piazza led them in a prayer for the people of Los Angeles, for the police, and for their brothers in Dodger Stadium, who had just finished up their own game and needed to get home safely.

The riots lasted almost a week, during which the LA Dodgers canceled their ballgames and Dodger outfielder Darryl Strawberry's brother Michael—a police officer—was grazed in the head by a bullet when his police car was ambushed. Lionel couldn't believe the stories coming over the television news channels and through the Dodger organization. News reports were sickening. He thought stuff like this only happened in

Haiti, and it unnerved him to see Americans losing their minds in aggression and violence.

When the worst of it died down, things got back to normal for the Dukes. Lionel's batting average crept up slightly, and by mid-May he was at .200. He stayed late to practice hitting and watched hitting videos in the coaches' offices whenever he had the chance. Coach, tired of waiting around for Lionel to watch videos every night, bought Lionel a small video-cassette player and told him to take it home and hook it up to his television so he could watch his videos there. Lionel went to Blockbuster Video and rented every baseball-related video he could find, scrutinizing the stance and style of other players in order to glean nuggets for his own batting technique. He spent his evenings practicing batting stances in his small living room.

While Lionel improved in the box, Cook's average began to slide. It seemed he would either knock one out of the park or strike out. He had no middle-ground. His anger flared in the dugout each time he didn't get a hit, and Russell was starting to tire of it. In the first game in a series against the division-leading Colorado Springs Sky Sox, Russell gave Lionel his chance to start.

In the first inning, Lionel caught two flies, including snagging a ball that would have landed foul in the stands. In the second inning, with two out and a man on base, Lionel got his turn in the batter's box. He didn't fall for the first pitch; which was high and outside. The second pitch, however, was a good fastball that Lionel wasn't ready for. He swung later than he wanted, and the ball went to the far right, foul. He noticed however, that the left-handed pitcher lifted the heel of his right foot ever so slightly before throwing that fastball, and he hoped he would do it again. As he waited for the third pitch, he watched. No heel lift, and the ball was slow and low. Ball two. Then, on the fourth pitch, the heel lifted. The pitcher wound up. Lionel was ready for the fastball and he belted it—nice and square—sending the ball out of the park for his first Triple-A homerun.

He finally had something to put in his notebook! "LHP Eric Bell, lifts R heel – fastball," he wrote, following his trip around the bags. Mondesí, the runner on base that also scored on Lionel's homer, came over and patted him on the back. "Gracias, amigo! Nice job!"

The Dukes won that series, and Lionel secured a spot in the rotation as a starter. Cook didn't like sharing the starting rotation with Lionel and showed it by acting like a jerk every chance he got. He'd slam his glove down, knocking over Lionel's water cup, or he'd swing his ball bag as he left the locker room, smacking it into Lionel's shoulders. Lionel largely ignored the passive-aggressive tantrums; the sense of belonging extended him by the other Dukes made up for them.

One Monday in June, Lionel arrived at the Albuquerque airport. The Dukes were headed to Vancouver, British Columbia for a game against the Canadians. When he checked in with Russell, he was handed his per-diem envelope and a copy of the Dodgers Organization's Summer Newsletter.

"Thanks, Coach," Lionel said.

"Have a look on page two," Russell said.

Lionel waited until he was seated on the plane to read the newsletter. When he opened it, his own face stared back at him from the page. A smiling headshot was accompanied by a larger photo of Lionel swinging the bat during a game. Sheer determination radiated from his face. It was the "Minor League Players to Watch" section, and Lionel couldn't believe—there he was!

Dominican outfielder Lionel "Push-ups" Bierto is a new name to the Albuquerque Dukes (AAA) line-up this season. Bierto played on the Caribbean Series Championship team Licey del Tigres and the Dominican Dodger Team before being drafted as a free agent with the Bakersfield Blaze in 1991. This year, Bierto plays for the Albuquerque Dukes, where he currently holds a .245 batting average. Coach Bill Russell says of Bierto, "This kid is on fire. He's not afraid to go after the hard plays that look like they're going into the stands or out of the park. He goes after them and grabs them all." Bierto was given the nickname Push-ups by his Dominican League fans because of the exercises he does in the outfield before each inning. Bierto says the push-ups help get his blood moving so he is ready to chase down whatever comes his way.

"Nice write-up, Push-ups," Piazza leaned over the seat and said to Lionel.

"Gracias," Lionel replied.

"What the hell kind of nickname is Push-ups?" Cook called out from across the aisle. "That's the dumbest nickname I've ever heard."

"Hey, can it, Cook," Mondesí called from his seat. "Don't be an a-hole."

The first game of the three-game series was stellar for the Dukes, as they put up five home runs in Nat Bailey Stadium. Its short center field helped them to best the Canadians twelve to three. Lionel was thrilled to get his second home run of the year, and on defense, he threw a rocket from far-left field to second base to get out a runner who thought he'd advance on a sacrifice fly.

They arrived for game two of the series feeling confident. Ashley was going to start, and Lionel planned to watch and take notes on the pitcher Alex Fernandez, as he hadn't seen him pitch before. Just as they put their bags down and began to get changed, the coaches walked into the locker room, trailed by four men in red shirts that bore the Canadian flag and the Pacific Coast League logo.

"Gentlemen if you could freeze what you're doing for a moment," Coach Russell said.

Cook, who was standing behind Bierto, leaned over and dropped something into Lionel's open bag. Lionel saw the movement in his periphery, but per instructions, he didn't move.

"These men are here from the Canadian arm of the league. They are going to do a bag check. All of you leave your bags where they are and step to the center of the room. Please don't touch anything."

"Damn Canadians," someone muttered.

Lionel wondered what Cook dropped in his bag. It wasn't long until he found out.

"Whose bag is this?" an official asked, holding up Lionel's duffel.

"Mine, sir," Lionel answered.

"You need to come with us," he responded.

The rest of the players continued to get ready for the game, while Lionel was ushered into a room with the League officials and Coach Russell. They found a brown pill bottle in Lionel's bag.

"What are these?" one of the men asked Lionel.

"I don't know, sir," Lionel replied.

"Would it surprise you to know they are amphetamines?" he asked.

"I don't know what amphetamines are, sir," Lionel replied truthfully.

"Son, these are illegal to have in Canada. Did you know that?" one of the men asked Lionel.

"No, sir," Lionel replied again. "Those are not mine."

"Did someone ask you to hold them?" Russell asked.

"No, sir."

"Then how did they get in your bag?" another one of the officials asked.

"I guess someone put them there. Maybe someone who didn't want to get caught with them," Lionel said.

"Do you know who that would be?" Russell asked.

Lionel didn't answer. Was he going to rat out Cook? He sure wanted to.

"Lionel," Russell said. "If you know whose drugs these are, you should tell us, son. Because as it stands, we have to send you back to the United States and conduct an internal investigation."

Lionel shook his head. "I'm not a snitch, sir. But those are not mine."

The official-in-charge looked at Russell. "I'm sorry, Coach. Make arrangements to send him home. We don't want him in Canada. He certainly can't be here at the ballpark. We'll be in touch with further information."

Russell gave Lionel one more chance. "Are you sure you have nothing to tell us?"

Lionel didn't reply.

Lionel was escorted back to his hotel room, where one of the Canadian officials went through all of his things, looking for more pills. Of course they didn't find any. Lionel packed up and was driven to the airport, then put on a plane bound for Albuquerque. At the other end, he was met by Erik the trainer. Erik and Angela took turns traveling with the team, and Angela was in Vancouver.

"What happened?" Erik asked. "Russell called me to pick you up and said I was to take you to your apartment, but I can't let you in until I go through your things, looking for drugs. You ain't on juice or anything, are you? I've got to get a urine sample from you."

"Of course not," Lionel answered. "The drugs they found weren't mine."

"Well whose were they?" Erik questioned.

"I can't say. I'm not a snitch," Lionel stated flatly.

"Jeez, man," Erik said. "They're going to find out eventually."

"Well, they won't hear it from me," Lionel said.

Erik went through Lionel's things, had him pee in a cup, and reported his empty findings back to Russell. Lionel was told to stay in his apartment and not to report to the stadium until called for. He ate dinner at the Mexican restaurant and only went out for his daily run.

From Vancouver, the team traveled to Portland for another three-game series. This series was not as successful, and the Dukes only won one game. It was more than a week later when Russell finally called Lionel to his office.

"Have a seat, son," Russell said when Lionel came in.

"Look. I don't know whose drugs those were. I don't think they were yours, but no one else has 'fessed up. Possessing that bottle isn't anything to get you kicked out of the league for, especially since you clearly don't take anything, but we've got to do something. It's a black smear on the organization to have a player sent out of Canada. We're sending you back to the Dominican to play summer ball for the rest of the summer. From there we'll figure out what to do."

"I'm done?" Lionel said incredulously.

"Unless you want to tell us whose drugs those were," Russell said.

"I can't do that," Lionel said.

"Then I'm sorry. I have no other choice."

Lionel did something he hadn't done in a while. He cried. Right there in Coach Russell's office, he bawled out the pain and frustration that had been building up. Russell was kind enough to let him get it all out, then Lionel stood and shook Bill Russell's hand. He walked out with his head held high.

CHAPTER 17

I t was a shameful walk back into Campo Las Palmas. Thankfully no one was around when he got there, and he could put his stuff on his old bunk without any questions. At least, until Avila caught sight of him.

"Bierto! My office," he said.

Lionel took a deep breath. He knew he'd have to face Avila, he just wished it wasn't so soon.

Lionel saw compassion, not anger, in Avila's eyes. "I know you, kid. You don't do drugs," Avila said as they sat down. "I'm not going to make a big deal out of this. You can join in the line-up starting next week."

"Sir, do you think I can make a trip to see my family first?" Lionel asked. He'd been thinking about it all the way there. He wanted—needed—to go back to Haiti, even for a short visit. He longed for the warmth and love of Elena and the assuredness of character that Jourdain gave him. He wanted to see whether Polo remembered their secret handshake, and he craved chocolate and Coca-Cola from Elena's store. He also wanted to visit Papa and Mama's grave.

Avila nodded. "Good idea. Take two weeks."

Lionel bought a plane ticket from Santo Domingo to Port-au-Prince. He took only his small suitcase with him, and before he knew it, he was riding a tap-tap from the airport to Elena's store.

"Elena!" he called as he stepped into the boutik. "Are you here? I need to buy some chocolate!"

"Is that you, Samféyo?" she squealed when she saw him and threw her arms around his neck in a bear hug. "You got taller!" she scolded. He hugged her tightly. "What are you doing here?"

Tears pooled up in his eyes. "I needed a little break. I just wanted to come home for a few days."

"Oh, Samféyo. I'm so glad you're here," she said cupping his face in both of her palms. "Say no more. Bring your suitcase upstairs. You'll stay in my spare bedroom."

He spent the rest of the day cleaning her store and chatting with her like old times. For dinner, she made them goat stew, and they ate a whole loaf of crusty bread that he picked up in the market. He told her stories from the places he'd seen in the United States, describing everything in as much detail as he could recall. She was fascinated with his description of Los Angeles, and in particular the picture he painted as he described the white living room and colorful kitchen found in the home of the Dodger player.

"I think you would have liked the Spanish styling and bright colors in the kitchen," he said. "It was pretty cool."

"Oh, Sam! Let's redecorate my kitchen!" Elena suggested, clapping her hands. "Make it look like the one you describe." He happily agreed.

Early the next morning, Lionel walked the familiar path to Jourdain's house. Jourdain was in the yard, sorting tobacco leaves. Wordlessly, Lionel took a seat next to him and picked up the knife. He began deveining the leaves. Jourdain waited a full minute before saying anything.

"Are you here for a visit or for good?" Jourdain asked, without looking up from his work.

"Just a visit. I really missed you guys," Lionel answered.

Jourdain nodded. "I've missed you, too." Lionel saw him smile.

They worked until the entire pile was deveined and sorted. Then they took a break and Jourdain fetched waters from his ice box.

"Elena wants me to redecorate her kitchen," Lionel said, after polishing off his entire bottle of water in one long gulp.

"Would you please help me get supplies?" He outlined his decorating plan to Jourdain.

"What a great idea. It would be my pleasure!"

They first visited the Matelec Ace Hardware in Pétion-Ville. Lionel chose a sunshine yellow color to paint the walls and a color called Bluebell for her cabinets. He bought a designer chrome faucet for her sink that had a sprayer feature he thought she'd enjoy.

"Very nice," Jourdain approved. "There's a flooring store next door. Let's find those tiles you mentioned."

"I can paint things, but I don't know if I can do the floor, Jourdain," Lionel worried.

"Pa gen pwoblèm," Jourdain assured. "I will teach you. It is easy."

Lionel walked through the stacks of precariously balanced tiles. He didn't think he would find anything like the tiles he saw in the ball player's kitchen, but in the last row, in the back corner, he saw them—large 12 x 12 rust-colored tiles, flecked with orange.

"Over here!" he called to Jourdain.

"These are nice!" Jourdain said. He picked out several boxes of them, and they carried them to the back of his truck. "We also need grout," he explained. He chose a sand-colored grout and picked up a few other things. "What else?" Jourdain asked.

"Decorations?" Lionel suggested.

Jourdain knew the location of a market that was similar to the fruit and vegetable market, but instead of food, vendors carried all kinds of things to decorate a house. Doorknobs, wall hangings, light fixtures... Lionel was amazed. He found a bin filled with painted cabinet knobs that he thought Elena would like. He did a mental count in his head of the number he would need and purchased them.

"What about this?" Jourdain asked. He held up a box that had a white ceiling fan with a light fixture attached to it.

"A ceiling fan!" Lionel exclaimed. "All of the places in America have ceiling fans! Yes!"

Lionel smiled as they carried their treasures up to Elena's apartment.

"What should I do first?" he asked Jourdain as they looked around.

"You should do all of the painting first. Then, we can do the faucet and ceiling fan. I'll help you with that. We'll do the floor last, once the rest is done."

"I had one more idea," Lionel said. He whispered it to Jourdain so Elena, who was down in the boutik, wouldn't hear.

"Great idea!" Jourdain said. "I will work on that."

It took Lionel three days to paint the walls and the cabinets, which weren't as easy as he hoped they'd be. There weren't many of them, but removing the doors took longer than he thought it would. Then, once they were painted, he couldn't remember which door went on which cabinet.

"Mercy!" he said, when he realized he got it wrong again. He kept Jourdain and Elena at bay during this process, wanting to accomplish it on his own. Once he finally got the doors in their proper spots, he put the new handles on in place of the old. He was pleased.

"Perfect!" Jourdain said, when he was invited in to see the end result. He showed Lionel how to shut the water off underneath her small sink, and it took no time at all to set the new faucet, with its fancy sprayer, in place.

The only hiccup with the fan was making sure it was strongly secured to the ceiling. Jourdain had to fetch a long board to make an anchor above the ceiling tiles so the fan had something to attach to. He showed Lionel how to add the beam and use his small power drill to tighten the screws. The fan and light worked beautifully.

Last but not least, Jourdain and Lionel put the new tile down on Elena's kitchen floor. They laid out the tiles first, to make sure they had enough. Jourdain brought a bucket from his house and showed Lionel how to mix the mortar and spread it over the old linoleum. They laid out the tiles which didn't need cutting first, then they made cuts on the tiles that needed to be fit around the cabinetry.

"Trè byen!" Jourdain exclaimed. "Now we wait. We will do the grout tomorrow."

Twenty-four hours later, the kitchen floor was finished. They had to wait another day before moving the table and chairs back in to show Elena the finished product. She had agreed to stay at Sissy's during the renovation so she wouldn't be tempted to peek.

While the tiles were setting, Lionel visited the marketplace again and found a set of three countertop canisters, painted with a blue and yellow Mexican design, to sit on her counter and hold her sugar, flour, and coffee. He was also thrilled to find a large bin of paper mâché fruits and vegetables. He bought several and filled a glass bowl with them that he placed as a centerpiece on her kitchen table. Brightly colored kitchen towels replaced the threadbare rags she'd had for as long as he could remember.

"Did you take care of the other thing?" Lionel asked Jourdain, as they rolled cigars in Jourdain's yard.

"I did. I took care of it today while you were out," he replied. "I think we are ready."

That night, after Elena closed the shop, they brought her up to her apartment. Lionel held his hand over Elena's eyes as they led her into her new kitchen.

"Get on with it already! The suspense is killing me!" she scolded.

"OK, Elena. One. Two. Three!" He removed his hand. Her eyes widened as she absorbed the transformed kitchen.

"Oh, my dear Lord!" she exclaimed. "This is beautiful! A ceiling fan! The cabinets! And—" She noticed Lionel's big surprise. "A new refrigerator and oven? Lionel! You can't afford this!"

"Do you like it?" Lionel asked.

"No, Samféyo. I love it," she said, wiping her eyes. "Turn on that ceiling fan."

Lionel had tried a couple of times to locate Polo while he

was there but had no luck. His mother said she didn't know where he was, and Polo's sisters were no help either. He noticed their shanty was larger than before, almost like a house now, with sturdy walls and a real front door with a lock. Lionel was happy for them, even though he was worried that Polo was nowhere to be found.

With his trip coming to a close, he visited Papa and Mama's grave. He sat cross-legged in the grass for a full hour, talking to Papa. On the way back, he stopped at Polo's one last time in an effort to connect with his old friend. He walked up the path as Polo was exiting his house.

"Polo!" Lionel exclaimed.

Polo's head whipped side to side, looking to see if anyone else was around.

"Sam!" he hissed. "What are you doing here?"

"I'm just here for a visit. I wanted to see you. What's wrong?" Lionel asked.

"Quick. Come in," Polo said. He practically shoved Sam inside and pulled the door shut behind them.

"Polo, what's going on?" Lionel asked. "Jourdain and Elena said they never see you anymore. Your mom and sisters said they didn't know where you were…"

"You can't be here, Sam," Polo said. "You have to leave. Especially before my ma and sisters get back."

"What do you mean, I can't be here? What's this about?"

"Macoute. If they find you, they'll kill you," Polo said.

"Macoute? Polo, it's been almost three years. Surely the macoute don't care about me anymore."

"Not true," Polo said. "Macoute don't forget. And I know for a fact you've been spotted in the marketplace."

"What? How do you know that?" Lionel asked.

Polo didn't answer. He looked at Lionel intensely, trying to find the words to explain.

"You—joined them," Lionel stated.

Polo shook his head. "Not macoute. The Soulèvman Jèn Yo. They are connected. Something I didn't learn until I was in too deep to get out."

"Why is my name on their list?" Lionel asked. "I never did anything."

"They think you were a part of the set-up that got Raul and the others killed. It was an unfortunate coincidence that the day Raul introduced you to his inner circle was the day someone set them up. But macoute don't believe in coincidence. It put you forever on their list. Till death."

Lionel breathed deeply. "So they know I'm here?"

Polo nodded. "One of the guys who had met you that day said he saw someone who looked like you in the market. They passed around your name and said they are going to put a watch out to see if you are seen again. If they know that I know you, we'll both be killed. So will my sisters."

"How'd you get involved?" Lionel asked.

"I started hanging out at Ricardo's when I wasn't working with Jourdain. It was nice to have some money and buy beer and chips whenever I wanted, you know?" Lionel nodded. "One day, a guy approached me, and we started chatting. I saw him there a few times after that, and after a couple of weeks he asked if I wanted to be a part of making Haiti better. I didn't know what I was getting into. Now I can't get out. Not without putting my sisters in danger. I stopped hanging around Jourdain and Elena because I didn't want to get them mixed up in anything bad. It was the only way I could protect them."

Lionel knew then that this was the last time he would see his old friend. They did the secret handshake one last time. Polo left first and headed toward town. Lionel waited five full minutes then slipped out, quickly racing back to Elena's, staying near the bushes the entire way.

"Samféyo! What's wrong?" Elena asked as he rushed in and ducked behind the counter.

Lionel explained quickly what he learned from Polo. Elena put her hand to her mouth in shock.

"Oh! Get upstairs. Don't come down. I'll get Jourdain; we'll figure out what to do."

Lionel didn't come out of Elena's apartment for the rest

of his trip. On Saturday morning, he and Elena ate breakfast together, then she went downstairs to open her shop while Lionel waited for Jourdain to arrive. He was not as concerned with his own well-being as he was with hoping anyone looking for him would not see him with Elena or Jourdain. Fear for their safety kept his stomach in knots.

As the clock neared ten a.m., Lionel heard the bell on Elena's shop door. Assuming it was Jourdain, he began to gather his things. A male voice he did not recognize stopped him.

"Good morning," Elena chirped brightly. "Can I help you?"

"Bonjou, ma'am," the voice said. "I was wondering if you could help me. I am looking for my nephew. He used to live in this area, and I heard he might be back. I think he lived around here."

"All of the locals come through here at some time or other. What is his name?" Elena asked calmly.

"Sam Bernard," the voice said.

"Oh, Sam! Sure, I remember Sam. He was a nice boy. He and his father moved away two or three years ago, I think," Elena said.

"Someone said he was seen around here last week," the man prodded.

"Yes, yes. He did come in. It was good to see him. Said he is living in Cap-Haitien now. He said they were only here for a day or two, so he probably is gone," Elena said.

Just then Lionel heard Elena's shop door open again. He held his breath, sweat beads of dread dripping from his forehead.

"Good morning, sister!" Jourdain said. "We are here to pick up the boxes for delivery."

"If you'll excuse me," Elena said to the stranger, "my cousin and his wife are going to deliver some boxes for me today."

"Yes, of course. Thank you for your help," the man said. Lionel heard the door yet again.

Wordlessly, Elena, Jourdain, and Sissy rushed up the

stairs.

"Do not worry, Lionel," Jourdain assured. "It is going to be alright."

Sissy wore a long orange muumuu, brown sandals, and had a bright yellow scarf wrapped around her head. From her bag, she produced an identical outfit and handed it to Lionel.

"Put this on over your clothes," she instructed. Sissy was tall and slender, and once they wrapped the scarf around Lionel's head, from the back they could be the same person. A pair of large feminine sunglasses completed the outfit.

Elena chuckled. "I know this is very serious, but you look fabulous!" She relayed the conversation with the man to Jourdain and Sissy.

"You did great!" Jourdain assured her. "If you had said you didn't see Sam, he would have known you were lying. You gave perfect answers!"

"I hope so," Elena said. "Sam—I love you! Be careful. Thank you for bringing a piece of your American adventures to my kitchen."

He hugged Elena and Sissy goodbye. Jourdain picked up the cardboard box that they'd put Lionel's suitcase into and carried it out to the truck. Sure enough, the mysterious man was standing just down the road, as if waiting for someone. He glanced over as Jourdain and Lionel—dressed as Sissy—exited the boutik and hopped into the truck. Jourdain made a U-turn and took off in the other direction, airport-bound.

CHAPTER 18

Lionel joined in with the Dominican Dodgers for the remainder of the summer and was signed to play again with Licey for the Winter League. No one mentioned what happened in Canada. He maintained his high work ethic and commitment to improvement and to his delight, found a way to further his education as well.

The University of Santo Domingo offered a night class. Following a successful fall semester, Lionel could take an exam to earn his *bachillarato degree*—similar to a high school diploma from an American school. He proposed his request to Coach Avila, who approved it heartily, as there was no need for Lionel to continue to take the English classes offered at the Academy. His classes began in September. As a result, when he wasn't practicing, he was either lifting weights, running, or studying. It kept him secluded from the other players, who didn't understand his ambitions.

"Come on out with us," Manny prodded Lionel one night. "We're going dancing."

"No thanks, man," Lionel replied. He picked up his books.

"You're no fun anymore," Manny whined. "You get moved up to Triple-A and suddenly you got no time for us lowlies."

"You know that's not true," Lionel said. "I want to pass my exam. Besides, don't forget, we have a game tomorrow night." Manny also played for Licey.

"Yeah, yeah. No one comes out to watch the games. No one cares," Manny shooed away Lionel's comment. "Probably will end in a brownout anyway."

"You won't get to Triple-A with an attitude like that," Lionel warned.

"Hey! *Vete a la mierda!*" Manny insulted Lionel and stormed off.

Lionel shook his head and went to find a quiet place to study.

Despite Lionel's personal commitment to baseball, the Licey team stunk it up that winter. Lazy plays drove them into last place, while the Águilas managed to stay ahead of the pack and make it to the Caribbean Series. The Tigres didn't even make it to the Winter League Championship game. Lionel's frustration at his teammates' lack of effort spilled over into his friendships, and by the end of the winter season, he hardly spoke to anyone except for Nick, who was thriving as a pitcher for the Águilas.

Lionel passed his exam, earning the equivalent of a high school diploma. The night he found out, he treated himself to a steak dinner to celebrate.

He was preparing to take a bite of his salad, when a familiar voice stopped his fork mid-air.

"Hello, son."

"Coach Lasorda! Hello," he replied. He hadn't seen Tommy Lasorda since the meeting in his office last year, when Lasorda spurred him on to maintain his integrity. He'd wondered if Lasorda had heard about what happened in Canada, and Lionel's subsequent banishment to the Dominican. He was about to find out.

"Mind if I sit?" Lasorda asked. He sat across from Lionel without waiting for a reply. "How have you been holding up, son?"

"It's been a long winter," Lionel said.

Lasorda nodded. The waiter came by and placed a salad and a large glass of water in front of Lasorda. They ate in silence, and once the salad plates were cleared and the steaks set in front of them, Lasorda spoke again. "I heard you took a class this winter."

"Yes, sir. Education was important to my mama and papa, and I'd always promised myself I'd get my secondary school certificate. This seemed as good a time as any."

"Congratulations," Lasorda said. "Your parents would be proud." His eyes were glassy. "One of the greatest joys a kid can give his parents is to make them proud." He ate several bites of his steak before continuing, "Did you know I had a son?"

"No, sir. I didn't know."

"I did. Tommy Junior. He died just over two years ago." Lasorda was quiet for several minutes before continuing. "That day I saw you on the hilltop, I was processing some bad news I'd learned about him recently. That was a rough time for me."

"I'm sorry to hear that," Lionel said.

"Thanks, kid," he wiped his eyes with his napkin. "It was good for me to talk to you that day. When you showed me your pictures, you gave me hope that the parent-child relationship is one that even death can't separate. The show goes on though, for the one left behind. And that's something I want you to remember when I tell you what I have to tell you." He took a long drink of water. "I know what happened in Canada last year. I also know whose drugs those were. It took a lot of inner fortitude not to speak up. I don't know that many guys would have kept quiet, especially considering what a dick that guy was to you. I'm going to do you a favor. I'm trading you to the Chicago White Sox."

"Sir? Trading me?" Lionel didn't feel like this was a favor.

"Cook is related to someone in the organization. That someone has soured on you. It is completely undeserved. It is complete bullshit—pardon my French—but nonetheless, that's what's happened. If we keep you on the roster, you will never make the Big Show. Not even with me as your cheerleader. You've got too much promise to spend it bopping around the minors. Do you understand what I'm saying?"

"I work my butt off," Lionel said. "I do everything that's

asked of me. I never complain."

"I know you do, kid. And you've got talent. And your head's on straight. That's a winning combination. But in this business, enemies can ruin the career of even the best players. I know that all too well." He looked down at his plate, and Lionel got the feeling he was thinking again about his son.

"The Chicago White Sox?" Lionel asked. "Do they want me?"

"The White Sox are hot this year," Lasorda said. "They've got Jack McDowell, Tim Raines, Frank Thomas, Robin Ventura, Ozzie Guillen. They're real contenders. I spoke with Tito Francona, manager for the Barons. They are light in outfield talent this year, and they are willing to sign you on. He's actually pretty glad to have you. His buddy, Pete, said he met you that night that Cruz got hurt and he was impressed with you."

"Pete?" Lionel remembered. "Oh, yeah. I never got his last name. But he was a pretty interesting guy. Had some great stories."

Lasorda laughed so hard he started to cough. "You never got his last name?" he managed to say between guffaws. "That was Pete Rose. *Junior*. He plays minor ball for the Sox. I bet he has great stories. He's been around the league since he was in diapers." Lasorda got to laughing again and his eyes started to water.

"But I thought there were only Dodger players there," Lionel said.

"Pete has friends on every team."

The waiter cleared their plates and brought two large chocolate mousse parfaits for dessert.

"Kid, trust me. This is for the best. For you, not for us. It's hard for me to let you go. Especially when I know you'd make a huge impact on our minor teams. The Dukes were looking strong, and I know you were a part of the growth. Russell loved you. You've got Major League potential. I have to let you go if you're ever going to get a chance."

"I understand, sir. I'm sorry," Lionel said. He really did

understand.

"You know, it would have been worse for you if you had ratted out Cook that day. As it is, your integrity saved your future," Lasorda said.

Avila called Lionel to his office the next day. Lasorda was there, as was the manager at the White Sox training complex. They signed the papers to trade Lionel to the White Sox organization. His salary was actually going to go up by two hundred a month, and he was being placed right on the Birmingham Barons AA team. His plane left for Birmingham the next day. He shook hands and thanked them all profusely, getting excited about his new adventure.

He called Jourdain that night to share his good news, promising to call whenever he could. He packed his things and said his goodbyes.

"I'm sorry for being a jerk," Manny said. "Guess I'm still mad cause you drew that big smiley face on my butt-cheek."

Lionel laughed. Manny had never mentioned that incident. "I understand. Hope to see you out there soon," Lionel said.

"Yeah," Manny said. "I'm going to change my attitude. Work hard and all that crap you're always doing."

"Glad to hear it," Lionel said.

Lacy, the administrative secretary for the Barons, wasn't able to take care of Lionel's apartment details on such short notice, so Lionel had to stay in the Moon Winx Lodge for a week until his apartment was ready. Lacy was full of apologies when Lionel arrived to check in at the Hoover Met.

"Your hotel is all paid for, just give them your name and they'll give you a room key," she explained. "Again, I am so sorry your apartment isn't ready."

"It's fine, really," Lionel assured. "I'm just happy to be here."

Lacy's kind face relaxed a bit. Lionel figured she wasn't used to guys being so easy-going when things didn't go their way. "Thanks for understanding. It's been a crazy week. Mr.

Francona is out at a meeting, but Mr. Barnett wanted to see you when you got here. I'll buzz him and let him know."

Lacy directed Lionel to the office of Mike Barnett, batting coach for the Barons.

"Lionel! Great to meet you," Barnett said. "Take a seat. Welcome to the Barons."

"Thank you, sir," Lionel said. "I'm happy to be here."

"Good! Practice begins end of next week. We'll have a team meeting at ten a.m. on Thursday. I've heard you've been largely self-taught with your batting techniques, is that correct?"

"Well, yes, sir, I suppose. I have watched a lot of tapes and I study the batting techniques of as many people as I can. I try and emulate the good stuff."

Barnett nodded. "We need a good outfielder. If we can marry that with strong batting, that's even better. Your outfielding is tremendous. I want you and I to spend a lot of time together getting that batting sorted out. As a switch-hitter, you can be a real threat. But no one seems to have maximized on that potential. Until now."

Lionel smiled. "I'd like that very much!"

"Good. See Lacy on your way out. She should have some of your gear ready. You'll get the rest next week."

Lacy handed Lionel a Baron's logoed duffel bag. "Wear the long-sleeved red shirt and grey pants to practice on Thursday. With your ball cap."

"Got it. Thank you," he said. As he turned to walk away, the duffel bag knocked a baseball off of her desk.

"I'm sorry!" he said, picking it up. Instinctively he looked at it. MADE IN HAITI was stamped on the bottom. "Where'd you get this ball?" he asked her.

"In 1979 my uncle Ted took me to my first Chicago White Sox game," she explained. "Chet Lemon hit a home run, and my uncle caught it! Barehanded and without even spilling his beer." She laughed. "It was great."

"Are you from Chicago?" he asked.

"Yes. I'm taking classes at the University here. I'm going to be a nurse. Oh! I almost forgot," she said. "What uniform number do you want?"

He'd stayed with number eleven at Bakersfield and the Dukes because that's what he'd been initially assigned. But looking at the baseball in his hand, he suddenly he got a new idea.

"I'd like number eighty-eight please," he said, tracing his fingers over the red thread.

His week at the Moon Winx wasn't so bad. The bed was comfortable, and the small family restaurant that occupied the corner of the parking lot was pleasant. His apartment was ready on Tuesday, so he once again visited Lacy at the Stadium to pick up his key. She drove him back to the hotel to get his things, then took him to the apartment, which was only a mile from the stadium.

"How will you get to the stadium?" she asked.

"I'm going to find a bike shop and buy a bicycle," he said matter-of-factly.

"You won't get a car?"

"I've never driven a car," he confessed. Her look of shock made him laugh. "I've never needed a car."

"Wow! How old are you?" Lacy asked.

"Almost twenty-two," he said.

"I can't believe it. Every twenty-two-year-old should know how to drive. I'll teach you!"

"OK," Lionel agreed. "Maybe one day. But first can we go to a store so I can get a bicycle?"

He'd given his bicycle from Albuquerque to the kind couple who owned the Mexican restaurant. They had a twelve-year-old boy who was thrilled with the gift. Lacy took him to a sports store, where he picked out a neon green mountain bike. She knew a lot about bikes, and she convinced him to get the upgraded model with front suspension and disc brakes.

"This is the fanciest bike I've ever owned," he said, as they strapped it to the top of her Honda Civic.

"If you ride your bike everywhere, you need to have good brakes. And you'll appreciate the suspension," she stated.

She was right.

His Birmingham teammates ushered him into their fold from the second he walked in. The practice schedule and basic rules of engagement were similar to what he was used to with other teams. Barnett asked him to stay late after the first practice.

"Which hand do you write with?" Barnett asked Lionel.

"Right," he answered.

"Not anymore. I want you to practice writing with your left hand for at least twenty straight minutes every day."

"What should I write?" Lionel wondered.

"I don't care. Write a letter, write a diary, write a story book. Doesn't matter. Just do it. Do you brush your teeth with your right hand?"

Lionel mimicked the motion. "I guess so."

"Don't. Left hand only. Got it?"

"Yes, sir."

"You should have been doing this stuff already, but better late than never. Switch sides for as many of your daily routines as possible. During regular B.P. split your time equally on both sides. We'll get together every other day to get in extra time. We've got four other switch hitters, so all of you will stay late together."

"Got it," Lionel said.

"The most important thing I can tell you is to remain open-minded. You don't change every little thing each time you have a bad game—but you have to be willing to try new things. You're young. The basics are there. You give me an open mind, I can help you bring up your batting average."

Francona practiced Lionel in both right and left field, and when the line-up for the first game posted, he was thrilled to see he'd be starting at right. Lionel was shocked when he rode his bike to the stadium on opening day to see that there were already a bunch of people there for the game. The Dukes had some pretty packed games—but they were never sold-out, as this game appeared to be.

When Lionel took the field at the top of the first inning, he dropped to complete his customary push-ups, and he heard someone cheer, "Hey! That's Push-ups Bierto!" He smiled, thrilled to be recognized.

Defensively, he played in top form, but he struggled in his first two at-bats. He struck out the first time and then popped out in the fourth inning. When the guy after him also popped out, Barnett grabbed the two of them and pulled them to the side.

"You're trying to launch that ball into the atmosphere. Stop it. Settle down. Hit a good hard line drive," he instructed.

Lionel took that to heart. He realized he was trying to prove himself with a home run. He took Coach's advice and on his next at-bat, took a deep breath and swung for a sweet line drive that got past the third baseman. The guy after him, however, did not listen and hit a big 'ol pop fly to right field. It did allow Lionel to tag up, even if it was unintended.

Lionel scored that inning, and in his fourth at-bat for the game, he used the same strategy. This time, an error by the left-fielder allowed him a double.

The Barons won their opener six to three against Memphis. After the game, kids were allowed on the field to get players' autographs in their programs. Lionel, who'd been practicing for this moment, signed his name with his left hand, and included a script S after writing his uniform number 88.

His first summer as a Birmingham Baron was the greatest summer of his life. He listened to Coach Barnett and learned to hit the ball anywhere in the strike zone, and his batting average crept up. He ended the season at .275. He became a confident batter, which made him a more consistent batter.

The joy he got playing with the Barons was nothing compared to the joy he got from spending time with Lacy. She was a breath of fresh air. His schedule and her nursing classes didn't allow for a lot of free time, but they made the most of the hours they could steal. He allowed her to teach him things—common sense things—that he had never experienced. He learned that summer that there was more to America than baseball. She took him to the Birmingham Museum of Art, the zoo, and she even taught him about the prominent place in history that Birmingham held during the Civil Rights Movement of the 60s. She gave him a tremendous gift by opening new windows of the world to him.

The Barons finished first in their division, then went on to win the Southern League Championships. The coaching staff was thrilled. This time, when he returned to the Dominican, Lionel would be staying at the White Sox complex that they shared with the Rangers.

"I'll miss you!" Lacy said, as she drove him to the airport.

He reached over and took her hand. "I'll miss you, too! But I will call you whenever I can."

They shared their first kiss at the airport, and Lionel left a piece of his heart behind in Birmingham.

CHAPTER 19

Former Chicago White Sox player Casey Parsons was named as coach of the Tigres del Licey that winter. Parsons was a good and fair manager, setting high expectations for work ethic around the team. The training complex had much to be desired though. If Campo Las Palmas was the créme de la créme, this place was the bottom of the barrel. None of the White Sox Major Leaguers who played Dominican winter ball stayed there. They opted to rent (or buy) their own places in Santo Domingo. After his first week on the saggy mattress and using showers that barely had enough water pressure to wash off the soap, he did a calculation to see if he could afford to rent his own place as well.

"This place is roach compared to Campo," Nick—who now played for the Rangers—complained one night when the power went out at seven p.m.

"I've been thinking of looking into renting a place," Lionel said. "You wanna go half with me?"

"Gotta be better than this!" Nick said.

They talked to Parsons—who himself didn't even stay at the complex—and he agreed to let them find alternate lodging.

"On one condition," he warned. "You can't be late for any practices or meetings."

"No worries, Coach," Lionel promised. "We got this."

"If we don't live here at the center, we're gonna need some transportation," Nick noted. "No way we can bike ten miles to and from each day."

"Do you know how to drive?" Lionel asked Nick.

"Are you kidding? Who doesn't know how to drive?"

Nick responded.

Lionel raised an eyebrow at him.

"You don't know how to drive?" Nick asked. "Shoot—I'll teach you."

Lionel smiled, thinking of Lacy. How surprised would she be if he returned to Birmingham next summer having learned all on his own? Nick's dad drove over from Barahona to deliver them a small blue five-speed they could use for the winter. Lionel's contribution was to purchase four new tires for it, a small price to pay for the luxury of living off-complex. Their apartment was actually the back-half of a small house owned by an elderly woman with four cats. She rented to them for hardly anything, if they promised to help with fix-ups around the house.

"The pedal on the far left is the clutch. You work that only with your left foot. If your left foot isn't on the clutch, it's not doing anything. Got it?"

Nick and Lionel were having their first driving lesson. They were in a large deserted lot, and Lionel sat in the driver's seat. "The middle pedal is the brake. The one on the right is the gas. You work the gas and brake with your right foot."

"Clutch with left. Gas and brake with right," Lionel affirmed.

"This is the gear shifter. There are five gears. One is for the slowest speeds. Five is for the highest. Moving around town here, I doubt you'll be driving higher than third or fourth gear. If you aren't moving at all—like stopped at a red light or parked—you are always going to start in first gear. The whole purpose of the clutch is to allow you to change gears. If the clutch isn't pushed down, the gears won't move."

Nick let Lionel practice pushing in the clutch and shifting through the gears with the car turned off. The gears on the Toyota were easy to find.

"You know when you're batting, how you want to find the sweet spot on the wood? Well, the clutch has a sweet spot. It's the point where the transmission engages with the new gear.

You'll take your foot off of the gas when you push down the clutch, shift your gear, then reengage with your gas pedal as you come off the clutch." Nick showed with his hands how the push-release would go. "The sweet spot is the point right in the middle there, where the clutch lets the gas pedal take over. If you are out of sync, the engine will either stall or not engage with the gear."

The concept was pretty clear for Lionel. He'd spent the summer watching Lacy navigate the clutch-gear shift relationship like a pro. "Let's do this!" he said.

He stalled on his first three attempts to start. "I'm trying to let the clutch out slowly, but it isn't working!" he said, frustrated.

"Check to see if you have it in first gear," Nick suggested.

"Idiota! It was in third," Lionel said, exasperated with himself.

"Put it in first. Try again," Nick coached patiently.

He rolled to a start smoothly. "Now what do I do?"

"To slow down, you push the brake with your right foot and push in the clutch with the left. The clutch and brake go together. Or else—" The car jerked to a stop. "You stall. Like that."

"Mercy!" Lionel said. "OK, clutch and brake go down together. Got it."

They practiced starting and stopping and driving around the parking lot in slow circles, all the while not getting the car out of first gear.

"You're a pretty good teacher," Lionel observed of Nick.

Eventually they worked their way up to road driving. Shifting became more natural for Lionel. What made him most nervous, though, was having to watch out for all of the speedsters on the streets of Santo Domingo. Cars zipped in and out of traffic with the drivers not even looking. It drove Lionel crazy.

"Look at that idiot!" he yelled after being cut off. "He didn't even use the turn signal."

"Not everyone follows the rules like you do," Nick said

with a chuckle.

"Well, they should! The rules are there for a reason," Lionel said, indignantly.

"Man, once you realize that every other driver is out to get you, you'll be a lot better off. You have to be defensive. Like when you play outfield. Anticipate what the others are going to do and make your move accordingly."

"Like in the outfield, huh?" Lionel thought this over. He began to view the other drivers as players on a field, and to his surprise, he got a lot less frustrated. Reacting to their mistakes with his own expertise became a challenge and built a source of driving pride inside of him.

The Tigres del Licey had a great season with Casey Parsons at the helm. Going into the Winter League Championship Series, they knew the previous year's champions, the Águilas Cibaeñas, would be tough to beat. The Águilas had Miguel Diloné as their manager and Manny Ramirez, Jose Bautista, Moises Alou, and other strong players on the field. It wouldn't be easy. Lionel admired Diloné, as he was a switch-hitter and played outfield, just like him. Even with such a power team for the Águilas, the Tigres won the Winter League, earning their spot in the Caribbean Series.

"We're headed to Venezuela!" Lionel told Lacy on the phone the night after their Winter League win.

"Venezuela! That's totally awesome!" Lacy said. "Oh, I'm so jealous. You'll have to get a camera and take some pictures for me."

"I will," Lionel promised. "I've never been there. It's been seven years since the Caribbean Series has been in Venezuela, so I think they're gonna do it up big."

"That's so terrific, Lionel," Lacy said. "I'm really happy for you!"

"Thanks," he paused awkwardly, as he usually did at this point in their weekly phone conversation. "I miss you," he said quietly.

He could hear her smile on the other end of the phone. "I

miss you, too."

For the seventh time in the history of the Caribbean Series, the Tigres del Licey won it all. It wasn't a shut-out, like the last time they were in the series with Roseboro, but it was a very respectable five wins, one loss record—made even more respectable considering the level of talent they were up against. But the Tigres' talent was nothing to sneeze at, with Raul Mondesí hitting for .450 to win the batting title. Lionel's personal batting average was .315 for the series and his fielding was error-free. In March, when he and Nick packed up their apartment and he left for the airport to fly back to Birmingham for Spring Training, he didn't think things could get any better.

"Michael Jordan?" he said incredulously, when Lacy told him the name of the newest player signed to the Birmingham Barons. "Are you kidding me?"

"They announced it in a staff meeting this morning," she said, tying her sneaker and stretching her calves. On the mornings she didn't have classes, she accompanied him on his morning run.

"Holy moly!" Lionel knew Jordan had been in Spring Training over in Sarasota with the Sox, and rumors floated around as to where he might play, but Lionel really didn't think the Barons would be the lucky winners. "That's going to bring some bodies out to the ballpark," Lionel stated. "Wow!"

He thought about it during their entire three-mile run. Michael Jordan! In Birmingham! On his team! He couldn't wait to meet him.

When Lionel arrived for practice that day, he could barely get through the crowd of press hounds to get to the locker room. Reporters shoved microphones in his face, asking stupid questions like, "So what do you think of Michael Jordan?" and "Are you excited to be playing with one of the greatest athletes of all time?" and "Do you think you'll win the Southern League this year?"

Lionel didn't open his mouth at all except to politely say,

"Excuse me." He parked his bike and found that inside the locker room things were in as much of an uproar as outside. The guys were all taking at once.

"Quiet down!" Francona called their team meeting to order. "It's a busy day around here, wouldn't you say?" The guys laughed. "Big changes for this year. Not in our ethics. Not in our goals. But I have a feeling we're going to be a bit more popular than we've normally been." More laughs.

"We're gonna sell-out every game!" someone said.

Francona nodded. "I assume we will. Ticket sales have already skyrocketed. They made the announcement at eight a.m. and by eight-oh-five we had a line forming at the ticket window."

"So when does the big guy arrive?" Coleman asked.

"The Sox have scheduled Jordan to play an exhibition game in Chicago. He will miss our opener but will join us after that. It's going to be a sell-out. This is going to be a big year for us, men. We're going to gain a whole lot of fans that have never heard of us but know who he is. Be ready. Buckle up, fellas."

Buckle up was indeed the right advice. Jordan's arrival in Birmingham was a spectacle Lionel hadn't experienced before. Lionel was called in to talk with Francona the day before Jordan was to arrive.

"I'm starting you at right field tonight, but when he arrives, I've gotta put Jordan in right field," he stated bluntly. "I'll move you to left for any games he starts."

"That's fine. I've played left before," Lionel tried to hide his disappointment.

"I know you have. I need your glove out there. I also need him out there. Right is his preferred spot."

"I gotcha, Coach," Lionel said. "Whatever it takes."

"Thanks, kid," Francona said. "Help him out however you can."

Lionel really didn't know what he could do for Michael Jordan. It seemed like this season was going to be all about what Jordan could do for the Barons.

Jordan's presence launched the Barons into superstardom. Every game was sold out. Fans lined the field, hoping for autographs. Jordan even helped the team acquire a flashy new bus for traveling around the south.

Jordan took every chance possible for batting practice, so Lionel—whose switch-hitting average was improving every game—got a lot of time with him there. He'd ask Lionel about tips for fielding, and Lionel was more than willing to divulge his technique for chasing down a fly ball while running backwards, how to stay fear-free when approaching the back wall, and how to track a ball in the sunlight. Jordan's rocky outfield start improved greatly as the season wore on.

"You made it!" Lacy said, as Lionel came into the apartment with Chinese food. It was his first time taking her car all on his own.

"Yes! I can successfully acquire dinner for us all by myself. That must make me a real catch," he said proudly. He plated their food and they sat on her sofa to eat.

"Great game tonight," Lacy said, using her chopsticks to eat a piece of broccoli.

"Yeah, we did alright," Lionel agreed. "He's getting better every game." He tried to use the chopsticks, but simply did not yet have the dexterity to get even the biggest piece of chicken successfully from the plate to his mouth. He gave up and unwrapped the plastic fork.

She laughed at his failed efforts. "I tell you, Lionel, it is so terrific seeing all the fans come out to the park. Even if they are only there for him. It's got to feel pretty good."

Lionel smiled. "When I was a little boy, we didn't have a television in our house. Any sports news I got came from stories my papa told me. He'd sit in the local bar for an hour or so to get caught up with what was happening here in America, and he'd come home and tell me all about it. I'd paint my own pictures in my mind, based on what he described. How things have been these last weeks is just the way I pictured it. This season. Right here. There is no better feeling than to have ten thousand fans cheering you on in a game you love. Nothing like it. If my baseball dreams ended tomorrow, I would carry this with me until the day I die."

Lacy reached over and touched his hand. "I like hearing about your papa. Tell me more. What was he like?"

For the next half hour, Lionel relayed stories of the lessons Papa had taught him. He left out the small detail that it all took place in Haiti, but she didn't seem to notice. He even told her about his one and only trip to the cockfights.

"People really do that?" she asked. "I can't imagine it!

"Oh, yea, they do. Men will gamble over anything in Haiti—and the Dominican Republic," he corrected himself.

"I'd like to go there someday with you," she said.

"I'd like that," he said. He leaned over and kissed her softly. "Thanks for listening to my stories. Talking about Papa makes me miss him just a little less."

"What was his name?" she asked.

"Eduard," Lionel answered.

"Eduard Bierto. That's a nice name," she observed.

Hearing those words come from her innocent lips stunned Lionel. His good feelings were gone. Here was a woman he was falling in love with, and he was being dishonest about one of the most important things in life—his family and his heritage. How could he continue to lead her in lies?

"I need to get back," he said. He practically dropped his plate onto the coffee table and stood. "I have to get up early tomorrow. I'll call you."

He rushed out before she could ask anything. As he walked out the apartment door, he heard her call him back, but he kept going. He knew he left her confused, and in all likelihood wondering if she said or did something to usher his exit, but his lies were too big to reel back in or to try and explain.

The next morning he received a phone call from Francona, requesting his presence at nine o'clock. The team was scheduled to leave on the bus at ten, bound for Greenville.

"Son, you aren't going to Greenville with us," Francona said with a frown.

"Sir? Did I do something wrong?" Lionel asked.

"You need to pack your bags," he paused for dramatic effect then broke into a smile. "You've been traded."

"Traded?" Lionel didn't understand. A minor leaguer? Traded?

"The White Sox did a deal with the new Florida team earlier this year for players to be named later. They've named their players. You and a few other moves within the organization are all part of the deal. You're headed to Florida."

Coach was only partially correct. When Lionel called to check in with the Marlins, he was told that he was being sent to help the newly established Portland Sea Dogs, the Double-A team for the Marlins. They needed outfielders who could hit, and they wanted him right away. Their next game was scheduled in New Haven, Connecticut the following night, and they expected their new number eighty-eight to be there.

As he packed his things, Lionel toyed over and over in his mind what to do about Lacy. He held his papa's and mama's wedding rings in his hand and wished he had more courage. There was no doubt in his mind that he felt love for Lacy. He would have asked her to marry him. To continue a relationship built on a lie would be unfair to her. To tell her the truth would end his dream of playing baseball in America—and possibly even cost him fines or jail time. And there was *no way* he could ask her to keep his secret. He would never put that weight on her shoulders. It was heavy enough on his. He had no idea what the penalty was for his kind of lie. He certainly would be sent back to Haiti, wouldn't he? With so many unknowns, he sat down and wrote her a letter, giving her as much of an explanation as he felt he could. He would not vanish without saying anything. Besides, he justified in his confused mind, she would be finishing up her schooling and looking to take on an internship soon. She deserved to follow her dreams without worrying about him. Right? He taped the letter to her apartment door and left his mountain bike on her doorstep.

Dear Lacy,

These last two summers have been the best of my life. I cherish every thought of the time we have spent together. You opened a world to me that I did not know was out there. You have shown me things and stirred feelings in my heart that I have never had before.

I have been traded to Miami. I have to leave right away. Our conversation last night brought up some things in me that I am not ready to talk about with you yet, but I hope that one day I will find the courage that I need in order to truly open up to you. I know that isn't very clear, but it is all I can offer right now. I will always think of you with love. Please take care of my bike.

Lionel

CHAPTER 20

Lionel barely had enough time to get used to his new teammates, when one of the worst things that could have happened to Major League baseball came about. All summer long, the players' union and the owners had been unable to resolve new labor agreement terms. Proposals rejected, benefits withheld, failed legislation—all contributed to the players' declaration that if things weren't taken care of, they would have no choice but to go on strike. The strike was initially set for September, but as summer rolled along with relationships worsening, the date was moved to August 12.

Lionel followed the news and listened intently to the locker room talk, but he was near the bottom of the Minor League totem pole. If he made the Majors, he'd be happy with *any* amount of money they would be willing to pay him—so he really struggled to get his head around the ins and outs of the problems.

On August 11, the Sea Dogs arrived in Trenton, New Jersey for a four-game series against the Thunder. Lionel had heard good things about this park. It was brand-new—which of course meant nice locker rooms—but the guys also said the fans were a lot of fun. Lurking in the back of everyone's mind, though, was whether or not the Major League players were, in fact, going to go on strike as of midnight that night, as they had threatened to.

His first game in the Mercer County Waterfront Park was indeed memorable for Lionel. Even though they lost to the Thunder with a score of seven to four, in the eighth inning he became the third player to hit a fair ball out of the park and into the Delaware River. The Thunder fans went crazy for it—even though it brought in two runs for the Sea Dogs.

When Lionel woke up the next morning, his roommate had the television on to sports news. Sure enough, the Major League players metaphorically walked out. There would be no games that day. Or the next day. Or the next…

The strike became the inevitable topic of conversation in any and all situations where players were gathered. For the minor leaguers who knew they would in all likelihood never get a shot at the Big Show, the talk was whether or not the league would bring them in as replacement players in order to complete the season. This, however, would infuriate the players who either had played in the Majors or were destined for the Majors, as their belief was that no respectable ball player would ever cross the picket line—not even for the chance to play big-league ball. Lionel was sick of it. When asked his opinion, he just said he wished it would all be over so things could go back to normal.

"You gotta pick a side, man!" one of his teammates chided him one day in the locker room following a game against the Bay Sox.

"I am on the side of baseball," Lionel insisted, his voice rising to a level of anger none of them had seen from him. "Baseball! Do you hear me? Isn't that why we are all here? I came to this country to play baseball. I came from a country where we played baseball because of the hope baseball brings to so many people. Not because we were paid. Not for perks. The only promise of a benefit where I am from is that I get to play the greatest game ever invented! Stop asking me which side I am on. A great man told me once that no matter what is going on around me, I need to be all about baseball. You guys played like crap tonight. There. I said it. You've been playing like crap for the past two weeks, since the walkout. Why? Because your focus is not on baseball. It's on the strike. How about you all go back to being here for baseball? Maybe then we'll win some games and give our fans something to cheer about. The fans deserve our best."

Lionel was panting when he finished his impromptu speech. He'd never spoken like that to any of his minor league teammates. He'd never spoken like that to anyone. Every man in the room was staring at him, dumbfounded. He turned around and saw that their coach and general manager were also present. He wondered how long they'd been there.

"Well," Coach Tosca said, "We were coming in here to chew your butts out for your poor performance tonight, but I see that isn't necessary." He tipped his hat at Lionel and they turned around and walked out. Lionel picked up his duffel bag and went home to his lonely apartment.

"Bonjou!" Jourdain said as he answered his phone.

"Hey, it's me," Lionel was glad Jourdain picked up.

"Alo! How are you? How's Portland?" Jourdain asked.

"It's pretty nice here. The season is winding down. I'll be headed back to DR soon."

"Do you have a date yet?"

"I think I'll be back by the tenth," Lionel said. "We aren't going to make the playoffs."

"I'm sorry," Jourdain said. "Let me know when you get back and I'll make a trip. I'll have cigars ready to deliver. The wet spring last year made things tough, but Elena and Sissy have revived the plants. They are producing like old times again finally."

"That's good news," Lionel said. "I wish I could help."

"Lionel, fulfilling your dream is all the help you need to give me. I promised your papa I would look out for you."

"Jourdain, I need to ask you something. What would happen to me if they found out I wasn't really Lionel Bierto?"

"If who found out?"

"The baseball people. If they knew that wasn't me, what would they do to me?" His voice cracked as the question was finally spoken aloud.

"Ah, Lionel. I don't know. But you ARE Lionel Bierto. The name is secondary to the talent inside of you."

"But it is a lie. And by pretending to be Dominican, the world will never know that a Haitian can make it in this sport. I am being traitorous to Haiti."

"Haiti has not been good to you," Jourdain said. "Haiti is not good to anyone. You don't owe Haiti."

Lionel thought about what Jourdain said. His feelings were all knotted up inside of him, like an unruly shoelace. He sat down to write a letter to Lacy. He had not heard from her, despite sending her his new address when he'd arrived in Portland.

Dear Lacy,
     The season will be over next week. I played my heart out, but the Sea Dogs will not make the playoffs this year. How's Michael Jordan? How are you? If I remember, you should be getting close to graduation time. You will be the greatest nurse ever. Do you know what hospital you are going to apply to? Will you stay in Birmingham?
     I am heading back to the Dominican in a couple of weeks. I do hope to hear from you, but I understand if you decide not to write to me.
                                   Lionel

He said a prayer over the letter before dropping it in the mailbox.

If last year's winter league was the greatest Lionel ever had, this year's was the worst. The Tigres struggled all winter long. Lionel—who had thrown all of his energy into improving his batting statistics—played exceptionally well. The problem was that his teammates didn't share his commitment. The strike in the United States wore on through the winter, settling a veil of discontent everywhere, including the Dominican.

The World Series had been canceled. Guys who were on track to have record-breaking years never saw the potential realized. Teams and media lost millions of dollars. What Lionel saw as the worst thing, though, was that fans were turning their backs on the sport. He couldn't bear to watch the news about it. He put his head down and determined to become the best switch-hitter he could possibly be. Baseball would eventually return to the Major League. He wanted to be ready.

He and Nick returned to share the small back-of-the-house apartment that they'd shared the year before. Nick had gone through a pretty decent summer pitching in the South Atlantic League with the Greensboro Bats.

Nick's friendship was the one bright light in the Dominican for Lionel. When they weren't practicing or playing, they spent time on the beach or watching the latest movies that had made their way to the Dominican from America.

Lionel tried calling Lacy a couple of times with no success. He never left a message on her answering machine, fearful of sounding stupid. One January night, however, he dialed her number on a whim and she shocked him by picking up the phone.

"Hello?" her voice answered. She sounded rushed.

"Lacy? It's me, Lionel." *So much for sounding stupid,* he thought.

"Oh. Hi."

"Did I catch you at a bad time?" he asked. "Because I can call back later."

"Did you need something?" she asked.

"I—uh, no. I guess not. I just—I don't know," he fumbled. "Did you graduate?"

"Yes," she replied. "In December. I start my new job in a couple of months."

"Hey, that's great!" he said, trying to perk up his voice. "Where will you be?"

"I'm moving back to Chicago," she said. "I got a three-year internship at Northwestern Medical Center."

"Wow." He was out of things to say. "Congratulations. I'm happy for you."

"Thanks," she said flatly. "Take care of yourself, Lionel."

She broke the connection before he could say goodbye.

He cried himself to sleep that night.

As winter play came to a close with no end to the Major League strike in sight, Lionel packed his things and planned to return to Portland. A phone call from Sal Rende of the Charlotte Knights altered his plans, and he was happy to hear he'd been moved up to Triple-A. Things just weren't the same in the Sea Dogs' locker room after his outburst. Even though he'd likely run into some of the same guys from Portland, he was thankful for a fresh start.

Lionel arrived in Charlotte in March, determined to have his best season yet. When guilt set in about Lacy or about his false name, he refocused and lifted weights or jogged. Lionel realized quickly that he was one of the best switch-hitters on the team, and the coach noticed it, too. He felt really positive about his chances as a starter.

Their first game was scheduled for April 6; a home game against Norfolk. When he got to practice on April 2, there was chatter throughout in the locker room.

"What's going on?" he asked.

"Didn't you hear? The strike is over! O-V-E-R!" one of the pitchers said.

"It's over?" Lionel clarified.

"It's over!" someone else called out.

Speculations about what would happen to the replacement players who showed up for Spring Training started to arise but were quickly hushed when Coach Rende came into the locker room.

"Listen up," he said. "I need Garces, Myers, Witt, Schall, and Bierto."

They trailed Coach into his office. "I guess you heard. The strike is over. They're calling you up, boys. Won't be much of a spring training—games are going to start up pretty quick, you might have about 3 weeks to get ready—but they asked for you all to show up. I'll have your flight information in a couple of hours. In the meantime, go home and pack. Be back here at two."

Lionel hung back. "Calling us up?"

"The Marlins, son. They want you to report for Spring Training."

Foggy-headed, Lionel cleared his locker of his personal things—of which there weren't many since he'd only just arrived—and pedaled home to begin packing. He'd need to call a cab to carry his stuff back to the stadium, but there was nothing he could do about that. Once again, he would have to abandon his bicycle.

His refrigerator held a meager amount of food, so after making a couple of cheese and salami sandwiches, chasing them down with a liter of milk, and then eating the remainder of a jar of sliced pickles, his food was gone.

In fifteen minutes, his things were once again in his suitcase. He looked for a long time at the smiling faces of the Tigres del Licey 1991 Championship Team before placing the photo carefully on top of his clothes. He carried that 8 x 10 everywhere since receiving it from Roseboro four years ago. It represented his first trip to the United States; his first chance to be a part of something successful. But something about it always unsettled him. As he stared at it now, while packing up to head again to Miami to play with the Major League Florida Marlins, he realized what rubbed him wrong.

As he read the names in tiny type at the bottom of the picture, he knew the name that corresponded with his place in the photo was wrong. He was that same faker who showed up six years ago at Campo Las Palmas. Despite the attempts to justify why he did what he did; people depended on him being who he said he was. And he knew a part of him just wasn't that guy. He also knew what he had to do. He dialed Jourdain.

"Bonjou!" Jourdain answered in his usual cheery tone.

"Hi Jourdain! It's me," Lionel said.

"Lionel! What's up? Where are you off to now?" he said jokingly.

"Well…" Lionel told Jourdain his incredible news about being called up to report to the Marlins.

"Will you get a big raise?" Jourdain asked.

"I don't know. I will find out when I get to Miami." He paused. "Jourdain, I feel like I need to tell them."

"Tell who? What?"

"I need to tell them who I really am. That my name is not my own," Lionel said. Saying it aloud cemented in his gut that it was the right thing to do.

"You know they might fire you," Jourdain warned.

"I know."

"They might make you pay them back the money they gave you."

"I know."

Jourdain sighed. "Lionel—Sam—I support you in whatever you do. Are you going to tell them now?"

"No. I am going to wait until I get to Florida. I want to tell Mr. Dombrowski and Mr. Lachemann to their faces. I want them to know how sorry I am. And if I ever get the chance, I am going to find Mr. Lasorda and tell him, too."

CHAPTER 21

From the moment Lionel and the others touched down in Miami, things were in full throttle. They were whisked to Joe Robbie Stadium, where each player was assigned an assistant to navigate them through all of the necessary details quickly, so they could join in with practice as soon as possible.

Lionel's assistant took him to the team doctor as a first stop and waited in the hall while Lionel was given a complete physical exam. Afterward, the doctor spoke briefly with the assistant, who then ushered Lionel into a small office.

"Your physical went great. So here is your contract, offering you $109,000 for one year as a free-agent with the Florida Marlins. Sign here, here, and here."

Lionel took the pen and scanned the document. He signed tentatively, not because of the salary amount, but because he'd hoped to talk with Coach Lachemann before signing anything, and it didn't look like that was going to happen anytime soon. From there, he was shown to the locker room and handed his number eighty-eight practice jersey and pants.

"Do you need your ankles taped?" the assistant asked.

"No, thank you. I'm good," Lionel replied. "Is Coach Lachemann around?"

The assistant shook his head. "No, sorry. He is running like a freight train today. Report to the batting cages. He will catch up with you when he can."

Lionel knew in his head that Major League clubs had more staff and heightened activity than the minors, but to see it firsthand was overwhelming. The hitting coach welcomed him warmly and told him to just get in the cage and swing, starting with his left side.

"I'm not going to give you any pointers or comment. I just want to watch. I'll tell you when to switch," Coach Morales said.

Lionel was in the cage for sixty minutes. After half the time, Morales had him switch to his right side. Lionel fought to keep a level, consistent motion on both sides—strong for hitting powerful line drives. In the last ten minutes Morales stopped him and said, "Good hits. Now I want to see you swing as if you were sending it to the Delaware."

Fielding practice and conditioning came after batting, and Lionel caught everything he was supposed to. He knew it was an illusion, but the field seemed larger. Or maybe it was that he felt smaller.

With everyone scrambling to get ready for baseball season, there was so much action happening every second of the day, it was impossible to get close enough to Lachemann to have a personal conversation. He asked one of the other players about it and was told that the best way to get a meeting with both the GM and Lachemann was to call the secretary to set it up. Without even asking his preferences for day or time, she told him that he could have thirty minutes at nine a.m. on the twenty-third. That was just two days before the Opener. He called Jourdain and told him to please pray for him that the meeting would go well.

The days flew by, and before he knew it, the roster was posted. Dozens of men would be cut to forty. Twenty-five of those would stay. Fifteen would go on reserve. When he saw the list of the chosen, he briefly hoped his name wouldn't be there. It would make slipping away from it all just a little easier.

"Hey! Congratulations!" Alex Arias, a short stop from New York, said, as they checked the list.

Lionel smiled. "Thanks." *So much for slipping away quietly.*

When they posted the opening day line-up, Lionel learned

that he would not be starting that game. Lionel was actually glad to hear it. If they threw him out on the twenty-third, they wouldn't be left in a jam.

On the day of his meeting, Lionel dressed in his good black slacks, a light blue button-up shirt, and his light-green tie. He carried his baseball stuff in his duffel. If he were asked to leave, it would be less embarrassing to hand over a duffel bag than to have to go and change out of his clothing. He slipped Papa's notebook into his pocket as a security blanket and to give him courage for the task at hand. As he did so, it fell to the floor and opened to a page with writing that he hadn't noticed before.

"*Sak vid pa kanpe*," Papa's Creole writing read.

"An empty sack cannot stand," Lionel said out loud. He'd been feeling like an empty sack since pushing the Haitian part of himself out of his life. It was time for him to stand again. "Thank you, Papa."

He arrived at eight a.m.—a full hour early. He took no chances that he'd miss this meeting. The secretary instructed him to sit in the waiting area. There was one other person—a woman—also seated in the orange leather chairs. Her kind face looked his direction.

"Hello," he said.

"Good morning," she replied. "My name is Liliana."

"I'm Lionel," he replied.

"You look sad, Lionel," she noticed.

"Ah. I am heavy-hearted this morning, ma'am," he said. "But I'll be alright soon. I think."

"A heavy heart is hard to bear," she agreed. "Usually it is not until we lighten our load that find we had many things in our knapsack we didn't need to carry to begin with."

He chuckled. "Yes, I suppose that can be true."

"I, too, am heavy-hearted," she said.

"Oh," he said. He sensed she had more to say. "Did something happen?"

"Yes," she replied. "Do you mind if I tell you a story?" She did not wait for him to answer. "When I was a little girl, my family was wealthy compared to most. I had toys and love and all of the things a girl could want. And when I was seventeen, I met a wonderful man who made me the happiest girl in the world.

"He swept me off my feet and invited me to live with him, to marry him, and to have a family with him. I always wanted five little girls that I could spoil and dress up like dollies. We got married, and we moved to be close to his job. However, I did not get pregnant so easily, and the time between my first and second children was ten whole years! Can you imagine?"

Lionel liked listening to her voice. "What happened?"

"Well! My children brought sunshine to me every day. My husband worked hard—he was an exporter—and we had a good life. But in the area we lived, things were rough. There was a lot of needless violence. You know how that can be?"

"Yes," he said. "I have seen there is violence everywhere." He thought about the Los Angeles riots.

"Yes," she agreed. "Evil has a way of reaching its ugly tentacles even into places that are supposed to be safe."

He noted moisture in her eyes. He took a tissue from a box on the side table and handed it to her.

"Thank you. Anyway, one Sunday morning, my family and I put on our best clothes and went to church. There was violence in our streets, but my husband thought we would be alright. He thought we would be safe in the house of God." She stopped briefly, deeply inhaling, finding the fortitude to continue her tale.

"We were not safe. Evil men, armed with powerful rifles, came into the church and began shooting. I saw the bullet pierce my husband's temple. I screamed and grabbed my eldest boy and told him to grab his little brother. He couldn't get him, though. We were briefly separated, then my oldest said, 'Mama! I will get William!' and he ran back inside. He never made it out."

Lionel took a tissue for his own eyes. "I'm so sorry," he said. Then a teeny lightbulb lit up in his brain. "Was this in Haiti?"

"Yes," she answered. "Almost seven years ago. I am Dominican. My husband was Haitian. We shared our time equally in both countries. Unusual, I know, but he was an exporter. My oldest preferred when we were in the Dominican because he loved to play baseball. That is why I am here today."

"What was his name?" Lionel asked.

"Lionel Albert Bierto," she replied.

Just then the door to the office opened and Coach Lachemann came out.

"Good morning, son," he said, shaking Lionel's hand. He also acknowledged Liliana. "Nice to see you again, ma'am. Please, come in."

Lionel followed dumbly, feeling like his world had just been turned upside down. There, in the office, sat Tommy Lasorda and David Dombrowski, the General Manager for the Marlins.

"Mr. Lasorda," Lionel said. "What are you doing here?"

"What do you mean, 'What am I doing here?' I hear you wanted to talk to me," Lasorda said.

Lionel shook his head. How did he know? Then he looked at Liliana, standing next to him. He processed all she'd said, all that has happened. "Jourdain?" he questioned.

Lasorda pointed for Lionel to sit. "Son, last week I got the weirdest phone call I've ever received in my life. He said his name was Jourdain and he had something important to tell me. I almost hung up on him, but my gut urged me to listen. I listen to my gut. The story he told me made me bawl like a baby. No bullshit. Pardon my French. He tells me all about a young boy, who loves baseball, and has to drop out of school to work in the baseball factory. Then he tells me how the kid's dad dies, and he has to keep working, then some bad guys come after him. He tells me how he helped the kid escape to another country. The kid works hard and earns a walk-on spot with a rookie baseball team and plays his guts out, leaving his guts all over the field every night. He also tells me how this kid is the nicest kid in the world, and everyone likes him.

"So I says to this guy, 'I want to meet this kid.'

"The guy says, 'You already have,' and he tells me that it's you.

"Then he asks me if I can go to Miami on the twenty-third to help you out of a jam. He said he'd even pay for my plane ticket. I told him I didn't need him to pay for the plane ticket, I was going to be here anyway for the season opener." He stopped and laughed. "Can you imagine the chances of that? It must be fate."

"Or God's will," Liliana said quietly.

"Yes, ma'am. God's hand on it all. Anyway. The Marlins guys here and I have been talking a lot about this. The league is cracking down hard on players—especially Dominicans—who have obtained false documents to play baseball. Most of them lie to make themselves appear older or younger. But that's not you."

"No, sir," Lionel said. "I am the age I said I was. Just not the name. My name is Samféyo Bernard."

"None of us want to see you go down because you were running for your life," Lasorda said. "But you gotta make it right."

"That's why I am here, sir," Lionel said. "To make it right. But I don't know what to do."

"Your friend Jourdain had an idea. That's where this woman comes in."

Liliana continued the story she'd started in the lobby. "Sam—I've known Jourdain for many years. We were childhood friends. When he asked me for Lionel's birth certificate, he told me all about you. I knew you were the one to carry on my Lionel's dream. I kept tabs on your baseball career over these years. I even went to watch some games. When Jourdain told me you needed someone to help you now, I knew I had to come. I spoke with these men, and I spoke with a local lawyer," Liliana said. "He said—if you wanted—I could adopt you legally. We can make your name permanently Lionel

Bierto. Then, you are legitimately who you say you are."

"You can adopt me? You *would* adopt me?"

"It would be an honor for me to adopt you."

"Then there are no more lies," Lionel stated.

"No more lies," Lasorda said. Then he added, "Kid, in the last week I talked to every manager you played for, and even many of the players. There is not a single more highly regarded minor league ball player than you. I know from personal experience what you did for our club. If anyone deserves a shot in the Major League, it's you. Let the woman adopt you. Hell, you're twenty-three years old. Take the name, make it legal. We all agree that we're all good. Nothing about this ever has to be spoken of again. Just get the paperwork done."

Lachemann and Dombrowski nodded.

"It is our honor to have you as a Florida Marlin," Dombrowski said. "But you can't go easy on the Dodgers."

"I promise. I won't," Lionel smiled. "Sorry, Mr. Lasorda."

EPILOGUE
THREE YEARS LATER

Lacy grabbed her purse and coat from her locker and hurried to her car, which was parked in the hospital garage. It was a cold Chicago night, and she pulled her hood over her ears, bemoaning the fact that she'd forgotten her gloves.

As she neared her car, she could tell that a person leaned against the hood. She pulled a small can of bear spray from her purse and called to the figure. "Get off of my car or I'll spray you!"

"Lacy," the voice said. She recognized it.

"Lionel? What are you doing here?" she walked quickly to him.

"Lacy. Can we talk?" he asked.

She considered this question. Lucky for him it was very cold outside. "Get in," she said.

She drove to a small diner on State Street. When they were seated and had ordered hot coffee, he finally spoke. "I need to tell you why I ran away." She let him tell her everything.

"I am so sorry for lying to you," he said.

She reached across and took his hand. "You could have told me," she said. "I would have understood."

"Are you seeing anyone?" he asked the question he was most afraid to know the answer to.

"No. I've dated a couple of men on and off, but there has always been a problem."

"What's that?" he asked.

"I've been in love with someone else." She smiled. "What

took you so long?"

"I did not want to interfere with your internship. I figured if you were meant to be mine, then you'd be available when it was over."

She grinned. "Congratulations on the World Series. I never thought I'd be a Marlins' fan. My White Sox friends thought I lost my mind. I saw you at the White House on the news."

"Yes. I had promised my papa long ago that when I got there, I would have a few things to say to the president."

"Did you get to tell him what you wanted?" she asked.

"I gave him a letter," he laughed. "I hope he reads it."

"What did it say?"

"I told President Clinton that he had a responsibility to help Haiti, that he needed to finish what he started, and if he would let me, I would be happy to work with him to find ways to make Haiti respectable in the eyes of the world."

"Wow! Impressive!"

"I've started to build a baseball field in Miami. In Lemon City, where many Haitian immigrants live. I want to teach the Haitian children to play baseball. I've named it *Eduard Bernard Field.*"

"That's beautiful. Your papa would love that."

"You know, the local hospital could use a gentle, caring, beautiful nurse." He pulled a ring from his pocket. "My friend Elena told me once that when you feel you have no one, God will always send someone. She and Jourdain were my *someones.* Liliana was my *someone.* Now, I would like you to be my forever someone. Lacy Turner, will you marry me?"

"Yes."

Other fiction by
Kimberly Soesbee

Maneeya
ISBN: 978-1-942508-27-4

The Cookie Tree
ISBN: 978-1-942508-43-4

CoCo's Bananas
ISBN: 978-1-942508-06-9

**order through Amazon, Barnes and Noble,
or your local book retailer**

www.KimberlySoesbee.com